ARISTOCRAT

The

PENELOPE WARD

Edited by: Jessica Royer Ocken
Proofreading and Formatting by: Elaine York
Allusion Publishing, www.allusionpublishing.com
Proofreading by: Julia Griffis
Cover Photographer: Alejandro Brito
Cover Model: Kacey Carrig
Cover Design: Letitia Hasser, RBA Designs

To Linda ♡

The ARISTOCRAT

" The purpose of
life is to love with all of
your heart and soul."

xo

Penelope Sky

CHAPTER 1

Felicity

Track 1: "Somebody's Watching Me" by Rockwell

"What are you looking at?"

I jumped at the sound of Mrs. Angelini's voice and put my binoculars down momentarily. "Did you know we have new neighbors across the bay?" I asked.

"Well, I saw some flashing lights coming from the house the other night. Figured someone finally moved in."

"Yeah. They were having a party, I think."

We lived on the bay in Narragansett, Rhode Island. Aside from the house next door, the only other residence in the vicinity was a sprawling estate across the small body of water that separated our land from theirs. You'd have to take a boat to get to it—either that or be a really good swimmer. The house had been vacant for several months, but now someone had either bought it or was renting it.

"Do you know anything about them?" she asked.

"Why would I?"

"Because you've obviously been spying."

I cleared my throat. "I was...birdwatching and happened to notice them. It's two guys. I think they might be gay."

"And how would you know that?"

"Well, they're both extremely good-looking. Many of the ones who look *that* good tend to be gay. It's not fair."

The wind blew Mrs. Angelini's long sweater as she grabbed the binoculars from me and lifted them to her eyes.

She laughed after a moment. "Wow. Well, I can certainly see why you've taken a sudden liking to... birdwatching."

Mrs. Angelini returned my binoculars and winked before she walked back into the house, leaving me alone to resume watching the new inhabitants. But this time when I looked, I saw something I was most definitely *not* meant to see. One of the men must have gone inside the house, because the other was now alone. He'd moved from his previous spot and was now buck naked under an outdoor shower. My mouth dropped. I should've looked away, but my eyes lingered on his bronze body. The water fell over him like a waterfall down a mountain of carved stone.

I felt awful for staring, but honestly...who showers in front of the neighbors? Although, in his defense, he probably thought he was alone. The only house facing the back of theirs was mine. He likely never imagined someone as far away as me would be watching him.

My guilt finally caught up with me. I put the binoculars down and took a long sip of my lemon water. Maybe I needed to pour it over my head instead. Trying to concentrate on anything other than the peep show across the bay, I picked up my phone and began to search for summer jobs. I didn't want anything too stressful, just something to earn a little cash for my move to Pennsylvania in the fall. Considering the most excitement I'd had lately was spying on a couple of handsome men, I needed something to occupy my time.

I'd graduated from college a couple of years ago but had stayed in Boston for work. I'd just turned twenty-four and had moved back home to Rhode Island for the summer before I was headed to law school. *Home* was an estate owned by Eloise Angelini, a widow whose husband had owned a string of seafood restaurants. I'd been living with Mrs. Angelini since my sophomore year in high school. After her husband died, she'd decided to become a foster parent, taking me in after my previous foster mother had moved away. Because of Mrs. Angelini, I was able to finish high school with my friends and didn't have to leave Narragansett. For that, I would always be grateful. And as if taking me in wasn't enough, she'd decided she wanted to help put me through college—although she never had to, since I got a full scholarship to Harvard.

Even so, Mrs. Angelini made sure I had a place to call home. She always made me feel like she needed me more than I needed her, though I knew that couldn't be the case. She'd found me during one of the loneliest times in her life, but *I'd* already been accustomed to a lonely life. I'd never known anything but being on my own, and I'd learned not to get my heart set on anything, not to get attached to anyone. I'd been in and out of many foster homes by the time I landed on Mrs. Angelini's doorstep at fifteen. I appreciated that she didn't try to mother me. She was a true friend and confidante. And we made each other laugh—a lot. Mrs. Angelini gave me a sense of security, and I provided her with a distraction from the loss of her husband. We were just what the other needed. Still, my life had conditioned me not to get too comfortable with anyone—even Mrs. Angelini, who'd done nothing but embrace me with open arms.

I wondered if it was safe to look back across the bay now. Lifting my binoculars to my eyes, I flinched when I found the sexy man now wiping his still-naked body down with a towel. His huge cock bobbed up and down, and after losing my train of thought for a bit, I moved my peepers off of him and over to the left.

I jumped. Staring back at me was the *other* guy—with binoculars of his own. He'd been watching *me* watch his friend.

Oh no.

Then, to my horror, he waved, flashing a snide smile.

What do I do?

These guys knew where I lived, and I'd likely run into them around town. I couldn't hide forever. Playing it cool was my only option. Rather than run inside the house—my first instinct—I tried to remain calm. I smiled and waved back.

I was just about to put my binoculars down when I saw him call Shower Guy over. The formerly naked man now had the towel wrapped around his waist. The guy with the binoculars said something to him, and they laughed. Then Shower Guy grabbed the binoculars and waved at me as well. He was enjoying this? They both apparently got off on my stupidity.

I awkwardly waved back and then realized I'd had enough. I turned and went in the house.

Mrs. Angelini was standing at the sink washing dishes. "What's wrong, Felicity? You're all red."

"Nothing," I said as I passed her to go upstairs to my room.

Despite ruminating about what had happened outside, I forced myself to once again focus on the summer-job search for the next couple of hours—not the most exciting Memorial Day weekend, that was for sure.

Later that evening, the doorbell rang, and I could hear Mrs. Angelini's footsteps as she went to answer it. The door shut before she called to me from the bottom of the stairwell.

"Felicity, you might want to come down here. You have a delivery."

Something came for me? I jumped off my bed and skipped down the steps. Mrs. Angelini was holding a bouquet of bright yellow flowers. Daffodils?

"Who are they from?" I asked.

"I don't know. But there's a card."

I took the flowers from her and walked them over to the kitchen counter. My heart nearly fell to my stomach as I opened the card and read the note.

Dear redhead across the bay,

We thought these would be a perfect way to say thank you for being a neighbor. This is a flower known as the Narcissus Peeping Tom. Need we say more? Enjoy them.

Love your neighbors, Sig and Leo

Hell.

Hell was the moment I stepped into the grocery store a few days later and nearly knocked right into him.

"It's you." He held up a long, phallic-looking baguette and shook it. "Remind you of something?"

My face felt hot. "Very funny."

"I haven't seen much of you outside over the last couple of days. Did we scare you?"

This was not Shower Guy, but rather the one who'd caught me peeping. He had a strong British accent and was extremely tall, with dark hair.

"I've just been taking a break from the backyard."

"Too *hot* outside for you, eh?"

"Look, I didn't intend to see what I saw. I've been into...birdwatching this summer. Then one day you two moved in, and I—"

"Whoa, whoa, whoa..." The other guy had appeared next to his housemate. "I'm sorry for anything he might have said to you just now. Rest assured, it's all shite. He's just playing around." He, too, had a strong British accent. "I don't believe we've properly met."

"Although, you've *improperly* met..." his friend chided.

"Put a sock in it, Sigmund."

Okay, so the asshole is Sig—or Sigmund. The previously naked one must be Leo, then. They were both tall and good-looking, but Leo, with his chiseled features, lustrous hair, and striking eyes was on another level—a total Adonis, and intimidatingly gorgeous.

Sigmund shrugged. "Surely she knows I'm just kidding."

"But you don't know when to stop. That's always been your problem. Can't you see how red her face is getting? You're embarrassing her."

Uh...how red is my face getting? This was mortifying. I couldn't control that about myself. After all, I was a redhead with fair skin covered in freckles. Whenever I got embarrassed, I basically turned red from head to toe.

Leo's tone softened. "I apologize for his rude behavior." He held out his hand. "I'm Leo Covington."

I took it, enjoying the warmth of his skin. "Felicity Dunleavy."

The other guy offered his hand. "Sigmund Benedictus. But please call me Sig."

Benedictus?

Been a dick-tus.

He sure had.

Fitting.

"Good to meet you," I said.

"And you, as well, Freckles."

Freckles? He couldn't have come up with a more original nickname? I was self-conscious about my freckles, and typically wanted to murder anyone who dubbed me Freckles.

"Do you mind not calling me that?"

"Do you prefer a different nickname?" Sig asked. "Peeping Tom, perhaps?"

Leo gritted his teeth. "Enough. Seriously."

"All right. I'll behave. Going in search of tapenade for this bread." He winked. "Be back."

Relief washed over me as he walked away.

"I'm...really sorry about him," Leo said.

"Well, given how you came to know of me, the ridicule is warranted. I shouldn't have been spying."

"I don't reckon you anticipated seeing me in my birthday suit. That was the first time I'd ever done that. I assumed no one was in the vicinity, of course. For the record, I don't make a habit of showering for all the world to see. I never had an outdoor shower in England. So it's a novelty."

Leo was simply striking. His hair was light brown with golden undertones. He had beautiful bone structure and full lips that were difficult not to stare at. There wasn't one thing I would change about his face. His eyes were a deep blue. They reminded me of a piece of sea glass I'd used to make a necklace once.

I cleared my throat. "What brings you to Narragansett?"

"I'm taking six months off from life. It seemed like a good location to get lost. We picked this place randomly on a map, actually. Sigmund and I have spent our time in a few different locales. First was California, then New York, and now Rhode Island."

"Are you two...together?"

His brow lifted. "What do you mean by *together*? We're rooming together. But if you mean *romantically* together, then no. Exactly what did you assume?"

"I thought you might be gay."

"If I were gay, I'd have far better taste in men than that wanker cousin of mine. What in God's name made you think we were gay?"

8

"I don't know. Two handsome men...living together in a big house..."

"So, if I'm a guy living with another man, I'm automatically shagging him?"

"You're right. That was a hasty assumption."

"Thank you for the compliment, by the way."

I just called him handsome, didn't I? Feeling suddenly hot, I looked toward the produce section. "Well, I'd better be going..."

"Before you do, I want to apologize for the flowers he sent your way the other night. I urged him not to. Not everyone appreciates that sense of humor."

I shrugged. "It was fine. And they were pretty. I was embarrassed, at first, but then I ended up laughing about the whole thing. Mrs. Angelini certainly got a kick out of it."

His brow lifted. "Mrs. Angelini?"

How do I explain who she is without unloading my history on this stranger? I kept it simple. "She's my roommate."

"Ah. Roommate. So she must be your lesbian lover, then." He raised an eyebrow, and I had to smile. "Anyway, why do you call her Mrs. Angelini? She doesn't have a first name?"

"Well, she's seventy. It's more of a respect thing. It's what I started calling her some years back, and it stuck. She's always asked me to call her by her first name, but I got used to calling her Mrs. Angelini."

"I see." His eyes seared into mine for a moment. "Your roommate is seventy. And how old are you, might I ask?"

"Twenty-four. What about you?"

"Twenty-eight," he answered. His eyes lingered on mine for a bit. "Listen, we're going to be renting the house across from you for the entire summer. We know virtually nothing about Narragansett. I'd love to pick your brain about places to go and things to do here. Maybe you wouldn't mind coming over for tea sometime this week?"

"Tea? You really *are* British, aren't you?"

"Guilty as charged." His white teeth gleamed.

Looking down at my feet, I said, "I don't know."

"I promise not to take off my clothes..." He added a crooked smile.

I let out a much-needed laugh. "Well, since you put it that way."

"Tomorrow at two, then? Or whatever time works for you."

A part of me wanted to refuse, but why? It wasn't like I had anything more exciting going on. I didn't quite understand whether he genuinely wanted my expertise on Narragansett, or if there was something more to the invitation, now that I knew he wasn't gay.

"Sure. Two tomorrow works."

"Brilliant. You know how to get to the house without having to swim across, I take it?"

"Yes." I smiled.

"Very well, then. And I promise, Sigmund will be on his best behavior."

"I can handle it if he's not."

This seemingly rich traveler had no idea just how much I could handle. I might turn red when I was embarrassed, but I'd grown a pretty-thick skin over the years.

That's the way it is when you always had to fend for yourself.

CHAPTER 2
Felicity

Track 2: "It's the Hard-Knock Life" by the Original Broadway Cast of Annie

"What exactly does one wear to tea?" I asked.

"I'll tell you what they *don't* wear. That raggedy 'gamer girl' T-shirt you've got on."

My best friend, Bailey, was entering her second year of grad school at Brown. She lived about forty minutes away in Providence, but was visiting me a couple of hours before I was set to head over to the neighbors' house.

"That's why I'm asking you. You have much better fashion sense than I do."

She sifted through my closet. "I'm thinking... something buttoned up and proper, yet chic."

"Really? Aside from their accents, these guys don't seem that proper at all. They're more wild."

"Think about it. Tea? That's like synonymous with high necks and buttons." She reached for a white blouse I often wore to interviews. "This looks nice. What do you have for skirts?"

"I don't really wear them."

"Seriously. Your entire closet is jeans, the same few T-shirts in different colors, and a couple of sweatshirts."

"Well, that's what I like."

"You need something for special occasions, though."

"I don't really go anywhere."

She managed to find the one skirt I had in the back of my closet. "What's this?"

"That's the skirt I wore to concert choir performances in high school."

"Does it fit?"

"I think so, but don't you think that's too formal?"

"Nah. Try it on."

I undressed, putting on the white shirt and buttoning it before slipping the long, black skirt over my legs.

Bailey looked me up and down. "You look nice." She continued searching through my closet. "What about this over it?" She took a gray blazer off one of the hangers. "You need something to spruce up the white shirt."

"It's June. Isn't it too warm out for a blazer?"

"Well, you'll be in the air conditioning, right?"

"Maybe. Not sure." I slipped the jacket over my shoulders.

"Why are these guys renting that house again?"

"He said they picked Narragansett randomly. They're on a six-month vacation here in the States."

"Weird. But cool at the same time." She beamed. "You think this guy likes you?"

I closed the last button on the jacket. "I don't know."

"Well, he has no clue he's invited the chess champion of Narragansett High over for tea."

"Yeah, I don't think that's something to advertise. It's bad enough I'm dressed like I'm going to a job interview. I don't need to highlight my nerd tendencies."

She laughed. "Okay. Well, I gotta run. Let me know how it goes, okay?"

"Will do."

"And Felicity? Come meet me in the city next week. Let's go shopping. I didn't realize how bad this closet situation was."

"Not necessary."

"Oh, believe me, it's necessary."

I parked my tiny car in front of the beautiful property, which had a circular driveway. The house featured wood-shingle siding and a stunning front porch with four white Adirondack chairs. This was the quintessential Narragansett house, yet most people could only afford it in their dreams.

Before I could walk to their front door, Sig came out to greet me. I faced him as I stood in front of my car.

He gave me a once-over. "I didn't realize we'd invited Mary Poppins to tea."

Great.

Is it that bad? I looked down at myself. *It is that bad.* Long, black skirt with a white shirt and blazer. The only thing missing was the umbrella. *Damn you, Bailey.*

Glancing at his shirtless chest, I understood now that this was most definitely a casual "tea." Leo, who happened to have a T-shirt on, finally appeared, running toward us as if to stop his cousin from doing further damage.

"There you are," Leo said.

"I've never been invited to tea before," I told him. "I assumed it was more formal. But clearly I was wrong."

Leo smiled. "I think it's adorable that you dressed up. And for the record, you look lovely."

"And you're a liar." I laughed, wiping some lint off my skirt. "But thank you anyway."

Sig looked over at my tiny, mint green Fiat 500. "Would you like to bring your toy car inside as well?"

"Leave my car alone. It's easy to park and good on gas."

"Sigmund can relate to being small and gassy," Leo joked. He placed his hand lightly at the small of my back, sending a chill down my spine. "Welcome to our humble abode. Let's go inside."

"Hardly humble." I chuckled, looking up at the massive property.

They led me through a large foyer to a spacious kitchen with cream-colored cabinets and sparkling granite countertops.

"What can I get you to drink?" Leo asked.

"I thought tea was the default beverage today."

"I bet you like it with just a spoonful of sugar, yeah?" Sig chided.

I rolled my eyes. "Spoonful of Sugar"—the famous song from *Mary Poppins*. This guy was a pill.

I don't think Leo got the joke. He just squinted at his cousin. "Well, when I invited you for tea, I was using the term loosely," he said. "I do have other options. But I can make tea, if that's what you want."

"In that case, I'd love some tequila. Have any?" I teased.

"*Tea*-quila. Coming right up, gorgeous."

"I was kidding, but I certainly won't turn it down."

"Tea-quila is much better than tea anyway." He winked.

Sig had left the kitchen, and Leo ventured into an adjacent room that must have been where the liquor was stored. For the brief time I was left alone, I gazed out through the French doors at the bay.

His voice startled me. "It's a beautiful day." Leo stood holding what I recognized as a bottle of Casamigos Reposado tequila and two shot glasses.

"It's gorgeous out, yes."

He gestured with his head. "Let's enjoy these drinks outside, shall we? I'm eager to learn more about you."

"About me? I thought I was supposed to be teaching *you* about Narragansett."

"Oh. Well, I suppose we can talk about that, too." He smiled.

Leo led me out to the large deck and placed the alcohol and glasses on a table. I sat in one of the chairs, and he sat across from me.

He opened the bottle and poured the tequila nearly up to the rim of my shot glass before serving himself.

He reached his glass toward mine. "Cheers."

We both threw back at the same time. The tequila burned my throat as it went down.

So much for tea. Bottoms up! Almost instantly, I felt the buzz, my cheeks tingling. Looking across the sparkling bay, I said, "It's weird to see my house from this angle. Mrs. Angelini's property looks even more beautiful from here. In fact, I think this view—the back of her house—is the best part."

"I think the best part of the house might be sitting across from me, actually."

His words left me feeling flushed. "What are you basing that on?" I asked. "You don't even know me."

"I was trying to be complimentary, but you're right. I don't know much about you aside from the fact that you're not very easily charmed."

Sig appeared and patted his cousin on the shoulder. "My boy here is not used to that. Normally he has women falling at his feet."

I addressed Leo. "So...you said you're traveling for six months. Did you get time off from your job or..."

Sig snickered.

Turning to him, I raised my brow. "What's so funny?"

"He thinks me needing time off from work is hilarious, since that's not really a consideration for me," Leo answered.

"Why is that? You don't work?"

"He comes from old money," Sig said. "Whether he works on a daily basis or not is inconsequential, although there *are* responsibilities."

Leo looked annoyed. "My father is grooming me to take over the family business," he clarified. "He owns a number of properties in the countryside where we live in England."

After taking a moment to process that, I said, "So this grooming includes a six-month jaunt around the US?"

"That might not seem to make sense, but yes, this trip was part of an agreement I have with my father. Being an only child, I've always had tremendous expectations placed upon me. Before I can begin to take things seriously, I needed a break from the pressure. I know what's expected of me, and I plan to fulfill his wishes. But I needed this time away first."

"Okay, so you made a deal with your dad…"

He nodded. "He gave me six months off from any and all familial obligations. And in return, I'll take things more seriously when I return."

"You don't want to take over the family business?"

His expression turned a bit serious. "What I want has never really mattered."

"With all due respect, why can't you just tell your father you aren't interested?"

Sig laughed under his breath.

I looked over at him and back toward Leo. "I'm sorry to pry."

Sig chuckled. "Believe me, he's *thrilled* you're asking these questions, because it means you have absolutely no idea who he is, and that's exactly what he prefers."

Leo's face turned a bit red.

"What is he talking about?" I asked. "Who *are* you?"

"Here? No one." He sighed. "But back home in the bubble? People think I'm a big deal because of the family I was born into. I'm the subject of much unwanted attention."

"Boo-hoo." Sig rolled his eyes. "I'd gladly bear some of that so-called burden, if I could."

Leo glared at him. "Anyway, enough about that for now. Can I pour you another?" He seemed eager to move this conversation elsewhere.

I held my palm out. "I'd better not. I can already feel this one going to my head."

"How about some *actual* tea, then?"

"That might be good."

Sig stood up. "I volunteer to make it. I can tell you've been waiting for me to get out of your hair for a second so you can talk to Freckles in peace."

"I believe she told you not to call her that," Leo scolded.

"That's right." He placed his hand over his heart and feigned regret. "Forgive me, Mary."

Such a dick.

"I apologize for him. Really, if we weren't related, I would've cut him off a long time ago. But he's quite a fun travel companion when he's not being an arse."

"It's all right."

He tilted his head. "Tell me more about you, Felicity."

"Well, I graduated from college a couple of years ago, and for the last two years I've worked for a nonprofit in Boston."

"Whereabouts did you go to school?"

"Harvard."

His eyes widened. "No big deal, then." He coughed. "Wow. Seriously, congratulations."

"Thank you."

"What's next?"

"Headed to Pennsylvania for law school this fall."

"Brilliant."

"Yeah. I'm trying to enjoy the summer before I have to buckle down again."

"I know you live with a roommate. Whereabouts is your family?"

Here we go. I came out with it. "I don't have one, actually."

Concern filled his eyes. "You have no family?"

"Nope. I grew up in the foster system, so I've lived with people who weren't my actual parents for a good portion of my life. Mrs. Angelini is the last such person. She took me in when I was fifteen, and that house across the bay has been my home base ever since."

He nodded, taking in my revelation. "I hope you don't mind my saying, but I find you even more remarkable now—all that you've accomplished. It couldn't have been easy for you growing up."

"It wasn't, but it's made me the person I am today. Made me strong."

"I can see that." His stare lingered a bit. "Are you too hot out here?"

I was. Not only because of the sun and my ridiculously heavy clothes, but because of my attraction to him. That was causing me to burn up in a way I hadn't in a while. Which made me uneasy.

"Yeah." I looked down at my ensemble. "This get-up wasn't the best choice."

"Shall we go inside? I can give you a tour of the house."

"That might be good," I said, standing.

We passed Sig in the kitchen, and Leo showed me around.

Eventually he led me back through the foyer to the living room. Floor-to-ceiling windows provided a clear view of the bay from a different angle, and streaks of sunlight streaming through glowed against the hardwood floor.

"I'd always wondered what this place looked like on the inside. It's even more beautiful than I imagined."

He stared through me. "Yeah."

Being inside really hadn't cooled me down. I fiddled with my collar, tempted to unbutton my blouse, even though I knew I wouldn't.

"You seem a bit uncomfortable," Leo said. "Am I making you nervous?"

I admitted something I probably shouldn't have. "I think maybe I still haven't gotten over the way we first... met."

He raised his brow. "The *birdwatching*, you mean?"

"No. I started out birdwatching, but after I spotted you guys, I was definitely watching *you*. I'm not going to deny that. I think very few people would've turned away. I'm only human."

His mouth curved into a smile. "That is yet another reason why I like you, Felicity. Most people might not have turned away—I certainly wouldn't have—but few are honest about such things. I spend my life surrounded by dishonest people whose number-one goal is to look good rather than be authentic. I hardly know you, but what little you've given me is purely you. And I appreciate that. It's refreshing."

"Tea is ready," Sig announced from the threshold, prompting Leo and me to turn to him in unison. He gave us a look as if perhaps he knew he'd interrupted a *moment*. "Made some crumpets, too, since she was clearly expecting a more *proper* tea."

"Thank you, oh domestic one," Leo said before turning to me. "He's definitely the cook in this relationship."

I followed them out into a grand dining room, where Sig had set up a formal-looking tea service. A mountain of crumpets were stacked atop each other on a plate.

"So, you actually made these?" I asked.

"Yes. From scratch."

"Impressive."

"There aren't many ingredients," Sig said. "Make sure you eat one before they cool. There's nothing like melted butter on them."

I grabbed one and buttered it. It was exactly as he'd promised, savory and delicious. Leo took it upon himself to pour me a cup of tea. That was sweet.

Sig crossed his arms. "So, Felicity, what is it that two single guys do for fun around here?"

"You're asking *me*?" I said with my mouth full of crumpet. "Seems like you two have no problems finding fun, with your parties and all."

Leo's eyes narrowed. "Parties?"

"Yeah, I saw the flashing lights coming from here one night, and I've heard music from across the bay more than once."

Leo shook his head. "There was no party. That was Sigmund playing his music and fucking with me. We haven't really met anyone since we've gotten here. The previous inhabitants installed those strobe lights and the sound system."

I chuckled. "Well, that's sort of bizarre. I just assumed you were party animals."

"Anyway, you never answered my question," Sig said. "What's hot around here?"

"Well, there's the bar by the beach. A lot of people hang out there, even on weeknights. Then there's the center of town. There are a lot of nice restaurants. But if you chose to spend a portion of your US trip here, of all places, you may not be looking for exciting night life."

"Sig and I have wanted different things out of this trip," Leo said. "Narragansett was his compromise to me since I put up with the other locations. And I'm most definitely looking for peace."

"I'm looking for a *piece* of something too." Sig winked.

Leo rolled his eyes. "Never mind tourists. Tell me, what do the locals like to do?"

"Things are pretty laid-back here. We mostly sit on our decks and drink beer, or watch the sunset over the bay. We might go clamming or fishing and see what fresh catch we can bring home for dinner."

Leo smiled. "You fish?"

"Occasionally. Although, I'd need a boat to get to some of the best parts of the bay for quahoging."

"Co-what?" Leo asked.

"Quahoging. The act of digging for quahogs. Clams."

"Ah. You need a boat to do that?"

"Well, there's a section of the bay where you can harvest a lot, but you need a boat to get there from here."

"I see." Leo licked butter off the side of his lips. "If I can get a boat, will you take us there?"

"Um...I don't know..." I stammered.

Leo's face fell. "I'm sorry. I didn't mean to volunteer you to be our tour guide. That's not your job."

"I just don't know if I can commit to anything right now. I'm in the process of looking for a summer job. I have a couple of leads, so I don't know my schedule for much longer."

He nodded, still seeming disappointed. "Fair enough."

I exhaled. "So...how long are you guys here exactly?"

"Until the end of August," Leo answered.

"Leaving sooner would be my preference," Sig interjected. "I'm more eager to return home than Leo."

"Then you guys head back to England?"

Leo sighed. "That's the plan."

"His family will have his balls if he doesn't come back by September," Sig interjected.

Leo chose to move on. "So, you said you're going to law school in the fall. Tell me more. Which school and what type of law are you looking to specialize in?"

"Drexel. And I want to use my degree to work in child advocacy someday, to help children who grew up the way I did. That's very important to me, to do something close to my heart where I can make a difference."

"If only everyone followed their passion, the world would be a better place." Leo smiled.

Sig looked between us. "Did I miss something? Children who grew up the way you did?"

"I told your cousin earlier that I grew up in the foster care system."

"An orphan?"

I hated that term. "Yes."

Sig blinked a few times. "Let me get this straight. You're a redheaded orphan. You live with an older woman. Is her name Miss Hannigan, by any chance?" He tilted his head. "Do you have a dog named Sandy?"

Very funny. I rolled my eyes. "I think it's pretty hysterical how well you know *Annie*, Sig. I wouldn't have taken you for someone so well-versed in musicals. First *Mary Poppins*, now this."

Leo's face reddened as he turned to his cousin. "You are an absolute buffoon."

"And you're...Daddy Warbucks, apparently."

Leo nearly spit out his tea.

"Actually, our nan took me to see *Annie* in London when I was a kid." Sig looked over at me. "I'm sorry. I'll stop being an arsehole for now," he said. For the first time since I'd met him, he seemed genuinely interested. "What happened to your family?"

Before I could answer, Leo said, "I don't think you need to be prying into her background right now. Let the girl enjoy her tea without having to give you her life's story."

"I don't have a problem talking about it," I insisted.

Leo nodded.

I braced myself to explain. "My mother died of a drug overdose when I was seven. She'd been estranged from her family long before I was born. When you're left without a parent at that age, you don't have people eager to adopt you. People prefer newborns, not scrawny seven-year-olds who don't talk much. So, I was placed in various homes, but for one reason or another, no one was ever able to adopt me. I got very lucky—made it through the system without being physically or emotionally harmed. That's not the case for many kids. So, bottom line, someday I'd like to be able to help those who are less fortunate than I was."

Sig nodded. "That's commendable."

"Is that a compliment from your snarky ass?" I asked.

Leo snorted.

I shifted my focus to him. "What is it that you do, Sigmund?"

"Besides lurk in the shadows of my much better-looking and successful cousin, you mean?" He stood suddenly. "It seems I might have matched with a gorgeous Persian girl who's approximately two miles away. I need to get ready." He lifted his teacup toward me. "Nice chatting with you, Freckles. I mean, Felicity." He winked.

"Good riddance," Leo muttered when he'd gone.

"That was kind of a random way to depart."

"That's typical Sigmund behavior. He's at a crossroads right now, unsure what he wants to do with his life. I think your question scared him off. Not to mention, this is the longest I've seen him sit in one spot since we got here. He's always had ants in his pants. He's never satisfied just being alone, or relaxing and enjoying life. He's always going in search of the next big thing, the next woman, the next adventure."

"Makes sense why he wasn't the one who wanted to come to Narragansett, then."

"The deal was, if we spent the first half of our trip in metropolitan cities, he had to go wherever I chose for the last half. And so far? This was just what the doctor ordered."

"Yet even here, he's still finding ways to get ass."

"Precisely." Leo bent his head back in laughter. "And I love that you don't mince words."

"I am a bit of a straight shooter once I get comfortable around someone. Life's too short not to be."

"I can't tell you what a breath of fresh air it is to talk to someone who isn't trying to be someone they're not. I envy you in many ways."

"Envy? How so?"

"Back home—the life I was born into—you're expected to act a certain way, conduct yourself in a way that's very mechanical, for lack of a better word. I never feel like it's okay to be my authentic self, not only because I'm constantly being watched and judged, but because no one will accept me unless I fit their expectations. As difficult as I know your upbringing was, clearly it allowed you to grow into yourself, a strong woman who says what she wants, who makes her own choices. A family who nurtures you can be a wonderful thing. But family can also be a burden... stifling."

I arched a brow. "You don't expect me to feel sorry for you..."

He shook his head. "God, no. I'm sorry if I came across that way—"

"No worries. I'm just teasing. I can't begin to understand your struggles, just as you wouldn't understand mine. Clearly we come from two different worlds."

Leo continued to stare through me as my heart raced. I looked away.

Then I looked down at my watch. "Well, it's actually later than I thought. I'd better get back." I got up from my chair. "Thank you so much for the tea, and the tea-quila."

Leo stood, his chair skidding against the ground. "You sure you have to leave?"

"Yeah, I'd really better."

He blinked, seeming taken aback. I couldn't say I fully understood this myself.

"I'll walk you to your car."

"Thanks."

My shoes clicked against the marble floor of the foyer as Leo led the way back to the front of the house.

We stood face to face as a light breeze blew my long, thick red hair around. It was neither straight nor curly in its natural state, just a fluffy mane of waves. A strand flew into my mouth, and I blew some air out to get it off my face.

I was just about to say goodbye when Leo surprised me with a question.

"Why do you not like your freckles?" His eyes fell to my cheeks.

I shrugged. "I don't know. When I was younger, people teased me about them, and I guess that made me hate them."

Leo glanced down at my neck. "I love them, especially how they continue down your neck. They give you character."

"A few give you character." I looked at my feet. "I'm covered in them."

"Yes, I know. It's beautiful." He paused. "*You're* beautiful."

I looked up and met his eyes.

While I hadn't felt beautiful coming here in my Mary Poppins outfit, the man in front of me, the way he looked at me, did make me feel beautiful, for some reason. And that made me feel...like fleeing.

I lifted my hand. "Well, I'll see you around town, I guess."

As I began to walk toward my car, Leo called after me. "Felicity, wait."

I turned around. "Yeah?"

He slipped his hands into his pockets. "Will you let me take you out sometime?"

My mouth opened, but all I could think to say was, "On a date?"

"Of course." He laughed. "What else?"

He looked so handsome as he stood waiting for my answer, the sun reflecting in his blue eyes. A part of me wanted to say yes. But I knew getting closer to this guy would be a bad idea.

So I forced the words out. "Thank you so much for the offer, but I don't think so."

He frowned. "Can I ask why?"

Despite my openness about certain things today, I didn't want to admit the reason I'd declined: he scared me. For some reason, I knew saying yes would lead to inevitable heartbreak by summer's end. I needed to protect myself.

"I'm just…not interested," I finally said. *Damn, was that ever a lie.*

He nodded slowly. "Okay. Fair enough."

"Thank you again so much for tea," I said before escaping to my car so I didn't have to experience the lingering tension. Except in my haste, I accidentally put the car in reverse. Stepping on the brakes fast, I waved awkwardly and laughed. When Leo's smile didn't reach his eyes, it kind of tore through my heart.

I pulled out of the driveway and made my way down the road. Not even a minute into my ride, I was second-guessing having rejected his offer to take me out. We obviously came from two different worlds, and dating him would be futile since he was leaving, but I was deeply attracted to him—not only his looks, but his down-to-earth personality.

Without realizing it, I had long passed the street that led to my house when I finally looked around. I found myself driving over a bridge, unsure where I was headed anymore. Sort of the story of my life.

CHAPTER 3

Leo

Track 3: "Hot Hot Hot" by Buster Poindexter

Sigmund emerged from the shower wearing only a towel. He looked around. "Where's the redhead?"

"She left," I muttered.

"Is that why you have such a long face?"

"You'll be happy to know I finally know how you feel."

"Why's that?"

"I got rejected."

His eyes widened. "What?"

"Yep."

"That's literally the first time in your life a woman has turned you down, isn't it?" He patted me hard on the shoulder, enjoying this a bit too much. "Well, welcome to the club, mate. We serve blue balls and stale beer in our neck of the woods."

"Brilliant."

Though I was doing my best to take it in stride, Felicity turning me down did hurt a bit. And it wasn't about being rejected. I was genuinely disappointed to not spend more time with her. I couldn't remember the last time I'd yearned to know more about a girl, yearned to count every fucking freckle on her body.

Sigmund shook me out of my thoughts. "I had a feeling that for some bizarre reason you fancied her and might go in for the kill, but I never imagined she'd turn you down."

"Well, maybe that was a smart decision on her part."

"I couldn't agree more," he said. "What's the point of messing around with someone like that?"

"What's that supposed to mean?" I snapped. "Someone like *that*?"

"Well, you know after speaking to her that she's not the type who's only interested in shagging. She's too serious for that. So what's the point of getting to know her, or taking her out? It can never go anywhere."

"You can't exactly choose who you fancy, Sigmund, even if that person doesn't fit perfectly into the stifling box that is my life."

"She's the opposite of anything that fits, actually."

"That's precisely why I like her."

"And your dick is probably even harder for her now that she's turned you down."

I couldn't deny that her rejection made me want her more. A chase was always arousing. Yet Felicity Dunleavy didn't care to be chased by me. Rather than making up an excuse, she'd very directly told me she wasn't interested.

"Anyway..." He laughed. "Now your children won't end up looking like they belong to Ed Sheeran." He chuckled. "We can find you a replacement for her tonight, if you want to come out with me."

Frustrated, I ran my hand through my hair. "Not interested in that right now."

"Mate, she's not even a ten. What are you worried about?"

"Are you serious?"

"She's plain. Okay, well, she's fit in her own way, I suppose."

"She's naturally beautiful. Not like the made-up women back home."

"I'll be more than happy to take some of those girls off your hands when we get back, since you don't seem to appreciate them." He sighed. "Seriously, cousin, I think you should forget about the F-word and come out with me and Shiva tonight."

"Shiva?"

"The Persian girl I met on the app."

"Oh...yeah."

"Maybe she has a friend."

No way was I in the mood for that. "I'm feeling kind of knackered. I think I'll stay in."

"Probably better for me anyway," he said. "No chance of you stealing my thunder."

After Sigmund took the car to drive to Providence, I decided to pay my mum a long-overdue phone call. I'd been avoiding her because she kept insisting on an exact date for my return. We had yet to buy our tickets home.

After three rings, my mother answered. "Well, hello, love. I thought I might never hear from you again. It's late here. Is everything okay?"

I lay back on the couch. "Everything is fine, Mother. Sorry, I forgot the time. Things have been a little hectic."

"Too much lying around on the beach wasting precious time away?"

"This is far from a waste. My mind is ten times clearer than when I left."

"Well, your father is certainly more supportive of this whole thing than I am. I'm just happy it's halfway over with, and that come September I'll be getting my son back."

The thought of returning home made my stomach a bit sick. "How's Dad feeling?"

My father had been battling cancer for several years. He was always certain that one of these days he'd succumb to it. Prior to my trip, he'd made me promise I would carry on our family name. Since I was his only child, if I were not to marry and procreate, the Covington name would end with me. He'd always indicated he wished to see me married with a child before he died. *No pressure or anything.*

"Dad's been pretty good lately," my mother reported.

"I'm happy to hear that."

"Do you want to talk to him?"

"Not if he's resting. Just tell him I love him."

"He's eager to have you back as well. I think not having this time to train you on the ins and outs of the business is stressful for him."

"That's not what he expressed to me the last time we spoke. I think it's stressful for *you.*"

"Well, I have a number of prospects I've been keeping my eye on, and I certainly can't guarantee they'll be able to wait around forever."

Prospects. My mother's term for women qualified to marry me based on their prestigious backgrounds.

There were two requirements of a member of the privileged upper class: Don't do anything to shame your family, and marry within your pedigree. While I'd never agreed to anything formally, deep down, I knew if I didn't marry someone my parents approved of, they'd make that person's life a living nightmare. And I didn't want that for anyone. So, I'd always hoped I'd miraculously fall in love with someone who happened to be acceptable in their eyes. It was hard enough connecting with someone, but to have the playing field whittled down to a mere handful of people deemed suitable made it nearly impossible to find true chemistry.

"Well, Mother, I'm not returning any earlier than summer's end, so losing opportunities with the boring women you've selected for me is a risk I'll have to take."

"Boring? Hardly."

"Has it ever worked out when you've chosen someone for me before?"

She paused. "I'm trying to help."

"Exactly. Look...I appreciate your efforts, but—"

"Whatever you do, make sure the shenanigans you're up to out there don't land you in irreversible trouble. Don't dip your pen in the wrong ink, if you know what I'm saying."

"I haven't dipped my pen in a while, so no worries, and when I do, I'm careful."

"You'd better be," she warned.

Unlike my cousin, I'd only slept with one woman on this trip. She was someone I'd met in a bar when we were in L.A., and while there was physical attraction, there was nothing special about it. When I was younger, I'd been perfectly fine with meaningless encounters. But at twenty-eight, I found myself needing to be intellectually stimulated, as well as sexually aroused. That combination was hard to come by.

"I'll let you get going, Mum."

"Well, this was a quick conversation. But I suppose I should count myself lucky that you called in the first place."

"Give Dad a hug for me."

"Kiss that nephew of mine, too. What is Sigmund up to tonight?"

"You probably don't want to know."

"Likely not."

"Bye, Mother."

"Goodbye, my love."

As the evening wore on, I found myself unable to shake what had happened earlier. It was rare that someone captivated me the way Felicity had. And her rejection *was* a bit of a blow to my ego.

I had the lights off in the living room as I sat on the couch and looked out toward the moon over the bay. I grabbed my laptop off the coffee table and typed:

Felicity Dunleavy - Harvard

A link to a video popped up as the first result of my search. It was titled *Harvard Polar Plunge: Nutsack.*

Well, that certainly had my attention.

It was some kind of event for charity where people took off their clothes in the middle of winter and jumped into freezing cold water.

Curious as to why it had come up, I pressed play. Several men and women emerged from a choppy ocean. It only took a few seconds before I spotted her. Felicity wore a red, one-piece swimsuit, and rubbed her hands over her freckled arms as she shivered. Her long hair was wet and stuck to her body.

A voice from behind a microphone asked, "How do you feel?"

Felicity's teeth chattered. "How do you think I feel? I'm freezing my nutsack off!" Then her eyes widened in a panic. "Wait, am I live on TV?"

The camera immediately cut back to two television personalities at a news desk who were trying to compose themselves. One of them snorted before straightening her papers and thanking the reporter for the story.

And then the video ended.

I read the description under the title.

Harvard student Felicity Dunleavy proclaiming, "I'm freezing my nutsack off" on a local Boston TV station after the college's Polar Plunge charity event. The original video went viral with almost ten-million hits.

This particular version of the clip had seventy-five thousand views.

I spent the next several minutes re-watching it, and each time was funnier than the last. My favorite part was the shocked expression on her adorable face when she realized she'd just said *nutsack* on live television.

It was too bad she wanted nothing to do with me, because this video made me want to hang out with her again. I shook my head, forcing myself to close the laptop. I eventually nodded off, counting freckles in my head instead of sheep.

A week later, I'd somehow let my cousin convince me to go on a double date at a local bistro. No part of me wanted to go out with someone I'd never met before, but I had been a bit of a recluse since arriving in Narragansett and figured it would do me good to at least get out of the house.

When we arrived at Jane's by the Water, Sigmund's raven-haired date, Shiva, and her blond friend, Melanie, were already waiting at a table in the corner. There was nothing wrong with the person who'd been assigned to me tonight, but she looked like any other girl. Nothing stood out, nothing made me *not* want to turn around and head right back home.

"It's so great to meet you, Leo." Melanie smiled as she stood from her chair.

"Likewise." I took her hand and kissed her lightly on both cheeks before sitting down.

"Sig's told me so much about you," Shiva said. "Glad we could finally get you to come out."

"I can only imagine what he's said."

Sigmund patted my shoulder. "All good things, of course. And I agree, it's nice of you to grace us with your presence. One can only hibernate for so long."

"This place has really good food," Melanie said, her eyes wide with excitement.

"Glad to hear." I placed the cloth napkin on my lap. "While Sigmund here is a pretty good cook, it'll be a nice change to sample some of the local delicacies."

The conversation over the next several minutes was stale at best. A busboy brought some waters and assured us our waitress would be with us shortly.

Then from the corner of my eye, I spotted her. And suddenly my night became a lot more interesting.

Felicity. What the hell is she doing here?

She wore a white, collared shirt and a black smock. *She works here?* Narragansett was clearly a small world.

Felicity seemed tense, whispering to herself as if she were memorizing something. Then she began walking in our direction.

When her eyes met mine, she looked like she'd seen a ghost. "What are you doing here?"

"Dining out?" I smiled.

"Oh, of course." She shook her head. "That was a dumb question."

"I suppose I should ask what *you're* doing here...but it seems you got the job you were looking for?"

"Yeah." She licked her lips. "It's my first night, actually."

"Well, lucky to have caught you, then."

Flipping back a piece of paper on her pad, she said, "I'm still learning the ropes, so bear with me."

"Take your time," I said, my eyes getting lost in hers for a moment.

My cousin took it upon himself to introduce Felicity to the table.

"Felicity, this is Shiva." He pointed to my date, sitting across from me. "And that's Melanie."

She nodded toward both women. "Good to meet you."

"Felicity is our neighbor across the bay," Sigmund said.

"You grew up in Narragansett?" Shiva asked.

"Yes," Felicity answered.

"We're from Warwick."

"Ah." Felicity moved a piece of hair behind her ear. "They have a nice...mall over there." She took a pen out of her pocket, but it slipped out of her hands. She bent to pick it up and said, "Anyway, have you all decided what you'd like to order?" She shut her eyes as if she'd made a mistake. "Actually, can I start you off with anything to drink?" She whispered, "I forgot I was supposed to ask that first."

"I take it you've never waitressed before," Sigmund cracked.

"How did you know?"

"Wild guess." He smirked.

She took our drink orders and returned about ten minutes later.

"Are you ready to order?" she asked.

Everyone nodded but me.

Wanting to prolong her presence at the table, I asked, "What do you recommend to eat here?"

She breathed out, as if my question caused her stress. "It's my first night, so I don't really have the expertise to make a recommendation yet. But I did hear someone say the red snapper tacos are good."

As she made her way around the table, taking the orders of our dates first, I couldn't help but notice how anxious she continued to seem, tapping her pen and bouncing her leg. I couldn't figure out if it had to do with this being her first night, or whether seeing me made her uneasy.

But I did know that my "date" didn't hold a candle to the fiery redhead in all her freckled glory before me. Seeing her tonight certainly wasn't going to help my efforts to forget about her.

Felicity's voice startled me. "And you?"

"Hmm?"

"What would you like?"

You, I wanted to say. *I fucking want you. Time with you. Time to get to know you, to count the freckles*. But I was pretty sure admitting that wouldn't go off too well.

"I'll have the snapper tacos, since you've heard good things. I prefer not to take my chances, although sometimes taking a chance might be worth it—just not with food."

Her eyes landed on mine and stayed there for a few seconds. My cryptic message might have gotten through to her.

She left the table to put in our orders, and immediately I yearned for her return, all the while pretending to be somewhat interested in what Melanie had to say about her job as a schoolteacher. My eyes kept wandering the room, waiting for any glimpse of Felicity as she made her way in and out of the kitchen in the distance.

Finally, she approached us, carrying a gigantic circular tray that I assumed held our food.

Once she arrived, her hands seemed a bit shaky; she was most definitely still on edge as she placed the hot dishes in front of each of us.

When she got to mine, though, somehow the tacos slipped off the plate—and right into my lap. I looked down to find a hot mess of red sauce saturating my crotch. And then came the burn.

Hot.

Hot.

Hot.

Sigmund broke out into hysterical laughter. "Not exactly the fire crotch you wished for from her, is it?" he whispered.

CHAPTER 4
Felicity

Track 4: "Rock the Boat" by Aaliyah

My heart raced. "Oh my God. I'm so sorry." Instinctively, I grabbed a cloth napkin and began wiping his lap. When it hit me how inappropriate that was, I whipped my hand away.

"Felicity, it's really all right."

Before Leo could say anything more, I ran to the kitchen and grabbed a towel. Taking it over to the sink, I wet it and added some dish soap.

"Gino, I'm going to need another order of the snapper tacos. The last one accidentally fell...onto someone. I'm so sorry."

The chef didn't look too happy, but what choice did I have but to ask him?

I took the wet cloth back to Leo's table and handed it to him. "Again, I'm so sorry."

"No need to apologize. It was funny, actually," he said, placing his hand gently on my wrist.

The contact sent an unexpected blast of arousal through me. "It's not funny to me." I pulled my wrist away. "I've put in another order. And it's on me. Not on you this time. By *on me*, I mean I'll cover the cost."

"Don't be ridiculous."

I walked away again before he could say anything further.

When I returned to the kitchen, I took a few moments to compose myself before Gino announced the replacement snapper tacos were ready. Sweating, I took the plate off the counter and headed back into the dining room.

Placing the plate down carefully in front of Leo, I refused to make eye contact with him, instead looking over at a smirking Sig.

The rest of the evening, I did my best to avoid the table of doom altogether. I suppose that made me a terrible waitress, but I couldn't risk making an even bigger fool of myself. Sometimes when I'd glance over at them, I'd notice Leo's eyes on me. He must have felt sorry for my pathetic ass tonight. Yes, this was my first shift, but I was mostly nervous because I hadn't been able to stop thinking about him since he'd asked me out that day at his house. And now, seeing him on a date with a gorgeous girl was jarring. But that's the way it goes, right? You snooze, you lose.

The following morning at breakfast, Mrs. Angelini seemed to sense that something was bothering me.

"Is everything okay, Felicity?"

I put my coffee mug down. "Why do you ask?"

"You haven't said a word all morning. How did your first night at the restaurant go?"

"Oh." I shook my head. "It was...weird."

"Why is that?"

"You know the neighbors across the bay? They dined at Jane's last night."

"The handsome boys from Britain? What's wrong with that?"

"Well, for one, I dropped a hot plate of tacos on Leo's crotch."

Her mouth dropped. "You what?"

"Yeah. It was a total accident, but nevertheless awful. I ordered him a replacement and left the tacos off their bill, but after they'd gone, there was a mound of cash on the table. They left me a huge tip."

"That doesn't sound like a bad thing."

"It's not. But..."

Mrs. Angelini's brow furrowed. "Did something happen when you went over there for tea the other day? You never filled me in. I feel like I'm missing part of the story."

I exhaled. "They were on a double date last night with two gorgeous women. It threw me off, particularly because Leo asked *me* out that day at their house."

She frowned. "So, you agreed to go out with him, and now he's dating someone else? The nerve!"

"No, no. That's not it. I told him I wasn't interested."

Her eyes narrowed. "You did?"

I hesitated. "I find him extremely attractive and charismatic. But I don't think it's a good idea to get involved

43

with someone who's only on this side of the Atlantic for a few months. That would be a recipe for disaster."

"But he's not looking to get involved. He just wants to have some fun."

Her response shocked me a little. It also made me doubt again whether I'd made the right decision.

"That's not my thing."

"Fun isn't your thing?" She chuckled.

"I like...fun. Just not with charming men who are leaving the country."

"That's fair. You're trying to protect yourself. I understand." She got up to pour herself another cup of coffee, then looked back at me. "You know, one of the biggest regrets I have about my youth is that I always played it safe. Henry was the best thing that ever happened to me, but I always wished I'd had a bit more fun before getting married."

"You think I should've said yes to him, even though it can't go anywhere?"

She stirred her java. "I do see your point in telling him no, and I certainly don't want you to get hurt. But I also recognize that you take life very seriously—too seriously for someone your age." She tapped the spoon. "You've hidden behind your schoolwork and other obligatory things for as long as I've known you. But you're only young once. This is the time in your life to make memories you can look back on when you're old like me." Returning to her seat, she said, "You have plenty of years to worry about monogamy and stability."

"You're not making me feel any better."

"I didn't mean to make you feel bad about your decision. I just want to see you have some fun. That's all.

You deserve it, Felicity. You've worked so hard. And you're about to embark on law school, where I'm sure you'll bury yourself in the books for another few years. Before you know it, your twenties will have flashed before your eyes. So maybe take this summer to let go a little."

My head felt like it was spinning. "I appreciate the advice."

After breakfast, I continued thinking about everything she'd said as I retreated to my room to organize my June planner. I was a total planner nerd, collecting various notebooks and stickers to organize my time. When I looked at some of the entries for this month, it hit me that there was not a single "fun" thing. Every item listed was some obligatory thing I needed to get done before leaving at the end of the summer: doctors' appointments I needed to get in, items for school I needed to purchase. This only supported Mrs. Angelini's argument.

I closed the planner and shoved it in my drawer, deciding to go outside and get some sun. I was fair-skinned and needed lots of protection, but I tried to make a point of getting at least fifteen minutes of good sunlight each day for the vitamin D.

Grabbing a can of seltzer from the fridge, I headed out back and planted myself in one of the Adirondack chairs. After a few minutes, I noticed something moving toward me in the distance. It was a boat, and with every second, it came closer to my side of the bay. I walked over to the edge of the water.

The boat was now close enough that I could see the driver. He waved. *Oh my God.* My heart accelerated. It was Leo driving this boat toward me.

"What are you doing?" I asked as he docked.

"What does it look like I'm doing?" He laughed.

"Did you buy this thing?"

"It's a summer rental."

"It's really nice."

"Well, I'm happy you think so, because I was hoping you'd want to take a ride with me, show me that place where you get those clams... What are they called again?"

"Quahogs."

"That's right." He scratched his chin. "I've convinced Sigmund that we should have something like a clam bake tonight. I was going to buy some lobsters from the food shop, but I thought fresh-caught clams would be a nice addition. What do you say?"

I rubbed my chin.

He seemed to sense my hesitation. "I don't have an ulterior motive here, Felicity, in case that's worrying you. You made it very clear that you weren't interested. I'm just looking to explore Narragansett a little. I think you'd make a fantastic companion, but I understand if you're busy."

He looked so adorable with that hopeful smile and the sun shining on his gorgeous, light brown hair that looked almost dark blond in the sun. My walls began to break down. He'd rented a gosh darn boat—an expensive one—to go "exploring" with me. There was no way I could say no.

"You know you can't go clamming without rakes and stuff, right?"

"This is the part where I show how clueless I am despite my attempt at seeming nautical. I've never driven a boat before this. I got a temporary certificate to operate it.

I've also never fished for anything other than information in my life. You're gonna have to help me out."

I pointed behind me. "Well, I just so happen to have rakes and shovels in the garage."

"Shovels? Are we burying a dead body, too?" He winked.

"No. But you're about to learn how to dig for clams from an expert. I sometimes use my feet, but I think I should teach you with equipment."

"It's my lucky day." Leo smiled.

"I'll be right back."

Chills ran down my spine as I entered the house on my way to the garage on the opposite side.

Mrs. Angelini stopped me in the kitchen. "Is that the Brit in the boat?"

"Yeah. He wants to go clamming."

She smiled knowingly. "Sure, he does."

I shrugged. "It's just clamming."

"Sure, it is."

My face felt hot as I kept walking. "Gonna go grab the rakes and shovels."

She called after me. "Have fun, sweetheart."

After I brought out the supplies, Leo helped me board before he started up the boat and began to drive. I'd expected him to go a lot faster.

"Is there a reason you're going so slow?" I asked.

"I guess I figured boating was somewhat...leisurely."

"No." I shook my head. "We have work to do. Let me at the wheel."

Seeming amused, Leo grinned as he stepped aside.

I moved the throttle and we took off at warp speed, our hair blowing in the wind as mists of water sprayed us.

He shouted over the sound of the motor. "Apparently I'm only equipped to operate paddle boats."

"It's okay, newbie," I yelled.

His teeth gleamed in the sunlight as he smiled wide. He was almost painfully handsome.

It had been a long time since I'd driven on the water. Boating was a popular pastime here, but neither Mrs. Angelini nor I owned a boat. So the only time I went out on the water was when a friend invited me or when Mrs. Angelini's brother drove his boat from Newport to visit us and go clamming. He sometimes let me drive it. The rakes and other tools were technically his.

When we arrived at the part of the bay where I normally dug for clams, Leo and I docked the boat and got out.

"You're going to need to roll up your pants," I said.

"But we just met," he teased.

That made me think how odd it was that I'd already seen him in the buff. That felt wrong. But maybe that's why I never stopped blushing around him. The memory of his glorious physique was never far from my mind. And right now, in his dark jeans, his ass looked just as good as it had the day I saw him naked. Leo's T-shirt was drenched from the spray of water that continually hit us on the ride here. The wet, white fabric clung to him, allowing me a clear outline of the sculpted chest underneath.

We started out in the water, digging for quahogs with the larger rakes.

"What is that thing?" he asked, looking down at the green plastic tool I held. It had a hole in the center.

"This is what we use to measure the size."

"Interesting." He smirked.

It looked kind of like a mini glory hole. But I wasn't going to point that out.

"We have to hold our quahogs up to it, and if one of them slips through, it's too small to keep. It's actually illegal to take those."

"Really. Well, you learn something new every day. I would've grabbed them all," he said.

"No. That would be like kidnapping babies. And there's a hefty fine if someone catches you."

We weren't having much luck in the water, so we moved over to the sand.

"You don't want to dig too deep," I said. "Five to eight inches...anything beyond that we won't find anything. And only lightly move the sand around, otherwise you can murder the clam if you break the shell."

"And they said this was fun and stress free."

"You'll get the hang of it. Just watch me."

"Got it," he said, though he kept unknowingly doing what I'd told him not to.

"These over here are too small," I said. "Let's move to a different spot. But we have to put the sand back first to help them survive."

After moving to a different location, we finally ran into some luck.

"We hit the motherlode here!" I announced. "It's a honey hole."

He scrunched his nose. "A...honey hole?"

"Yeah. A sweet spot. A honey hole. That's what Mrs. Angelini's brother, Paul, calls it when you find a bunch of clams all convening together. Pretty sure he made up that name."

"I love it." Leo grinned.

About an hour into our adventure, Leo was finally getting the hang of things. Before I knew it, we'd filled an entire bucket with clams.

After our work was done, we took some time to relax on the sand.

Leo rested his arm on the top of the bucket. "That was a lot of work, but it was worth it."

"Yeah, I like that it takes my mind off stuff when I get into it."

"What's on your mind? Something stressing you out?"

Should I be honest? I laughed. "You."

His eyes went wide. "Me?"

"A little. Yeah," I admitted. "Last night...was weird."

"Ah." He nodded. "Let's talk about that. I wasn't going to bring it up, but since you did..."

I shrugged. "I don't know what to say about it. I guess I was nervous because I wasn't expecting to see you, and then the fact that you were on a date was awkward, for some reason."

"It was awkward for me, too," he said.

"Running into me?"

"No. The date. I had no desire to go, but I gave in to my cousin's prodding."

I blinked. "You're not seeing her again, or...?"

He shook his head. "I'm not interested in her."

"I would imagine she's disappointed, then."

"I don't know. And I don't really care." His eyes pierced mine.

"I lied to you the other day when I said I wasn't interested in going out with you," I admitted after a moment. "My rejecting you had nothing to do with a lack of interest. I just have a bad habit of avoiding things that come with risk. I don't want to grow to like you and then have to deal with you leaving and all that. So I said no, even though I wanted to say yes."

Leo smiled. "Thank you for your honesty. I understand completely." He threw a rock toward the water. "And now I'm going to be honest with you and admit that my renting this boat had nothing to do with wanting clams for dinner." He turned to me. "I don't even know what they taste like. I just wanted an excuse to see you again."

"Well, this was a lot of work for someone who didn't even want clams," I teased.

"I suppose. But without this guise, I would've had to admit right off the bat that I couldn't stop thinking about you. I wasn't sure you wanted to hear that."

Rubbing my bare feet into the sand, I asked, "Who *are* you, Leo?"

"How do you mean?"

"I mean…Sig alluded to the fact that you're someone important. Is it just based on money, or is there something more you're not telling me?"

For the first time since I'd met him, I noticed a look of true discomfort on Leo's face.

"My father is a duke. The sixth Duke of Westfordshire," he finally said. "It's a title he inherited from his father, the fifth Duke. As the only child, I'll inherit it from my father someday as well and become the seventh Duke of Westfordshire. Along with that title comes ownership and control of my family's vast estate."

Wow. Okay. "You're a royal?"

"No. Not a royal. We're more like landowning, rich pricks."

"Oh my Lord…"

"Literally."

"Jesus, you're right." I covered my face. "Oh my Lord, literally."

"Lord Covington, yeah. But please never call me that." He chuckled.

I blew a breath up into my hair. "This is definitely bigger than I imagined."

"It's not something I wanted to advertise the second we met. I much prefer people to see who I am beyond all that. That's just not possible back home. And your shocked reaction only proves my point—once people know, they see me differently. Spoiled and entitled, perhaps?"

"I'm sorry my reaction made you uncomfortable. I didn't mean to give you the impression that I see you differently. I swear, I don't."

"I just want to forget about it for a while. That's all. I'm not trying to hide anything. Talking about it takes away the point of this reprieve. But you have every right to ask who I am."

Suddenly, I felt oddly bonded to him. "I can relate to wanting to forget. It's like…when I tell people I've been on my own most of my life, they definitely see me differently. There are so many preconceived notions about growing up in the foster-care system. They assume I must be troubled or unstable in some way because I didn't have a solid family foundation. Because of those weird reactions, I prefer not telling people, too. But you can't exactly lie when people ask, you know?"

"Yep."

"Thank you for your honesty," I said. "You could've totally lied to me or downplayed it, and I would never have known the difference."

"You can ask me anything, Felicity. I'll always be honest."

When our eyes locked, I felt an urge to escape. Standing up, I brushed my butt off. "Well, we should probably take our catch back."

He got up as well. "Will you come over for dinner?"

He watched me carefully as I struggled with my answer.

"I can see the wheels turning in your head," he said. "You're not sure whether to say yes. It won't technically be a date, if that makes you feel better. My arse of a cousin will be there to ruin any chance of privacy. It's just dinner, because quite frankly, there would be no clams without you, and you should at least get to enjoy the fruits of your labor."

When he put it that way, it was hard to say no.

"Okay. Just dinner. I can live with that."

He lifted the heavy bucket. "Are you driving back, or shall I?"

"Well, if we want to make it for dinner before nightfall, I probably should take the wheel, Grandma."

Leo shut his eyes. "Ouch."

After spending the afternoon with Leo, I felt much more comfortable around him than before. He'd shown me his vulnerable side today, and that made it hard to be afraid of him. I was mainly afraid of my own feelings. But ultimately, I wanted to enjoy tonight and not analyze it. So that was the choice I made.

I stopped the vessel on my side of the bay, and Leo got out to help me return the clamming tools to the garage.

Back out by the boat, he said, "How about eight for dinner?"

"That works."

"Shall I pick you up in the boat, or will you drive?"

"I can handle the drive over."

He winked. "See you then, love."

I stood and watched as he turned on the boat and made his way back across the bay to his house. As he disappeared into the distance, a little panic set in. I could feel my heart beating out of my chest. I wanted to tell it to quiet down, to not get its hopes up about a man it couldn't have. But I knew I had little control over what caused it to beat in such a way. It would probably beat harder the more I tried to stop it.

My legs felt wobbly as I made my way back into the house, my body still used to being on the choppy boat, apparently. Or maybe this insane attraction to Leo caused the weakness in my legs.

Mrs. Angelini came downstairs when she heard me enter.

"Well, you were certainly gone long enough."

"Yeah. We got a ton of clams. I'm going over to their house tonight for dinner."

"Good." She smiled. "I'm glad you're letting go a little."

I had no clue what to wear. Bailey and I were supposed to go shopping soon, but we hadn't had a chance yet.

"Mrs. Angelini?"

She turned around. "Yeah?"

"I need your help. I want to look nice for this dinner tonight, but I have nothing but jeans and T-shirts in my closet. I don't want to wear the same long skirt I did when I went over there last time. His cousin called me Mary Poppins…"

"He what?" She laughed.

"Yeah. But I kind of deserved it." I shrugged. "Anyway, I want to wear something nice—not too dressy, but not as frumpy as jeans and a T-shirt."

"I would let you borrow something of mine, but I'm far too portly." She looked over at the clock. "I have a better idea. My friend Helena owns the boutique in town. It closes pretty early. We don't have much time, but I bet she'd keep it open a little later for us. We'll make sure we get you something that accentuates your beauty but isn't over the top."

I never asked her for much, but when I did, Mrs. Angelini always came through. I tried to block the emotions that bubbled inside of me right now, because her coming to my rescue yet again reminded me of exactly something a mother would do.

CHAPTER 5

Leo

Track 5: "The Lady in Red" by Chris de Burgh

Carrying the heavy bucket into the house, I said, "Please tell me you know how to cook clams."

Sigmund narrowed his eyes. "What in God's name did you bring back here?"

"Felicity and I took my boat out to dig for these."

"*Your* boat?"

"Yeah. Have a look outside. It arrived while you were out earlier. A rental, of course."

"Have you lost your mind?"

"Maybe." I smiled. "Yeah."

"When have you ever touched a boat in your life, aside from stepping onto your father's yacht?"

"This time here in Narragansett is all about exploring new things, Sigmund."

"And I'm sure exploring *the water* was exactly what you were aiming for with this boat today, eh?"

"We had a nice time."

"I was sort of hoping you'd forget about her after she dumped that fish on your crotch and made a mockery of our date last night."

"The only mockery about that date was the brain-dead conversation."

"Okay, so now what? I'm roped into Operation Woo Carrot Top by having to learn how to cook these things?"

"You're the cook. It's what you do. Figure something out that won't embarrass me."

"You're going to owe me big time for this."

I arched my brow. "I suppose footing the bill for this entire trip counts for nothing, then?"

"Solid point."

"I also told her we were having lobster."

"So I'm supposed to make an entire seafood feast for you both?"

"I'll head out and get the lobsters. You figure out what to do with these clams."

After jetting to the shop and picking up three, one-pound lobsters, I returned to the house to find Sigmund had removed some of the clams from their shells and was cutting them into tiny pieces. He'd texted me to pick up some Portuguese sausage as well.

"What are you doing slicing them? I thought we were supposed to crack them open and eat them that way?"

"Is that what you'd like to do to the redhead? Split her wide open and eat her?" He snickered.

"Can you please stop?"

"Why are my innuendos suddenly bothering you so much?"

"Because my attraction to her has nothing to do with sex." That was partly a lie. "I mean, I *am* sexually attracted

57

to her, but it's not *all* about that." I wiped sweat off my forehead. "Anyway, answer my question. What the hell are you doing to those clams? Why aren't they in the shells? You'd better not be ruining them."

"This is a recipe called stuffies. I figured it was appropriate considering you'd like to stuff Pippi Longstocking."

I rolled my eyes. "Seriously, what are you stuffing?"

"Relax. It's why I had you buy the sausage."

"Please tell me the sausage wasn't some kind of sick sexual thing, too?"

"No, you bloody wanker. Who's the one with the dirty mind now?"

"Clearly I don't trust you."

"The sausage will be mixed with the clams and some breadcrumbs, then put back in the shells and baked. It's apparently quite a popular way of making them, despite your assumption that I'm working to taunt you or sabotage your dinner."

I relaxed a little. I should have more confidence in him. The one thing he rarely screwed up was food.

Looking over at the clock, I realized there wasn't much time before Felicity would arrive at eight. My clothing still smelled like the salty ocean from our jaunt earlier today. Leaving Sigmund in the kitchen, I went upstairs to shower and get dressed.

When I returned downstairs, the counters were empty. "Where's the food?"

"Will you relax? I didn't ruin anything. The stuffies are in the oven. And the lobsters are boiling. Everything is under control—except you. Calm your balls."

"Also, can you not be an arse to her tonight? Is that too much to ask?"

"I can't promise I won't slip up. But I'll try. Unless you'd prefer I leave altogether?"

"No. I told her we would be getting together as a group. I don't want to freak her out. This isn't supposed to be a date."

"Ah. I see what you're doing. Very clever. Reel her in by making her believe you're no longer interested in dating her, all while charming her slowly."

The doorbell rang.

"That's her now. Turn on your manners button."

He pressed repeatedly on his chest. "Bugger. It must be stuck. Looks like you're out of luck."

I sighed and went to the front door. When I opened it, the breath nearly left my body.

Her flaming hair was down, styled into long, loose tendrils. She wore a bright red dress that wasn't formal, but rather made of thin cotton with a tie around her neck. It was short, simple, and sexy as all hell, accentuating her long legs. Her lips were painted a matching shade of red. This was a different look for her, but I loved it. My favorite part was the ability to see for the first time just how far the freckles traveled down her chest.

"Felicity, you look…" I cleared my throat. "Incredible."

"Thank you. I thought it might be nice if I actually dressed up for once. You know, not quite Mary Poppins, not quite tomboy—somewhere in the middle."

"You look lovely no matter how you're dressed. But you're particularly stunning tonight." I shook my head, realizing I'd been so mesmerized I hadn't invited her inside. "Come in. Come in."

As she entered the foyer, she took a deep breath. "Something smells good."

"He's making...stuffies?"

"Oh yes. Good choice."

The fact that she'd heard of them brought me relief.

When we entered the kitchen, my cousin's eyes widened. "Felicity, you look absolutely gorgeous."

"Why, thank you. I think that might be the first nice thing you've said to me."

"Well, it's deserved."

His compliment irked me. And I didn't like the way he was looking at her now, either—like he was finally seeing what I had been all this time. But it didn't matter to me whether she was in a red dress or a baggy T-shirt; she was beautiful.

"What can I get you to drink?" I asked.

"Surprise me." She smiled.

Back home, they always served white wine with seafood, so I figured that might be the best choice for this evening. Then I remembered the bottle of Dom Pérignon chilling and opted to open that instead. After preparing two flutes, I handed her one and watched as she took a sip. When she licked her lips, I swore my cock moved.

"Mmm... Good choice. I love champagne. Thank you."

Sigmund opened the oven and placed the tray of stuffed clam shells on the counter. I had to admit, they looked and smelled delicious.

Felicity leaned her head over the tray. "Had you ever made stuffies before, Sig?"

"This was my first time."

"Impressive."

"If food is the way to your heart, love, my cousin doesn't stand a chance." He laughed.

She patted me on the shoulder. "Well, he's a great boat captain. At least he has that."

I cleared my throat. "What she really means to say is, I put in a good effort before she had to take the wheel from me because I was driving it like Nan."

She smiled from behind her champagne. I loved her smile, especially when it was focused on me.

The voice in my head seemed to come out of nowhere. *"What are you doing?"* The answer was certainly: falling for someone I had no right to be. I just didn't know how to stop. I shooed the negative voice away.

Sigmund grabbed a beer from the fridge. "You know, it wouldn't kill you to set the table, Leo."

He was right. I should've at least offered to do that. I'd been a little distracted.

Felicity put her glass on the counter. "I can help."

"No, you're the guest. You'll do no such thing," I said.

She wouldn't listen and began rummaging through the cabinets for plates. We ended up setting the table together.

After we'd laid everything out and settled into our seats, Felicity looked around, as if we were missing something.

"Do you have...bibs?"

My cousin looked horrified. "Bibs? As in a baby bib? No. Afraid not."

"Yes. Lobster can be quite messy." She stood and disappeared into the kitchen before returning with three dishtowels.

She came around to my side of the table and tucked one of the towels into the top of my shirt before patting her hand over it gently. That simple touch stirred something in me.

She then handed the other towel to Sigmund, neglecting to place it on him. That pleased me to no end. My cousin ignored the towel and started eating without it.

A few minutes into dinner, it was clear Felicity was no stranger to cracking open lobster with precision, and she was certainly unafraid to make a mess.

She sucked juice out of one of the shells. "This is amazing. Thank you. It's not every day I get to have lobster. This is a special treat."

"I would've thought you got to have it all of the time, considering it's a local delicacy," I said.

She shook her head. "Mrs. Angelini is allergic to seafood. Which is incredibly ironic, since her husband owned a chain of seafood restaurants before he died. But we never have lobster, and I don't typically get it when I'm on my own, since it's quite expensive."

Her words were a wake-up call. Not everyone could afford the luxury of eating whatever they wanted, whenever they wanted. *You idiot, Leo.* She probably saw me as coming from another planet.

"I'm sorry. That was stupid of me to say. Of course, lobster is expensive."

"Not stupid at all. Mrs. Angelini is wealthy. She would buy me lobster anytime I wanted, if I asked. But I wouldn't enjoy having it in front of her. I also try not to take advantage of her generosity. She tries to give me money for school, but I don't feel like she should have to pay for that. I've always insisted on paying my own way. It makes me feel more secure, knowing I can."

I nodded. "I'm sure most people *would* take advantage."

"I don't get too comfortable anywhere. Once you start depending on someone and they're gone—then what? You need to be able to fend for yourself."

My chest felt tight as I realized the deeper meaning behind her not wanting to accept help. The helpers in her life had always left her. That was what she was used to, and the reason she was so strong.

The mood soon lightened when a deluge of lobster juice shot out of Sigmund's shell and onto his three-hundred-dollar shirt.

"Bollocks!" He shouted as he looked down at himself.

"I'm not gonna say I told you so." Felicity laughed.

He pretended not to care, but the grumpy look on his face told me he regretted not covering up.

I spent the rest of dinner asking Felicity things I was curious about, such as what life was like at Harvard. I learned she'd been a member of the extreme Frisbee team there. She talked more about her plans to become a lawyer so she could use that opportunity to help people. She knew what she wanted and exactly how she was going to get there. I admired her desire for independence, but also realized her apparent need for no one else came from a place of self-protection.

I cringed when she turned the tables on me.

"So, enough about me," she said. "Tell me more about your situation back home in England. What's it like where you live?"

"The countryside is beautiful, but I escape to London a fair amount on the weekends. Before I left to come here, my days were spent shadowing my father, for the most part."

"You went to college, right?"

Sigmund snorted, all too amused by her question. "I can see how you might have doubted that."

She turned to him. "I didn't mean that to be an insult. He just never mentioned it, and I didn't want to assume."

"Yes, I did go to university." I glared at Sigmund. "Despite the fact that many things are handed to someone in my position, I got my master's degree from London Business School."

"Nice." She tilted her head. "How many properties does your father own?"

"Too many to count, honestly."

"Half of England is owned by less than one percent of the population," Sigmund explained.

"God, that's a tremendous amount of responsibility, and a lot of pressure, I'm sure."

"It's also why half of the eligible women in our neck of the woods try to dig their claws into him," my cousin added.

"And here I was thinking it was just my looks," I said, growing angrier by the second. "Thank you for the newsflash, although it wasn't necessary."

"Actually, I'm a little interested in knowing about all that," Felicity said, fidgeting in her seat. "Is there a lineup of debutantes waiting in the wings for you back home or something?"

"He has to marry someone his parents deem suitable," Sigmund offered before taking a sip of his beer.

Why the fuck would he bring this up right now?

Her expression darkened. "Like an arranged marriage?"

"No," I clarified before my cousin could say another word. "Not an arranged marriage. I would never go for that. Ultimately, the decision is mine. But the expectation has always been that I would marry someone from a similar background."

"What happens if you don't?"

Sigmund chuckled. "His parents would probably disown him."

"That's not true," I retorted.

He squinted. "Really?"

I knew why he was doing this. He'd been against my pursuing Felicity from the very beginning, and he was trying to derail things. Even if some of what he'd divulged was *partly* true, I'd hoped for a little time with her before she ran for the hills.

"Don't you have somewhere to be tonight?" I asked him.

"No, actually. No plans at all."

I glared at him.

After he took his plate into the kitchen, I picked up Felicity's, and then mine. "I'll be right back," I told her. "Can I get you more champagne?"

She shook her head, seeming a bit unnerved by our conversation. "No, thank you."

In the kitchen, I gritted my teeth and whispered, "Great job trying to scare her away."

"I'm doing you a favor. How is it fair to get her hopes up when you know damn well you don't have a future with her? Look at how she came here tonight. She's clearly dressed to impress and not exactly playing hard to get anymore."

"You don't have a right to manipulate things. I planned to be honest with her about my situation. But it wasn't your place to throw everything out there in the span of one dinner."

Felicity appeared, entering the room holding the tray of empty clam shells. From the concerned look on her face, I could tell she'd either heard everything we'd just said or suspected we'd been arguing.

"Please sit and relax," I said, holding my palm out. "I'll take care of that."

"It's okay," she insisted.

Together, we brought everything from the table into the kitchen in silence. After, we took turns washing our hands at the sink.

Handing her a towel, I said, "Let's go out back for a moment, shall we?"

"Sure."

I grabbed our champagne glasses, along with the bottle of Dom, and some strawberries from the fridge, and carried them outside.

"Are you okay?" she asked once we stepped onto the back deck.

"Sure." I placed everything on a table. "Why do you ask?"

"You seemed uncomfortable when I was asking about your life back home, particularly when Sig took it upon himself to speak for you. Why do you seem ashamed of who you are?"

"Because it's *not* who I am. Who I am has nothing to do with where I come from or the expectations placed upon me." My tone was harsher than I'd intended.

"I'm sorry. You're right. That was a dumb way to word it. What I meant was…you shouldn't feel like you have to hide anything just because your life is different than the norm. Most people would be quite impressed, actually."

"You're not most people, though, are you? None of that impresses you in the least. In fact, if anything, it's a deterrent in getting to know you better."

She stayed silent, neither confirming nor denying.

I exhaled. "The dilemma of my life has always been balancing what I want with what my family wants for me. The latter typically wins." I looked up at the starry sky. "I know I'm fortunate in many ways, but there are days when I wish I could just live a normal life, not have to take anyone else into account when it comes to my own happiness. With you today—out on that water—I was happier than I've been in a very long time." I shook my head. "Sorry. You didn't sign up to be my therapist tonight. I'm supposed to be entertaining you."

Felicity placed her hand on her chest. "Are you kidding? Out of all the brief times we've spent together, this moment is my favorite. Today I feel like I've gotten to experience the real you. The vulnerable side. Vulnerability is…sexy."

"Sexy, eh?" I laughed. "Should I start crying, then?"

"You don't need to go that far."

"Okay." I smiled.

Our eyes locked, and I wanted nothing more than to kiss her.

She shivered. "It's chillier tonight than I thought. I should've brought a sweater."

"Be right back." I ran inside and grabbed one of my jackets.

I returned to the deck and wrapped it around her shoulders.

"Thank you. That was very sweet."

"Well..." I grinned. "I wouldn't want you to freeze your nutsack off."

CHAPTER 6

Felicity

Track 6: "Blowing Kisses in the Wind" by Paula Abdul

I can't believe he knows about that. "You Googled me. Congratulations."

"The day you turned me down, I was feeling a bit low. That night, I missed looking at your face. So, yes. I went online, searched your name, and found that unexpected pot of gold."

"That's my one claim to fame."

"It was hysterical."

"Seriously, what is wrong with people? They have no lives. I mean, it was funny, but it wasn't *that* funny. To get millions of hits?"

"It wasn't just what you said. It was the freaking adorable look on your face when you realized you were on live television. It's also the fact you're beautiful. That's why it went viral."

"I don't see myself that way," I said. "I never have."

"That doesn't change the truth."

"I feel like I look different from everyone else. I mean, there are other people with red hair and freckles all over their body. But how many do you run into on a daily basis? Very few. We're a rare breed."

"Precisely. You're uniquely beautiful. But it's not just your skin and hair that set you apart. It's your eyes, the way they seem to pierce through everything with genuine wonder and interest. I can see the good in you just by looking into them. And you have so many features I love. Your nose has the slightest ridge in the center. Your lips and their natural red color, even when you're not wearing lipstick. And yes, the freckles. Don't get me started on them. They are my weakness."

I rolled my eyes, feeling my cheeks heat. "You're insane."

"I'm *insanely* attracted to you, yes."

His blunt admission caused my entire body to heat. I had to look down because it was too much—not just the way he was looking at me, but because I was incredibly attracted to him, too. Leo wasn't just handsome. He was scorching hot from head to toe. The more I looked at him, the more out of control I felt. The more I wanted him to kiss me. Every time my eyes landed on his full lips, I could feel my tongue buzz with the need to taste them.

"Did what I just say make you uncomfortable?"

Adjusting his jacket around my shoulders, I said, "It's not what you said about me. It's how you make me feel, how attracted I am to you, too. It's very mutual."

His breath seemed to hitch, and before he could respond, I decided I needed more champagne.

I reached for the bottle on the table. "Do you mind if I have some more of that?"

"Let me," he said as he poured. "Would you like a strawberry?"

"Sure." I immediately downed half my glass.

Instead of simply handing me one, Leo took a strawberry. With a glimmer in his eye, he placed it between his lips and spoke through his teeth. "Come get it."

Is he serious? My palms grew sweaty as I considered whether to go for it. I leaned in with a racing heart and carefully used my teeth to retrieve the strawberry. Our lips didn't even touch, but I could feel the heat of his erratic breaths, which sent a jolt through my body.

"Holy fuck. I didn't think you'd do it." He licked his lips.

As I chewed the berry, I looked down and wondered if I was losing my mind. Because that? What I just did? That was not like me at all. It was freaking erotic, though. Leo was so intoxicating that he impaired my judgment. I needed to be careful, because I was setting myself up to get hurt. Mrs. Angelini thought I should let go a little. But this night didn't feel like letting go. This felt like my feelings were becoming entangled with this man. I wasn't sure I was capable of just enjoying the present with someone who would inevitably be leaving.

It was all I could think about, even with the summer still ahead of us.

"How long do you plan to look down at your feet and not at me?" Leo asked.

Finally meeting his eyes, I shook my head. "I'm sorry. I don't know how to handle this. When I told Mrs. Angelini I had turned you down because I didn't think it was a good idea to go out with someone who would be leaving, she suggested that I let go, not worry so much about what might happen in the future. I decided to try that tonight. But I don't think it's my nature. Because as you're standing here in front of me, I'm supposed to be letting loose, and all I can think about is the fact that I'm already sad, and you haven't even left yet." I stared into my champagne. "I can't get out of my own head long enough to enjoy being with you."

"You're level-headed and practical. There's nothing wrong with that."

"There's nothing wrong with it, but it makes for a very boring life."

"You've graduated from Harvard, you're a master boat captain and fisherwoman, Frisbee player, not to mention a viral superstar—that's far from boring to me." He grinned.

I smiled. "You like me because I'm different than what you're used to."

His smile faded as his stare burned through me. "I like you because you're you. Not just how you look, but how you look at *me*. You see me as the person I am, not my title or social status or where I come from. But more than that, you're as intelligent and real as you are beautiful. God, Felicity, I've thought about little else since I met you." He continued to examine my face. "What are you thinking?"

"I'm thinking about some of the things Sig was saying in there, to be honest."

"All right." He swallowed. "What questions do you have?"

"So...say you told your parents you met a girl this summer in Rhode Island. You really like her. What would their reaction be?"

He scratched his chin. "You want the honest answer, I assume."

I nodded.

"They—my mother, in particular—would make my life very difficult. They want me in England, settled and focused on continuing my father's legacy, not focused on anyone outside of the bubble they live in."

I swallowed. "And hypothetically, if you met someone here in the States or from anywhere else, and took them home to England, that wouldn't be acceptable to them?"

A look of pain crossed his face. "They wouldn't be able to stop me, but they might make that person's life miserable. And I wouldn't subject someone I care about to all that. It wouldn't be fair. That's the answer. I can't change how *they* are, how they act, and what their expectations are."

Defeat washed over me. "I'm sorry if my questions are too intrusive. I mean, we've only been on one date..."

He smiled. "So this *is* a date?"

My eyes widened. "It wasn't supposed to be?"

"I'm teasing. I wasn't going to call it that because I didn't want to scare you. But I certainly intended it to be a date."

"Oh." I looked down at my shoes.

"Can I ask you something?" he asked.

"Sure." I looked up, straightening my posture.

"When was the last time you had a boyfriend?"

It seemed like forever. I finished the last of my champagne before setting the glass down. "My freshman year in college, I met a guy—Finn—who I dated for about a year. He ended up unable to handle the pressure of school and dropped out. He had some serious anxiety issues. And it sucked because I'd hoped I was reason enough for him to stay, but when someone has an internal struggle, there's nothing you can do sometimes. I never took it personally because I understood it for what it was. His leaving still sucked, though. I just ended up focusing even more on school after that. My sophomore year, I joined the Frisbee team and did everything I could to convince myself it was best to be alone. That's sort of where I still am."

"You never dated anyone else after?"

"No. I also had one serious boyfriend in high school, but we broke up before college. So, I've had two relationships. In the years since, I've gone out with guys here and there. But nothing that lasted beyond a couple of dates. Nothing that mattered, you know?"

"Nothing that mattered…" he muttered. "I can relate to that. I've been with my fair share of women. But I can't say any of them mattered." He took a few steps toward me. "I know we hardly know each other. But from the moment we met, somehow I knew you *mattered* to me, Felicity. Does that sound strange?"

"This whole thing has been a little strange." I laughed as I looked up at this striking man whom I would have assumed was unattainable were it not for the fact that he clearly liked me. "Not in a bad way. Just a different sort of experience. And I'm sorry if I turned this night into something too serious. We were supposed to be having fun."

"You're not crazy for thinking about the future. By that, I mean my leaving. It's not that far away. We could choose to ignore it or acknowledge it, but it doesn't change the fact that I'm not here forever. So, the bottom line is, you have every right to protect your heart, just as I have no right to toy with it. Tonight, at dinner, when you were talking about how you look at everyone in your life as a temporary player..." He paused, pointing to his chest. "It hit me hard. Because I don't want to be yet another person who comes into your life and leaves you hurt. The last thing I want to do is hurt you."

My stomach was in knots. "Yeah, so this situation sort of sucks, doesn't it?"

"I wasn't expecting this, to find someone here I truly wanted to get to know better, spend time with. That wasn't part of the plan." He closed his eyes briefly. "At the same time, I wish I'd met you at the very beginning of this journey and not the last leg."

I wanted so badly for him to lean in and kiss me. But I also hoped he didn't. Confusion tore through my heart as a soft evening breeze sent his delicious, masculine scent toward me. I felt like this moment of silence was a crossroads, one where I decided whether I'd escape getting my heart broken or dive headfirst into the fire. Ultimately, fear won out.

Say it. "I think it's best if we don't continue to see each other," I finally managed. "I feel something inside my chest whenever I'm with you. And it's telling me we'd better not take things any further."

He looked deeply into my eyes, then took my hand and placed it over his heart. "Feel that. I think we might be feeling the same thing."

His heart beat so fast against my hand.

"Wow," I whispered.

"That's what's happening almost any moment I'm with you. For that reason, I fear you might be right about this whole thing...as much as I don't want to face that."

I took my hand away and looked down at myself. "I was hoping this red dress would magically transform me into a carefree woman for a night."

"I don't want you to be anyone other than who you are, Felicity."

Every additional second made it more difficult to leave, but I knew it was the right thing to do.

"I think I should go home."

The disappointment on his face was clear. "I'm sorry this night turned awkward."

"It wasn't awkward. It was real. I appreciate your honesty so much. And dinner was amazing. Thank Sig for me."

When I started to walk away, he followed. "This is it, then? We won't see each other at all? Even just as friends?"

My eyes stung as I turned to face him. "I think it's easier if we don't."

He blinked like he was searching for an answer but couldn't find one.

We resumed walking in silence to the driveway where my car was parked.

"I have a favor to ask," he finally said.

"Okay..."

"I want to see you one more time before I leave—even if it's just for tea. I don't know offhand when you're leaving for school?"

"Probably the end of August."

"That's around the time we're leaving, too. We don't have an exact day. It's still up in the air. But would that be okay? To see each other once at the end of the summer?"

I didn't know how that was going to help, yet I didn't have the heart to say no. "Yeah. That will be okay." I smiled, looking down at my phone. "I just realized we don't even have each other's numbers."

"Well, who needs numbers when you have a boat to travel across the bay, right?"

"That's right. I'm just a ten-mile-an-hour boat ride away." I winked.

"Might be quicker if I swam, yeah?"

The tension in the air felt thicker by the second.

"May I?" He reached for my phone and entered his phone number. When he placed it back in my hand, he folded his fingers over mine. The warmth of that touch resonated throughout my body. I'd never been more terrified of someone kissing me in my life. I didn't want to know what that was like, if we were parting ways. It would haunt me. Yet I craved it as well.

But alas, instead of moving closer, he let go of my hand, and a coldness seeped in.

After I handed him back his jacket, I rushed to open my car door.

Leo looked morose as he stood and watched me enter.

I turned on the ignition and offered a simple wave. My heart clenched as Leo touched his hand to his mouth and blew me a slow and gentle kiss. *There it was*. The kiss I was sure he'd wanted to give me but chose not to. I would cherish it, even if it never physically reached my lips. It had reached my heart.

I knew I'd made the right decision, but as I drove away, I felt more and more unsettled and incomplete.

CHAPTER 7

Leo

Track 7: "Hello Again" by Neil Diamond

"Where's Little Red Riding Hood?" my cousin asked as I entered the house.

"She's gone."

"Gone? Where did she go?"

Feeling bitter, I gritted my teeth. "She went home. It's done. Your plan to scare her away worked. Are you happy now?"

His eyes widened in shock. "She left because of what I said at dinner?"

"Wasn't that your intent?" I shouted. "Laying out all of my dirty laundry to scare her away? She asked me to elaborate out there, and it led to a conversation about how feasible it really was for us to keep seeing each other if she'd only end up getting hurt by my leaving. She came to the conclusion that ending it before it started was best."

"And *you* don't think that's best?"

It likely *was* for the best. But right or wrong didn't change how I felt about her. "I was hoping for some time with her before the inevitable. Ultimately, I agreed with her decision. But none of this should have been influenced by anyone other than her and me."

"Well, I'm sorry. It wasn't my intent to make her leave."

Beyond pissed off, I moved past him and made my way up to my room. I knew we'd probably made the right decision not to pursue things, but it didn't *feel* right. How could I be so broken up over someone I barely knew? My gut told me I'd just let someone important go.

I couldn't let this deter me from enjoying the last of my respite here in the States because I needed to return to England with a clear head. Plain and simple, I needed to get over Felicity, whether I liked it or not.

Two weeks passed. Depending on how you looked at it, you could say I'd done a good job distracting myself—or you could say I'd gone insane.

Sigmund had just returned from a trip to the liquor store when he walked into the kitchen to find me practicing my new hobby.

He put the paper bag on the countertop. "What the hell are you doing?"

I pressed pause on the YouTube video. "Painting."

"I can see that, but why?"

The other night I'd come across some videos of a bloke named Bob Ross. Apparently, his painting tutorials were legendary. But I'd never heard of him. After an hour of watching him paint, I was transfixed by the movements of his brush and his simple instructions. I'd somehow convinced myself that I might be able to paint just as well under his tutelage. He made it look so easy. Yet when I tried to execute the steps myself, it didn't work out the way I'd imagined.

I stepped back and crossed my arms to get a look at my painting, which featured a number of green blotches that were supposed to be trees. "It's coming along, don't you think?"

"For a primary school art project, perhaps, yes. Is this what you do when I'm not home?"

"I've actually been practicing for days—just up in my room, not out here. But I needed a change of scenery. So I brought everything into the kitchen. Better lighting."

He looked over at the video. "Are you going to grow your hair into a giant puffball to match his as well?"

"I might."

"Whatever floats your boat, cousin. It's better than you moping around doing nothing at all. Only slightly better, might I add."

I'd been in a funk since the night Felicity and I decided not to see each other anymore. I hadn't seemed to be able to enjoy anything other than being alone and practicing my new hobby. I couldn't even categorize it as enjoyment, really. It was purely distraction. Sigmund had tried to get me to go out with him, but I had neither the interest nor the energy. For the first time in my life, I understood what depression felt like.

After he left me alone, I ripped open a bag of saltwater taffy and resumed my painting. That was the other odd habit I'd developed, an affinity for this chewy candy that seemed to be popular here and would likely rot my teeth in no time. Incidentally, it tasted nothing like salt water.

When my phone rang, I put down my brush to pick it up. Looking down at the number, I smiled.

"Grandmother," I answered.

"Leo, how are you, my boy?"

"I'm…" I paused, looked at my painting and laughed at myself for a moment.

Hesitating, I thought about whether or not to tell her the truth. Nan was the only person in this world I could open up to. Even if it wouldn't change anything, she was the one voice of reason and understanding in my entire family.

I finally settled on, "I've been better."

"Tell me what's wrong. Is this about a girl?"

I pulled on my hair as I paced. "I…met someone, yes. A very special, wildly intelligent, beautiful, and nonjudgmental person. But I decided not to pursue things, as it wouldn't be wise…for obvious reasons."

"You didn't tell your mother about this, did you?"

"Of course not."

"Good. You don't need the additional stress. What she doesn't know won't hurt her."

"Agreed."

"So, you know you made the right decision, but you can't stop thinking about this girl, I assume? Tell me about her."

I spent the next several minutes describing Felicity to my grandmother. At heart, my nan was a romantic.

"An orphan? Your mother would crucify that poor girl."

"That's one of the many reasons I have to move on."

"How much longer are you there?"

"The end of August was my plan."

"Would you consider another destination? Perhaps if you left town, it might be easier to forget her."

I'd thought about leaving Narragansett. Sigmund would certainly be all for it. But for some reason, I couldn't pull the trigger. We had already paid for our stay here through the end of the summer—not that money mattered if I truly wanted to leave.

"I have no desire to go anywhere else right now. It's peaceful here and—"

She finished my sentence. "You're not ready, because a part of you still wants to be near her."

I hesitated. "Maybe on a subconscious level. She agreed to see me one more time before I leave and before she moves away to law school."

"And you haven't run into her in the meantime?"

"I haven't left the house much—except to buy taffy and painting supplies."

"*Taffy* and painting?" She laughed. "What are you painting?"

I popped another piece of taffy into my mouth and chewed. "Happy little clouds."

"What?"

I chuckled. "Never mind, Nan."

"Well, that sounds like a strange existence, my dear. You need to give yourself a good, swift kick in the arse. I realize the pressure your parents have placed on you. And I don't entirely disagree that you have to follow through with your responsibility to carry on the Covington name and marry someone appropriate for that responsibility, someone who understands our world and can handle the stress. But I wouldn't be opposed to you doing whatever it took to be happy despite it all."

"I don't understand what you're getting at."

"As I said before, what your mother doesn't know won't hurt her. Someday you'll marry a woman your parents approve of. But what you do behind closed doors is your own business. Perhaps you can make an arrangement with someone—someone who may need to hide behind appearances as well."

"Are you suggesting I enter into a sham marriage someday and proceed to live my life the way I want otherwise?"

"I'm just saying...there are options. Not everything is black and white, certainly not in the world we come from."

While my grandmother's suggestion was interesting, to say the least, I ultimately concluded that she was crazy for suggesting such a thing. It would be difficult enough to find a woman I cared about who also met my parents' criteria. The only thing more difficult might be finding a woman willing to enter into a loveless marriage so I could be free to entertain any dalliance I wanted—not to mention reducing someone else I *did* care about to a virtual concubine.

I had to give Nan credit for thinking outside the box, though. She was a rebel. And creative, if nothing else.

The following evening, Sigmund took off on a weekend trip to Newport with yet another woman he'd met on the dating app. When she arrived to pick him up, he tried everything to get me to go along, but I refused.

Seeing as though he wouldn't be home to cook dinner, I forced myself to put my paintbrush down long enough to head to the food shop.

It's a cold reality when you realize that all the choices available at the store mean little because you can't cook to save your life. I settled on a box of macaroni and cheese, something I'd been meaning to try since arriving in the States, and grabbed a can of SpaghettiOs while I was at it. I'd been spoiled my entire life with personal chefs, and never ate any of the processed foods I'd heard about. Junk food was a novelty.

I'd just exited one of the aisles when a flash of red caught my eye. My heart sped up at the sight of Felicity standing in the bakery section, looking down at the glass display. She hadn't noticed me. I wasn't sure if I should say hello or just keep walking. I knew the latter would be wiser, all things considered, but then the universe made the decision for me when Felicity turned and met my eyes.

Her mouth opened slightly. She looked like she didn't know whether to run or say something.

I smiled and took a few steps toward her. "Fancy meeting you here."

She let out a breath. "Yeah."

"Are you buying a cake?"

"Yes, actually. It's Mrs. Angelini's birthday."

"Ah. Very nice."

Felicity looked down at my basket. "Some healthy choices you have there."

"Sigmund is in Newport for a couple of days. So I'm planning a processed-food fiesta tonight. If it doesn't come out of a can or box, it's not allowed at my party."

"Looks like you're missing some SPAM. I think I saw that in aisle five."

"Thanks for the tip, but I need to pace myself."

She smiled nervously. "So...how have you been?"

"Keeping busy," I said, noticing her fidgety hands. "You?"

"Same."

A long moment of silence ensued.

Although it felt unnatural, I forced myself to leave her be. I assumed it was what she preferred. "Well, pass along my birthday wishes to Mrs. Angelini."

"I will."

I nodded. "I'll see you."

My chest felt tight as I walked away. I stood in line in a daze, refusing to allow my eyes to search for her again, keeping them fixed on the conveyor belt. The old woman in front of me seemed to have an endless number of coupons. I'd definitely gotten into the wrong line.

By the time I'd checked out, I found myself leaving the shop at the same moment as Felicity, who was now carrying a white cake box.

"Long time no see," I said.

"Yeah." She exhaled, her body tense as we walked together through the sliding glass doors.

As we were now heading together toward the carpark, I made conversation.

"Which cake did you settle on?"

"Just a white cake with whipped-cream frosting and strawberries on top."

"Strawberry on top—just like you."

God, that's fucking horrible. It sounded like something Sigmund would say, and I should've been shot. My nerves apparently made me stupid, on top of everything else. I rolled my eyes. "I'm sorry. That was pathetically corny."

"It's okay." She smiled. Felicity stopped in front of her vehicle. "Well, this is me." She shook her head. "Of course, it is. You know that. Who else has a mint green Fiat in this town, right?" She placed the cake box atop her car.

"I'm parked over there," I offered stupidly. She hadn't asked where I'd parked. Why the fuck did it matter to her?

We stood facing each other, neither of us moving or saying anything.

Wanting to keep looking into her eyes, I knew I wasn't going to be the first to leave this spot. I reached into my pocket, taking out a wrapped candy. "Do you like taffy?"

She scrunched her nose. "I hate it, actually. It's like chewing plastic to me."

"Well, see, if you hate taffy, it could never have worked between us anyway." I winked.

I'd expected her to laugh, but her reaction was just the opposite. While she smiled, it somehow looked sad.

"What's wrong, Felicity?"

She shook her head slowly. "I don't know."

"Yes, you do. Talk to me."

She didn't say anything. She just kept staring into my eyes. And the longer she did, the more I needed to taste her lips more than I needed my next breath.

CHAPTER 8

Felicity

Track 8: "Kiss Me" by Ed Sheeran

I didn't know how many seconds passed while we stared at each other. The sounds of the parking lot seemed to fade into the distance.

We slowly moved closer until Leo's lips were inches from mine. How had we gone from a casual and awkward conversation to this moment—so intense that I could hardly breathe? I'd missed him, thought about him every moment of every day for two weeks as I gazed across the bay. And now that he was in front of me, I didn't know how to hide my feelings.

I couldn't have told you who kissed whom first. It seemed to happen spontaneously. Our lips got so close that they attached, if by magnetic force. The moment his hot, wet mouth enveloped mine, all the breath I'd been holding escaped into him. Leo let out a slow and sexy groan that vibrated at the back of my throat. I opened wider to let his tongue in, relishing the taste of this beautiful man.

It had been so long since I'd been kissed, but only a few seconds in, I knew I'd never been kissed like *this*, kissed to the point that my knees went weak, that I felt it in every fiber of my body.

We started out tender and easy, but it soon deepened. I felt the metal of my car hit my back as Leo leaned his body into mine. His hands threaded through my hair as my fingers dug into his back. We were lost in each other, neither of us aware that we were still in a very public place. He smelled and tasted so good that I never wanted to stop, nor did I care who might have been watching this go down.

My body buzzed as his warm hand slid down my back, landing just above my ass. I pressed myself into him, aware of the erection against my abdomen. Our tongues sought each other's taste with reckless abandon. I reached up to rake my fingers through his silky hair.

It wasn't until a rogue shopping cart powered by the wind came crashing into us that we were forced to break the kiss.

He pulled back suddenly as his hands wrapped around my face. "Are you okay?"

"Yeah." I blinked as if coming out of a trance.

He looked dazed, as well, as he moved the cart away and rested it against a barrier.

When he returned to me, he ran his tongue along his bottom lip, still seeming a bit shocked. "I, uh, don't know what came over me. I just... That wasn't supposed to happen. I wasn't supposed to run into you. And I certainly wasn't supposed to maul you in a ShopRite carpark."

I rubbed my fingers over my mouth. "Are you sure you mauled me, or did I maul you?"

We shared a smile.

After a few moments of silence, he said, "Felicity... I know we agreed to not see each other. But I haven't been able to stop thinking about you."

I nodded. "I've been thinking about you, too."

"You have?"

"Yes," I whispered.

"I've spent the past two weeks doing nothing but painting with Bob Ross and eating saltwater taffy."

"Bob Ross?" I laughed. "What?"

"Don't ask." He shook his head. "And I don't think I actually like taffy, either. But it was better than drinking, or worse, getting in the boat and crossing the bay to make a fool of myself by begging you every day to reconsider spending the summer with me. So I opted not to, only to make a *bigger* fool of myself in this carpark the first chance I got."

I was just as much to blame for the PDA fest that just happened. But how was I supposed to go on my merry way now and forget about him after that kiss?

His eyes seared into mine. "Tell me what to do, because I don't want to leave you right now."

I knew I'd live to regret the words I uttered next. "Do you like cake?"

His mouth curved into a smile. "Only white cake with whipped cream and strawberries."

My pulse raced. "Would you want to come over tonight for Mrs. Angelini's birthday? We were gonna order pizza, which isn't the healthiest thing, but it's a step up from your mac and cheese party."

"An evening with you would be a huge step up from that."

"Want to say seven, then?"

"What can I bring?"

"Just yourself."

"What does Mrs. Angelini like to drink?"

"Fireball." I laughed.

"Really? All right. I'll pick some up."

I nodded. "See you later."

Just as I was opening my car door, he stopped me. "You might want to take the cake off the top of your car before you drive away."

Shutting my eyes briefly, I cringed. "Right. That would be a great idea."

After I got in my car, I put it in drive when I should have been reversing, nearly hitting a barrier before catching myself. Why could I never seem to drive around Leo?

He stood there smiling as he watched me take off. I had butterflies and a feeling of dread all at once. I knew this invitation meant way more than just pizza and cake. I'd officially thrown caution to the wind and invited him into my life. And before I knew it, he'd be gone just as fast as he'd entered.

The doorbell rang promptly at seven.

"There's the aristocrat." Mrs. Angelini smiled.

My palms were sweaty as I walked over to open the door for Leo.

Mrs. Angelini had seemed surprised that I'd invited the Brit across the bay to her birthday, but she didn't question my sudden change of heart. I think the situation entertained her, to be honest—and that was without me divulging what had happened in the supermarket parking lot.

Leo stood behind a massive bouquet of flowers. In his other hand, he held a bottle of Fireball.

"Hey," I said.

He moved the flowers out of the way so I could catch his beautiful smile. "Good evening, gorgeous."

I stepped aside. "Come in."

Mrs. Angelini came up behind me. "Hello, Leo."

"You must be Mrs. Angelini. It's lovely to meet you."

"Likewise."

"Happy birthday." He handed her the flowers and the alcohol. "These are for you."

"Flowers *and* Fireball? Truly a man after my own heart. And I suspect a little bird helped you with the choice of liquor."

"Indeed." He smiled over at me.

"Well, that was amazingly generous. Thank you. My three favorite things start with F: flowers, Fireball, and Felicity."

"I think we share the last one in common." He grinned.

Damn him and his charm.

Mrs. Angelini went to put the flowers in the kitchen, leaving us alone in the living room. His eyes fell to my lips. I suspected he was still thinking about our parking lot kiss. I certainly hadn't been able to think of much else.

The doorbell rang again, giving me a moment to escape the tension as I answered it. The pizza delivery man removed two large pies from his insulated carrier. I handed him a tip and closed the door.

"What can I do? Put me to work," Leo said.

"Everything is all taken care of. The table is set. The pizza is hot. We can just eat. I made a salad, too."

The three of us sat down to dinner. Despite my nerves, I had a pretty big appetite, devouring three slices of pizza and a heaping bowl of salad. The red wine I was drinking helped relax me as the evening wore on.

Leo spent a good portion of dinner answering Mrs. Angelini's questions about England. He seemed comfortable talking to her, though I knew going into the details of his life in the aristocracy wasn't something he loved to do. But Mrs. Angelini always made you feel like she understood where you were coming from. She never made assumptions about people just because her personal experiences were different. I think Leo could sense that about her, and it made him more comfortable.

At one point, Mrs. Angelini changed the subject.

"How's the fundraiser for Mrs. Barbosa going?" she asked me.

"I'm not sure we're gonna hit the goal this summer. We're debating starting anyway, but then we run the risk of leaving it incomplete."

"What's this?" Leo asked, looking between us.

"Felicity is trying to raise money for a local woman who fosters a few kids. Her house is very small, so Felicity thought it would be a good idea to try to help her build an addition."

"What's your goal?" he asked me.

"Thirty grand. We've raised about twenty since I started the campaign last year."

He looked a bit confused. "Thirty grand sounds low for an addition to a house."

"Well, it's technically a garage renovation. The structure is already there. One of her kids has autism. So once we raise the money, two others and I are going to redo that space and have it insulated. Her foster son is Theo. It will be where he does his therapies and has some sensory equipment. Apparently, it gets too noisy in the main house, and it's hard for him to calm down and focus. So, it's not like a true addition, more like a glorified shed with electricity and heat."

"That's amazing of you to want to do that. Who's doing the work?"

"It's cheaper if we do it ourselves, but we're going to have to hire out for the plumbing and electricity."

"Who's *we* exactly?" he asked.

"Well, me and a couple friends from high school."

"But you've raised enough to get started?"

"Yeah. I think so."

"I would love to help while I'm here."

"Are you handy?"

He arched a brow. "Do I give off a vibe that I wouldn't be?"

"I don't know," I admitted.

"My father put me to work a lot on our properties. And I actually helped build a small structure in Tanzania on a volunteer mission. So yeah, I'd love to help."

Accepting his help meant committing to spending regular time with him. That was risky, but how could I refuse?

"Well, that would be great."

"Good, then." He smiled. "I'd also like to contribute to the fundraiser."

"Don't feel obligated."

"I don't. I'd just like to."

"Okay. I'll text you the information."

"Thank you."

Opening my phone, I scrolled down to his name and sent him a link to the fundraising page I'd created.

Then I stood. "I'm going to go set up the cake."

He stood from his chair. "Let me help you."

"No. Please. Stay and finish your drink."

After I went into the kitchen, I took the box out of the fridge and set the cake on a large, round plate. I opened the package of candles and placed them around the edges. I could hear Mrs. Angelini and Leo laughing in the dining room.

A few minutes later, Mrs. Angelini snuck up behind me. "He's adorable," she whispered.

"And dangerous..."

"Because he's leaving, yes. But that doesn't make him any less adorable."

"I'm trying not to overthink things right now."

"You absolutely shouldn't."

Blowing a breath out, I carried the cake into the dining room.

We sang "Happy Birthday" and spent the next several minutes devouring our generous slices of cake.

Leo reached his hand to the corner of my mouth at one point, causing me to flinch.

"Sorry to have startled you. You had some whipped cream on your face."

Licking the edge of my lips, I said, "Thank you."

Mrs. Angelini smirked. I knew what she was thinking. It was the same thing I was: I was completely screwed.

CHAPTER 9

Leo

Track 9: "Shout Out to My Ex" by Little Mix

Felicity insisted on taking our dishes to the kitchen. She wouldn't let me help, and I didn't push the issue because I suspected she needed a breather. The intensity between us that had spiraled in the carpark today hadn't waned in the least. I knew I made her nervous. I only hoped that was because she liked me and didn't know what to do with those feelings. I didn't know what to do with all of this, either.

Our kiss earlier today had knocked me on my arse. I'd replayed it every second of the afternoon. And now that I was here with her, the need for a repeat felt even more urgent than I'd anticipated.

Mrs. Angelini interrupted my thoughts. "You seem smitten with my girl."

I stopped mid-sip. "How can you tell?"

"You haven't taken your eyes off her." She laughed. "I suppose I haven't taken my eyes off you, which is how I've noticed."

"I guess it's obvious how much I fancy her."

She smiled. "Felicity is the whole package. She's as beautiful on the inside as she is on the outside. And she really has no clue just how beautiful she is."

"That's part of what fascinates me about her. And she's so smart."

"She's also very guarded. But when she opens her heart to someone someday, I know she'll give that person all of it."

I nodded, and an uncomfortable tightness developed in my chest. Maybe because I knew that person wouldn't be me. And I envied him—whoever he was.

"It's clear you and she have a great relationship," I said. "I think it's interesting, though, that she insists on calling you Mrs. Angelini."

"I've tried to get her to call me Eloise for years. Not doing so is a protective mechanism on her part, I think. I'm sure she's told you about her background. As a child, she allowed herself to get close to caretakers a time or two, and that backfired. I do hope by now she knows I'm not going anywhere. She's an adult, obviously. Technically, I'm not responsible for her in any way. But she's the only family I have aside from my brother. So I'd be lost if she ever left me. I need her just as much as she needs me."

"That's beautiful. Truly. I'm glad you found each other."

"Don't hurt her too badly," she said after a moment.

Unsure of how to respond, I simply told the truth. "I don't want to hurt her at all."

"But you will. She's going to let you do it. The fact that she invited you here tonight tells me that."

Felicity walked in at that moment, interrupting any further insight I might have gotten from Mrs. Angelini, whose words had left me uneasy. Although, the message was certainly nothing I didn't already know.

Mrs. Angelini stood. "Thank you for the birthday dinner, folks. The Fireball is calling me. I'm gonna pour myself a nightcap, head to my room, and read my steamy book." She winked. "Why don't you show Leo the rest of the house?"

Felicity turned to me. "Would you want a tour?"

"I'd love that," I said, finishing the last of my wine.

She then took me through all of the rooms on the first level, which included an impressive library with built-in shelves and an ornate, wooden desk.

I wasn't going to suggest she show me her bedroom, but when she began walking up the stairs, I followed.

We passed Mrs. Angelini's room and continued down the hall until we reached the end. Felicity opened the door and led me inside. I was glad she trusted me enough to bring me to her bedroom. I was going to remain on my best behavior tonight, but she had no way of knowing that, especially after the way I'd attacked her mouth earlier today.

Felicity's room was much more feminine than I might have imagined—not that she wasn't a feminine beauty, but she'd never come across as a girly girl. I was surprised to find it decorated in pastel colors.

"So, this is my room. I haven't changed it up in years. But I love it. It's spacious and looks out over the bay."

There was something very calming about this space. It was organized and held the same quiet elegance she did.

A series of notebooks in every color of the rainbow caught my eye. They were lined up on a shelf.

"What are all these?"

"Those are my planners. They're all for this year."

"I thought most people had one planner, not twenty."

She laughed. "I collect them. I don't know. They make me happy. Planners and stickers. I know it seems crazy."

"Crazy? You're talking to a man who's been painting with the intention of becoming the next Picasso, when the reality is more like paint by number."

"That's true." She sighed. "Well, I suppose like your painting, the planners are...therapeutic for me. I feel more aligned when I know what I'm doing and where I'm going on a particular day. Growing up, it was always important for me to feel like I had control over my life, even when I never quite knew where I'd end up. Somehow if I took one day at a time, and wrote down everything that was going to happen, it brought me some solace and lessened my fear about the future as a whole. Like, I'll check my planner and tell myself, 'Today, Felicity, you're going to do XYZ. You don't need to worry about anything else.'" She shook her head. "And then, of course, that habit transformed into a superficial addiction to colorful planners and stickers. I'm making this sound way deeper than it should be."

"No. It makes perfect sense. And I'm learning that when it comes to you, nothing is superficial. There's deeper meaning behind almost everything." My eyes wandered to a photo collage on her wall—a city at night, two hands with fingers intertwined, more colorful planners. I walked over to it. "What's this?"

Felicity seemed hesitant. "It's a vision board."

"What does that mean?"

"These are all things I envision in my future, things I want in my life. Visualizing them on a board like this is supposed to help you manifest them."

I leaned into the picture. "Is that New York?"

"Yes. I'm a city girl at heart, even though I grew up by the water. I'd love to live downtown in the midst of all the action someday. In Boston, I lived in Cambridge, which wasn't quite downtown. It doesn't have to be New York, though. That was just the example I used."

"I don't have to ask about the planners. I know all about your addiction to those now." I smiled.

"Yeah. I don't know why I threw those in there. For good measure, I guess."

The image of the interlocked hands had me most curious. "Tell me about this. What does that mean to you?"

"It's not obvious?" She blushed. "Someday I want a partner in crime. The hands represent...trust, not letting go."

Of course. The opposite of abandonment.

"So, even though you've said you don't want to depend on anyone, you *do* want a life partner."

"Of course. I didn't mean to imply that I want to go through life alone, just that I don't want to feel like I *can't* survive alone."

"I understand completely," I whispered. That feeling in my chest from earlier was back—the one that had developed when Mrs. Angelini spoke about Felicity giving her whole heart to someone someday.

"If you had a vision board," she asked, "what would be on it?"

At the moment? Your face. That's pretty much it. Letting out a long breath, I took some time to ponder an answer. "I guess when your future seems mapped out, there's little room for imagination. I've never really thought about what I might *truly* want if there weren't any restrictions." I stared at her collage. "But I suppose my board might look somewhat like yours—minus the planners, of course. The bright lights of a city, maybe some pyramids—you know, representing the possibility of traveling the world with no obligations. That would be my ultimate fantasy—to indefinitely have the freedom I'm affording myself right now."

"But ultimately, Leo, everything is a choice," she said. "On some level, you're *choosing* your fate for the sake of your family, aren't you? I respect you for that, even if I can't relate. I don't have anyone who depends on me to carry on a family name. I have no responsibility toward anyone but myself. If I were in your shoes, I would probably do the same thing."

I'd never looked at my decision to carry on my father's legacy as a choice. But I suppose it was. There were no shackles on me.

I nodded. "Thanks for sharing that perspective. It's a different way of looking at it. There's no such thing as a total lack of choice, is there?"

Her phone chimed, and she looked down at it. Her eyes widened.

"What is it?" I asked.

"I get notifications when someone makes a donation to Mrs. Barbosa's fund." She looked up at me. "What did you do?"

When Felicity had been cleaning in the kitchen earlier, I'd clicked the donation link and sent the rest of the money—ten-thousand dollars—that would allow her to meet the goal.

"I've donated to far less important causes in my lifetime," I said. "I wanted to make sure we had what we needed to get started."

"You didn't have to give *that* much. It's crazy."

"It's not, really. We'll be helping someone in need, and I get to spend scheduled time with you. I can't put a price tag on that."

"Well, normally, I'd be angry at you for giving so much, but it's so needed, and it's for a good cause. So I really appreciate your generosity. Without your donation and Mrs. Angelini's, this probably wouldn't have happened for at least another year or two, if ever."

"It's truly my pleasure, Felicity." Sitting down on her bed, I looked around. "Being here..." I paused. "It feels so...nice. This warm, inviting room. This house, in general. Mostly the beautiful girl who lives here." I winked. "You're all right, too."

She laughed. "Good one."

"Seriously, Mrs. Angelini is a gem. It was great to meet her. Thank you for inviting me over tonight."

"You're welcome. And yeah, I know. I'm a lucky girl to live here."

"From what I gather, Mrs. Angelini feels lucky to have you in her life as well."

"She's the best."

"You think she'd foster me, too?" I teased.

"Well, then, you'd be like my stepbrother, and that would be creepy."

"Because I'd be trying to sneak into your room at night?" I smiled mischievously.

"I read a book like that once. It didn't end well."

"Interesting." I put my feet up, sinking into her pillow.

"Feel free to make yourself more comfortable," she said, eyebrow raised.

"I'm sorry. Does this bother you?"

"I'm kidding."

I tucked my hands behind my head. "I notice you're keeping your distance. Perhaps a good idea after what happened today?"

"Probably." Felicity blushed.

"You're smart to do that, because I would probably try to kiss you again."

Her cheeks reddened. She looked so beautiful, dressed in a peachy shirt that complemented her hair and skin. Her hair was a bit straighter than its usual fluffy texture.

"By the way, Mrs. Angelini gave me a warning tonight," I said.

"She what?"

"Yeah. She said to make sure not to hurt you too badly."

Felicity shut her eyes. "I wish she hadn't said that. I'm sorry."

"Don't be. She's right. Which sort of makes me wonder *why* you invited me over. You'd previously decided it was best that we not see each other anymore. Did my kissing you change things?"

She tilted her head. "Did you kiss me, or did I kiss you?"

"Come to think of it, you might've initiated it." I smiled. "Wait—did you take advantage of the pathetic state you found me in at the food shop?"

She shrugged. "I felt bad for you. The mac and cheese and SpaghettiOs? It *was* pathetic. I had to do something."

I straightened up against her headboard. "Okay, in all seriousness, aside from the kiss, what made you invite me here tonight?"

Felicity continued to keep her distance across the room as she looked down.

"At Harvard, I used to play extreme Frisbee, right?" she said, looking up. "I was one of the worst players on the team, and we didn't win very often. I always knew most of the time I was going to lose. Yet I was okay with that because the invigorating experience was worth the loss. As long as I didn't *expect* to win, I was okay. I could just enjoy the experience." She exhaled. "Falling for you is a losing game."

"But one you're willing to play?" My heart raced. "I'm game if you are."

"If we're gonna spend time together, I have to let you know that I...can't sleep with you."

All right. Fuck.

I certainly hadn't been expecting her to mention sex right now, even if the thought of it was never too far from my mind these days.

"I understand." *Even if it kills me.* But she had reopened the possibility of spending the summer together. I stood up and walked over to where she had her planners lined up on the shelf. "Do you have one of these to spare?"

She squinted, seeming perplexed. "Um...sure. The ones on the right aren't written in yet."

I pulled a blue one off the shelf. "I'll return it at the end of the summer. Is that all right?"

Felicity shrugged. "Okay."

The last thing I wanted to do was leave her tonight. But since she'd resigned herself to letting me hurt her, my gut told me to pace myself in doing so.

"Thank you for a lovely evening, Felicity."

"You're leaving?"

"I think it's best if I do. Especially since we have a long day tomorrow."

"We do?"

"Unless you're working at the restaurant?"

"Not until the following night."

"Brilliant, then. I'll pick you up in the morning, and we'll head to the store to start purchasing supplies for the renovation. How many people did you say are able to help?"

"My friend Bailey and her boyfriend both live in Providence. I know they're definitely in. I'll contact them tonight and see who can make it tomorrow."

"It's okay if they can't. We can get started ourselves either way. But the more the merrier. What do you have already in terms of tools? I'm wondering what we'll need to purchase."

"Our next-door neighbor works in construction. He has a ton of power tools in his garage—probably almost everything we need, aside from materials. He told me to just let him know when I need to borrow stuff. I can text him." She smiled. "I can't believe this is actually happening."

As we descended the stairs, excitement raced through me. I'd be spending the day with her tomorrow. And working on this project would be a better way to expend my energy than painting art I was too embarrassed to show anyone.

We stood facing each other at her front door. I chose not to give in to the need to kiss her again.

"In case there's any question, Felicity," I said as I turned to go, "it was most definitely *me* who kissed *you* today."

The following morning, I picked Felicity up bright and early, and we went to the nearest home improvement store. We were able to borrow a lot of tools from Felicity's neighbor, Hank Rogers: an air compressor, pneumatic nailer, and chop saw, among other things. So the first step would be getting the framework up. I'd rented a truck, so we'd be able to transport the wood we'd use to start framing the inside. Then we'd have to hire out for electrical and plumbing before resuming the last of our tasks—things like drywall, painting, then flooring.

Mrs. Barbosa was out when we arrived at her house after our shopping trip. Felicity and I went straight to the old garage structure we'd be renovating and got started. Luckily, I remembered much of what I'd learned from my father when he'd brought me with him on a volunteer mission in Tanzania a few years back. That trip, we'd built an addition to a schoolhouse.

Felicity held the studs while I put them in place. I also taught her how to cut the wood properly. Our team of two was off to a pretty good start, if I said so myself.

But a couple hours into it, our private partnership was interrupted when her friends arrived to help. Two guys and a girl entered the garage.

"Sorry, we're late," the girl said.

"I didn't know you were back in Narragansett," Felicity said to one of the guys.

He nodded. "It's been a long time, Felicity."

Getting a strange vibe, I looked between them.

Felicity seemed uncomfortable as she turned to me. "Leo, this is my best friend, Bailey."

"Great to meet you," I said.

"You, too." She smiled.

"And this is her boyfriend, Stewart."

"Stewart, how's it going, man?" I shook his hand.

Then she turned to the other bloke. "And this is Matt."

I nodded toward him as my suspicions grew. "Hi."

"Hey," he said, seeming just as wary of me.

Matt was a couple inches shorter than me, with dark hair and dark eyes. I'd have to ask Felicity about him later.

She showed them around the space for a few minutes. "If one of you wants to handle cutting the wood, that would be great," she said. "That way I can continue to help Leo."

Matt volunteered to handle the wood cutting while Bailey and her boyfriend worked on clearing out some of the residual junk out of the side of the room opposite where I'd been working.

At one point, Felicity stopped me. "I think Mrs. Barbosa just pulled up. We should go say hello."

I put down the piece of wood I'd been about to affix on the wall. "All right…"

We left the other three in the garage and headed toward the main residence.

Before I could blink, a large boy ran out of the house and landed straight against my chest, nearly knocking me over. Without saying anything, he took my hand and led me to the backyard as he ran at warp speed.

"What's going on, mate?" I asked.

He shrieked but said nothing. Within seconds, I realized he wasn't typical. This must have been the special-needs child we were renovating the therapy space for. I laughed, relieved that I hadn't had a knee-jerk reaction to nearly being clobbered by a kid almost as big as me. I knew he was only about thirteen or fourteen.

The boy led me to a bench swing, and we sat down. He began swinging us with his legs as he continued to hold my hand. There's a first time for everything in life, I guess.

I spotted Felicity running toward us.

"So, okay, you've met Theo," she said, out of breath.

"I certainly have. We've become quite acquainted in a matter of seconds."

A woman, whom I assumed was Mrs. Barbosa, appeared. "Leo, I'm so sorry. Theo loves it when we have fresh faces over to the house, especially guys. He's so used to all the female therapists who come work with him. I guess he got a little excited to see you."

I looked at him, and he gazed over at me before placing his head on my shoulder.

"I hope you're not uncomfortable," she said.

"Of course not."

Theo was like a nearly two-hundred-pound teddy bear. There was certainly nothing to be uncomfortable about.

"Thanks for humoring him. He's not verbal, but I can see he likes you, even if he can't tell me. And believe me, he can sense the good ones."

"His radar must be off today, then," I joked as he continued to swing us.

She smiled. "I can't thank you enough for your donation that helped make all of this possible. Felicity told me. I don't know what to say."

"No need to say anything. I'm happy to do it. You'll be seeing a lot of us over the next few weeks."

"I understand you're from England, and you're only here through the summer?"

"Yes. And being able to work on this project will bring important meaning to the last leg of my trip."

Mrs. Barbosa looked back toward the house. "I wish I could stay and chat, but my other kids need me inside. It's time to make lunch." She waved at the boy. "Come on, Theo."

Theo didn't budge. He seemed very comfortable as he continued to lean his head on my shoulder.

"It's all right. He can stay with me. I'll make sure he gets inside safely."

"Are you sure?" she said.

"Yes."

It didn't look like we had much choice; this kid wasn't letting go of me anytime soon.

After she left, Felicity beamed as she looked at me. "You're very sweet to let him do that."

"Every man can use a ride on a swing once in a while."

She chuckled. "Do you want me to stay here with you?"

"No. We'll be fine."

"Okay." She smiled.

"Hey…" I called as she walked away.

"Yeah?"

"That guy…Matt. Who is he?"

Felicity let out a breath. "Did you sense something? Is that why you're asking?"

"Yeah, I did. You seemed nervous around him from the moment he arrived."

She glanced toward the garage. "He was my high school boyfriend. I had no idea Stewart was going to bring him here. They're good friends. The last I heard, Matt was living in Pennsylvania. I never expected to see him."

That gave me pause. "He lives in Pennsylvania. The same place you're headed?"

"Yeah. That's just a coincidence, of course. He ended up getting into UPENN after high school. That's why we went our separate ways. At the time, I was pretty broken up about it. I didn't see why distance had to matter. But I guess he realized he wouldn't be able to keep it in his pants at school or something."

"I see."

"I haven't seen him in a while. He doesn't usually come home in the summers. I've maybe seen him twice in the years since we broke up."

My suspicions grew. "Interesting that he decided to come help all of a sudden." *Damn.* I could feel this odd jealousy rising to the surface. I had no right to feel territorial about her, but I felt threatened by her ex.

"Well, he's good friends with Stewart."

Is she that naïve? "Make no mistake, he came here because of you."

"I don't think so."

"Trust me. He's using this as an opportunity to reconnect. He missed your beautiful face." *Just like I will.*

"Well, that's too bad for him, isn't it?" She shook her head. "Anyway, I'd better go help them."

My eyes remained glued to her as she walked away, but I stayed on the swing with Theo. I had only a limited view of the garage from here.

At one point, as Felicity walked from the garage to the house, Matt stopped her. They talked for a while. I was certain he was happy to have cornered her.

She kept looking down at her feet. He definitely had an effect on her.

I turned to Theo and muttered, "If you weren't cockblocking me, I could have rescued her from this, you know."

He laughed and began to move the swing faster.

Hanging on to the edge, I warned, "I don't think these swings were meant to go this fast, mate."

He laughed harder.

All in all, I spent nearly an hour on that swing with Theo before he randomly bolted toward the house. I chased after him to make sure he got safely inside.

When I returned to the garage, I locked eyes with Felicity, who seemed less anxious than before as she chatted with Bailey and gathered trash into garbage bags.

I went back to my task of putting up the framework. From time to time, Matt would bring me the appropriate-sized pieces of wood, and I'd pretend to be cordial while sizing him up.

After our work was done for the day, Felicity and I packed into my rented truck while the other three took off in Stewart's Jeep.

As we headed down the road, I turned to her. "I think we got a lot done for the first day, yeah?"

"Way more than I thought."

"What did Matt want when he stopped you earlier?" I asked. "I watched you talk to him while I was swinging with Theo."

"He asked me what I was up to, and he said we should get together when I move to Pennsylvania, but I brushed it off. I'm not going to do that."

I knew it. "Nor should you, if he's hurt you in the past," I said, swallowing the lump in my throat. He'd only been back into her life for a matter of minutes and had tried to make a play for her. "How long is he here for?"

"Not sure. He's on vacation in Narragansett, visiting his family. He has to return to Pennsylvania for work, I assume." She turned to me. "He also asked if you and I were together."

"What did you say?"

"I told him we were seeing where things go."

"That's the truth, I suppose." I tightened my grip on the steering wheel. "Anyway, I'm sorry he showed up if it dampened your spirits today at all." Glancing over at her again, I paused. "The fact that you were so affected made me wonder if you still have feelings for him?"

She shook her head as she twirled her silver ring around her finger. "The only thing that bummed me out about seeing him was that it reminded me of how things ended—of the fact that almost *all* relationships end. I'm not into anyone right now but you, Leo, if that's what you're wondering. And that really sucks for me."

Some of the tension that had been building inside my body all day began to lift. "I guess we're one fucked-up team, then. Because all I could think about was how lucky he is to get to live where you'll be. And the way he was looking at you made me a bit uneasy, even though I don't have a right to be."

Felicity remained quiet for several seconds as she looked out the window. "Matt was my first...everything. I gave way too much of myself to him at a very young age. It's why when the other relationship I had in college ended, it almost didn't faze me. I'd already been there and done that with Matt and had lost some capacity to be hurt by then."

"Do you really lose the capacity, or do you just block it out?"

"I'm definitely a good blocker of emotions. It's a practiced talent." She flashed a sad smile. "Have you ever had your heart broken?"

I shook my head. "I've only had one serious girlfriend... in secondary school. I ended up cheating on her. I was too young for a relationship at the time. I wouldn't stay with someone today if I were going to do that. But back then, I was just a stupid teenager."

"And beyond her you haven't had a girlfriend?"

"I've dated a lot, but nothing serious, no."

"You're a playboy. Am I right?"

"I was. But it's not a bad thing if you're not leading anyone on, right?"

"You said you *were*...in the past tense. You don't consider yourself a player anymore?"

"Since arriving here I'm not living the playboy lifestyle, nor do I care to at the moment."

"You seem to care so much about what your parents think. They don't care that you play the field back home?"

"There's an unspoken rule where I come from that anything you do before marriage, while it shouldn't be spoken of in great detail, is fair game. But the closer I get to thirty, the more pressure there is to settle down."

"Why thirty, specifically?"

"It's always been a magic number in my family. Every man has gotten married by the time he was thirty. My father seems to expect the same from me."

"Thirty is still so young."

"The thing is, I don't believe I've told you this, but my father has been battling cancer for several years. He doesn't think he has all that much time left. I sometimes feel this pressure to get settled in case something happens to him, so that he'll die in peace, knowing things will continue as they should."

"I'm sorry to hear that. I didn't know." She paused. "Why does he care so much whether you're married as long as you can continue to do his work for him?"

"It has to do with continuing the family name. He wants to be assured that I will, in fact, marry and have a male child someday. It seems to be all he cares about. My father's entire side of the family is adamant that there's no use for me if I don't procreate. Not to mention, one of my father's sisters and her kids are very bitter that the family inheritance will go to me and not them. It's just the way it's written, not my choice. So they try to make my life miserable when they can."

"Like how?"

"One of my cousins is a real pill. She tipped off the press once when I was on vacation, and they printed photos of me tanning naked."

"Ugh." She cringed. "That's not Sig's family, is it?"

"No. Sigmund is my cousin on my mother's side. A much nicer, but crazier, bunch."

"I'm sorry you've got to deal with that."

"There are worse lives to live. I know I'm privileged. I don't have a right to complain."

"No, but it's *your* personal struggle. Even if it doesn't compare to what many people have to go through in this world, you have a right to be angry or frustrated, especially when it comes to your family betraying your trust."

"Thank you for always making me see things in a different light." I reached for her hand. "It's why I can't help wanting to be around you." I considered asking her to dinner tonight, but didn't want to overwhelm her, since we'd spent the entire day together. I pulled my hand away. "Today was a long day. I'm sure you're dying for a shower, just as I am."

"Are you saying I need one?" She chuckled.

"No, you smell delicious even when you're sweating." I'd lick every ounce of sweat off her body right now, if I could.

When we pulled up to Felicity's, I ached to lean in and kiss her. But it had been a weird day with her ex showing up and all, and I didn't want to push anything right now. So as much as I yearned to taste her lips again, I simply said, "I'll call you."

"Uh...okay." She flashed a hesitant smile.

Is she upset?

Her eyes fell to my mouth, and it occurred to me that maybe she'd *expected* me to kiss her. But before I could rectify anything, Felicity exited the truck. I waited to make sure she was inside before taking off.

Sigmund was in the kitchen when I entered the house. "Where the hell have you been? I've been texting you all day."

"Sorry. I've been busy and didn't check my phone."

I'd forgotten that he was returning today from his trip to Newport.

"Busy? What the hell have you been up to?" he asked.

For a split second, I considered keeping my reconciliation with Felicity to myself, but my astute and annoying cousin would figure it out soon enough.

"I was with Felicity."

His eyes went wide. "Ginger? She's back in the picture?" He rolled his eyes. "I should've known."

"Why's that?"

"Well, clearly you were on the verge of insanity before I left, what with your painting and taffy consumption. I knew you wouldn't go much longer before giving in and groveling for another chance with her."

"I actually hadn't planned to see her again. We ran into each other at ShopRite yesterday, and one thing led to another."

"You shagged her?"

"No. That's not happening. She made that clear. But we had a moment. We kissed—in the carpark."

"For Christ's sake, you couldn't have picked a different place to lay one on her?"

"It was like spontaneous combustion, really. I hadn't a moment to contemplate whether it was appropriate or not. And I didn't give a fuck. That was amazing. It was the best kiss I've ever experienced. Then she invited me over for dinner. I met Mrs. Angelini. And today, we spent the entire day helping renovate a local foster mother's garage. We're turning it into a therapy space for her special-needs son."

"Well, that's a noble way of getting into her pants."

"That's not what it's about."

"All right. If you say so." He smirked. "In any case, that's certainly a lot to have happened in one weekend. I hope you know what you're getting into."

"What I'm getting into is none of your concern." I opened the fridge and grabbed a lager. "Anyway, how was your trip?"

"It was wild."

"Yeah?" I took a sip. "You had a good time with... What was her name?"

"Maria."

"That's right."

"Yes. I had a great time with Maria...and Maria."

"There were *two* Marias there?"

He wriggled his brows. "Her friend."

"They're both named Maria?"

"Yes. Apparently, half of the Portuguese girls out here are named Maria. I had an equally good time with both of them."

My eyes nearly bugged out of my head. "Wait, you messed around with her friend, too?"

"We all messed around together."

"Jesus Christ."

"Or even better, Ave Maria." He winked.

I rolled my eyes. "And you accuse *me* of moving fast?"

CHAPTER 10

Felicity

Track 10: "Maria" by Blondie

Driving home from work at the restaurant, I thought about the past few days. Because I'd had to work the last three nights, I hadn't gotten to spend any real time with Leo, aside from working over at Mrs. Barbosa's during the day.

Matt had only shown up again one of those days. I got the impression that working alongside Leo wasn't what he'd had in mind when he volunteered to help. Leo had also seemed uncomfortable around Matt, so it was just as well that Matt skipped out. I doubted I'd see him again before he returned to Pennsylvania.

Each time Leo drove me home from Mrs. Barbosa's, we'd say goodbye, and I'd hope he'd kiss me. I'd longed for that since that day in the parking lot and wondered why he hadn't tried it again. Was it because I'd told him I wouldn't have sex with him? Did he think I meant *all* physical contact was off the table? And did I even mean what I'd said about not sleeping with him? Or was I just scared that taking that step would mean feeling even more hurt when he left?

I was pretty sure it was the latter, considering sexual fantasies of Leo had been keeping me up at night. I wanted him so badly. More perplexing than him not kissing me was the fact that he hadn't asked me to hang out after my shifts. Maybe he assumed I'd be tired? I sighed.

It was 10 p.m. by the time I got home and showered. Sitting alone in my room, I itched to see him. Looking out the window in my bedroom, I could see the lights at Leo's house were on across the bay. Feeling restless, I opted to take a chance and head over there. If I delayed long enough to change into something nicer, I knew I'd change my mind. I looked down and cringed: a Hello Kitty T-shirt and denim shorts. But this getup would have to do because I had no time to think this through.

Grabbing my keys, I ran down the stairs and out to my car. Mrs. Angelini had already turned in for the night, so I didn't bother letting her know where I was going.

My pulse raced as I pulled up to the front of Leo's house. Exiting the car, I looked up at the dark night sky and got goose bumps. I knew what showing up here unannounced at this hour would look like. *Can you say booty call?* But the message I sent didn't matter; I just needed to see him.

I knocked on the door, and a few seconds later, it opened. But the person greeting me was neither Leo nor Sig.

"Can I help you?" A petite brunette tilted her head.

I swallowed. "Is Leo here?"

"Yeah. He's upstairs taking a shower."

My stomach churned as my eyes found another dark-haired girl sitting on the couch. What exactly had I interrupted here? I wasn't about to stay and find out.

Completely at a loss, I was about to turn around and head back to my car when the sound of Sig's voice stopped me.

"Ginger! Where are you going?"

I turned around to face him. "Uh...home. It looks like you guys are pretty busy."

He smirked. "Just dinner and an orgy."

My eyes widened. "What?"

"Felicity!" Leo came down the staircase. He wore a T-shirt and jeans and his hair was wet.

Our eyes locked. "I can see you guys are busy, so I'm going to get going."

Leo shook his head almost frantically. "Wait, what? No. Busy? I'm not busy at all. These are his friends, not mine."

I looked over at Sig, then back at Leo. "He said there was an orgy tonight, so I didn't know what to—"

"What?" Leo's eyes shot daggers at his cousin. "What the fuck did you say to her?"

Sig turned to me. "There *is* an orgy happening tonight. Just not involving Leo. You didn't give me a chance to clarify, Ginger."

His friends laughed.

"Have you formally met the Marias?" Sig asked.

I blinked. "The who?"

He wrapped his arm around one of the girls. "This is Maria Josefina." He turned to the other one over on the couch. "And that's Maria Isabel."

I nodded. "Nice to meet you both."

Sig laughed. "I'm sorry to have alarmed you, Ginger."

"Is that your permanent name for me now? You've just used it three times in a row. Are you getting lazy about coming up with new ones?"

"I think Ginger suits you. Yeah. I quite like it."

Rolling my eyes, I conceded. "I guess it's better than Freckles."

Leo continued to glare at Sig as he placed his hand at the small of my back. "Let's go out onto the deck, Felicity."

Once outside, he pulled at his hair. "I'm so fucking sorry about that. I'd been outside taking a dip in the bay when he arrived with these girls, so I escaped upstairs to take a shower, and when I came downstairs, there you were."

"I'm not gonna lie. I had a mini panic attack, thinking I'd interrupted something."

He shook his head. "I'm sorry. I can only imagine what that looked like."

"Especially since you haven't asked me to hang out the past few days. I didn't know what to think."

Leo placed his hand on my cheek, sending chills through my body. "You think I haven't *wanted* to see you?"

"I don't know."

He exhaled. "Felicity... The moment you agreed to spend time with me this summer ended any chance of me hooking up with anyone else. I know we're not technically exclusive or anything, but I wouldn't do that to you. Is that clear?"

His words, while comforting, still left me with questions. "You're a self-proclaimed playboy—at least you said you were in the past, so…" I covered my face. "Never mind. I feel stupid. I'm sorry."

"Don't be." He reached for my hand and threaded his fingers with mine. "I'm happy you came over. I wanted to see you tonight, but I assumed you'd be too tired after a long day. I didn't want to overwhelm you, since we've been spending our days together at Mrs. Barbosa's. I've been trying to pace myself, but I've been fucking dying to spend more time with you."

"I really wanted to see you, too, so I figured I would chance it and just come by."

"And then as luck would have it, Sigmund has his harem over."

"Is he really with *both* of those girls?"

"Apparently, yeah—the Marias. He started seeing one of them, and she brought a friend along to their weekend getaway in Newport. That was Maria, too. And the next thing you know, it's a party of three."

"Are you sure he's not hiding a third Maria somewhere?" I chuckled.

"With Sigmund, anything is possible."

We laughed, and I narrowed my eyes. "Have you ever had a threesome?"

Leo's pupils flared. "Okay, that came out of nowhere."

"It really didn't. We were on the subject."

"True." He hesitated. "Yeah. I've had one. Once."

Jealousy coursed through me as I pulled my hand away from his. "I see."

"I won't lie if you ask me something. I'll always tell you the truth."

Taking advantage of his promise, I added another question, a slight bitterness in my tone. "Did you enjoy it?"

"You may not believe this, but I didn't like it as much as I thought I would. It was too much choreography—worrying about pleasing them equally. And I found myself gravitating toward one girl over the other. It was awkward. The experience made me realize I much prefer being able to give my everything to one person." He brushed his hand along my cheek, studying my face. "And Jesus, you're turning so red. Did I upset you?"

"No, it's not that." I breathed out. "When you mentioned giving more attention to one girl, the visual of you in that situation just made me a little... I don't know." I stopped before I could vomit out the rest.

He moved a step closer. "A little what?"

"Flustered, I guess. Jealous, maybe." I chewed my bottom lip. "Never mind."

A few moments of awkward silence passed. "Did it turn you on?" he asked in a low voice. "To think about me fucking?"

My nipples hardened. God, that word coming out of his mouth.

"Not the thought of you with other girls...just the thought of *it*."

"Of course. That's what I meant."

"The idea of you, yeah."

He moved closer. "The idea...of me and you..."

"Maybe," I admitted, feeling hotter by the second.

He wiped the sweat from his forehead. "It's warm out tonight, yes?" He looked toward the water. "Let's go sit on the boat. We can go for a ride, if you like. I've never taken it out at night. The lights on it are supposed to be awesome, according to the guy who rented it to me."

I nodded. "That sounds nice."

"We should grab water from the kitchen, in case you get thirsty."

I followed him back into the house. As we entered the kitchen, both Marias were hanging off of Sig as he cooked.

"Are you two joining us to eat?" Sig asked.

"No, we're going out on the boat," Leo said, pulling two waters from the fridge.

"This late? You can't even navigate that thing during the day, Leo."

"We're not going far. Just getting out of here."

"Very well, then," Sig said as he turned to me and winked. "Goodbye, Kitty."

Kitty? "I thought you called me Ginger now."

He pointed to my shirt. "Hello Kitty? Goodbye, Kitty. Get it? Also...are you twelve years old with that shirt?"

His girlfriends snickered.

"Bugger off," Leo said, placing his hand at the small of my back to usher me out of the house. "I'm so sorry about my fucknut of a cousin," he said as we made our way back outside.

"I actually find him entertaining. It's fine."

"He's even worse when he's pissed like he is tonight."

"What's he upset about?"

Leo looked confused. "What do you mean?"

"You said he's pissed."

He laughed. "Pissed where we come from means drunk."

"Ah."

We stepped onto the boat, and he turned on the lights. He didn't turn on the boat, though. We just sat on opposite ends of the bench seat and floated.

Leo's gaze landed on my chest. "Fuck whatever my cousin says. You look adorable in that shirt."

"I'm sure people look at the way I dress sometimes and roll their eyes. They would never know I graduated from Harvard and am about to enter law school. But I like cute and whimsical things that make me smile. So sue me."

"It's all part of what makes you unique. You don't give a fuck. At the same time, you look amazing in whatever you wear—even with a cartoon kitty face on your shirt, all I see is the beautiful woman inside of it." His eyes moved over me before he looked out toward the water. "Do you want to take a ride, or…"

"I think we should just sit here. I want to be able to talk, and we can't do that if the motor is running."

"Okay." He smiled.

I looked down at my shirt. "So…there's a bit more to Hello Kitty, actually, than just me liking it."

"What's that? Tell me."

"It reminds me of my mother…before she died." I looked up at the stars. "There was a Sanrio store at the mall. She'd take me there and let me pick out Hello Kitty trinkets. That's one of the few memories I have with my mother. Whenever I look at this cat, it reminds me of that innocent time in my life. You'd think it might make me sad, but for some reason, it doesn't. It takes me back to those simple moments before everything changed."

"That makes sense. Nothing is ever shallow when it comes to you."

As he looked into my eyes, I summoned my courage. "Why haven't you kissed me?"

His eyes widened. "You think I haven't *wanted* to kiss you?"

"I don't know. It seems like you're intentionally staying away. You haven't asked me to go anywhere, either. I just thought—"

"You're right. I'm a bit scared to kiss you again. Because the last time I did, I wasn't even on this damn Earth anymore. I'd never felt anything like it. That carpark didn't exist. You told me certain things were off limits, and I don't trust myself not to take things too far." He exhaled. "I've been walking on eggshells because I don't want to push you into something you'll regret."

The only regret I had at this point was having made him feel that way. "I'm struggling with what I said to you in my room that night—the boundary I set. Sometimes I blurt things I'm worried about before I think them through. It's like I'm afraid I'll change my mind, so I make sure I get it out."

"You've changed your mind about what you said?" he asked in a low voice.

"I don't know," I whispered. "Sometimes the things that scare me the most are the things I really want."

He swallowed. "You know what I think, Felicity?"

"What?"

"I think we shouldn't worry about it so much. Boundaries, no boundaries. I think we need to let life happen and see how it goes." He reached out his hand. "You with me?"

I took it and smiled, enjoying the warmth of his skin a little too much.

He looked out at the water again. "I'm not gonna promise I won't hurt you. I think we've already established that's a given. We're both going to end up hurt. But I promise to make every moment with you matter up until that time."

I needed to trust him. "Okay."

"There's something else I need to say," he added.

I nodded.

"I know we previously compared what we're doing together this summer to a losing game. But I want to make something clear. As long as I'm here, as long as we're together, this is a relationship, not a game, to me. And even if it has to end, it's no less valuable than if it lasted forever. We have a tendency in life to judge the value of a relationship by how long it lasts. But some of the worst ones are the longest-lasting. A connection between two people is no less valuable if cut short by circumstances." His eyes glowed in the moonlight. "You already mean so much to me."

Emotions bubbled up inside me; I'd really needed to hear that.

"I'm so glad you came over tonight," he said.

"Me too."

He looked toward the house. "After they eat, I'm certain he's going to take the Marias upstairs. Maybe it will be safe to go inside then. We can have the living room to ourselves."

I shrugged. "Either way. I don't care if they're there as long as we get to hang out."

"Hanging out with you is becoming one of my favorite things," he said.

His admission made me feel guilty. Something I'd done last night before bed started to weigh on me. "I have a confession, Leo, and I don't know if you're gonna like it."

His body went rigid. "All right."

"Remember how you said you Googled me once?"

"Yeah?" He gulped.

"Well, I did the same to you. It started because I wanted to learn about the peerage system and the world you come from without having to ask you a million questions. That unfortunately led to other internet searching."

His expression fell. "Find anything interesting?"

"Lots, actually," I said.

"I'm sure." He scrubbed his hand over his face, looking frustrated. "It sucks that getting to know me has to involve history lessons and research."

Shit. "You're upset at me."

"No. No, of course not. I'm surprised it took you so long, to be honest. It's just...all of that is not a representation of who I am. Not the history, of course. But the gossip part. It's lies, mostly. Some paparazzo snapping a photo of me and some girl they think is my future wife, when in fact, we'd probably just met. Or saying I'm buying cocaine when it was weed, which I rarely smoke, but of course they'll make me out to be a massive drug addict. Basically, it's rubbish ninety-nine percent of the time. So it's useless."

"I understand that."

"Do you?" He searched my eyes.

"Yes. I do."

"Well, then, you're smart. Many people aren't. They just believe what they read. You'll never get to know me through some high-society gossip rag."

I hated that I'd upset him. More than that, I hated that I'd disappointed him.

"Your mother is very beautiful," I added.

"That she is. Thank you."

"I can see a lot of her face in yours."

"Are you saying you think *I'm* beautiful, then?" He winked. "So, what other things did you dig up?"

I was afraid to ask the next question, but he seemed open to further inquisition.

"Do you have a brother?"

His expression darkened. "Where did you read that?"

"There was this website that listed the family trees of a bunch of landowning, aristocratic families. You know how it is with internet searching—it leads you down one rabbit hole to the next. Anyway, it listed both Leo and Thomas as the children of your parents, Leo and Scarlet. You had said you were an only child, so I was curious."

He nodded slowly and looked down at his thumbs as he twiddled them. "Thomas is my brother, yes," he finally said.

"I didn't know you had—"

"He died in childbirth."

My heart clenched. "Oh no. Gosh, I'm sorry."

"It's okay," he whispered.

"Was he older or younger?"

"Neither. He was my twin."

My chest felt heavier by the moment.

"There were some complications. Apparently, something can happen where one twin essentially donates blood to the other. It's called twin-to-twin transfusion syndrome. And the recipient can suffer complications. It doesn't always end badly, but it did in our case. They tried surgery to save him, but he was stillborn. My parents had made the mistake of announcing they were having twins ahead of time, so they couldn't mourn in private. The press was all over it—the burial and everything."

I felt absolutely nauseous for having initiated this conversation.

Tears formed in my eyes. "I should have never brought this up." I reached for his hand. "I'm so sorry, Leo."

"It's okay." He looped his fingers through mine and squeezed. "It is what it is. I can't change it." He was silent for a while. "Can I ask you a personal question, too?"

I nodded.

"Do you have any idea who your father is?"

He must have assumed this was a sore subject for me, but I was pretty numb to the idea of my father. At least that was how I'd trained myself—not to feel anything.

"Not a clue."

"Have you ever tried to find out?"

I grabbed a water and took a long sip before closing the bottle. "When I was really young, I just believed whatever my mother said. She told me she didn't know who my father was, and there was no way to figure it out. As I got older and understood the nature of her lifestyle as a junkie—that she might have used her body for drug money—I realized that was probably true. I guess I could've hired a private investigator, but I never pursued it. Whoever he is, he's probably either a drug dealer my mother got involved with, or some poor, unsuspecting soul who has no clue he fathered a child. I don't want to put anyone through the shock of finding out they have a kid twenty-four years later."

Leo smiled sympathetically. "What if he wasn't disappointed? What if he looked at it as a blessing?"

I shook my head. "I don't think I want to know the truth. I know that sounds odd, but I don't think I could handle being rejected by him—whoever he is. It's why I've never done one of those genealogy tests that match you with relatives. Maybe I'm missing out. Maybe I'm not. It's a risk I've decided to take. Or not to take. However you look at it."

"Fair enough."

"Do you think I'm dumb for shutting the door on the possibility that I could find my father someday?"

"There's absolutely nothing about you that's dumb, Felicity. You know who you are, and you know what you can handle."

The boat rocked gently as we continued to talk.

"It's amazing how comfortable I am around you," Leo said. "Back home, I feel like I'm two people—the one others see, and the one I really am, my authentic self. I trust almost no one. But I trust you. It's a good feeling to let my guard down." He looked up at the sky. "At the same time, I feel this pressure to experience so much more with you in the little time we have because I'm leaving. I want to know everything about you."

"There's not that much left to tell. I've told you almost everything. What else do you want to know?"

His eyes burned into mine for several seconds. "I want to know what you ache for..."

Despite the now-cool night air, I felt a rush of heat.

"This," I finally said. "I hadn't been worried about you leaving until you reminded me just now of how little time we have. I've been lost in our conversation tonight. I'm loving being here with you. It's peaceful and exciting at the same time. I ache for more moments like this."

He took my hand in his. "Do you want to know what I ache for?"

"What?"

"More time." He squeezed. "More time with you. Or maybe I ache for time to stand still."

"Yeah," I muttered.

When I rubbed my hands over my arms, he said, "It's chillier than I thought out here. Do you want to go inside for a bit? I'm thinking they're probably upstairs by now. Maybe we'll have some privacy."

"That sounds good."

We exited the boat and made our way inside. Thankfully, the kitchen was empty. I could hear footsteps upstairs and laughter in the distance, but it seemed we were in the clear from having to deal with the trio.

"Are you hungry for a late-night snack?" Leo asked. "I feel like I should make you something to eat."

"Actually, I skipped dinner. I wasn't that hungry earlier, but now it's catching up with me. So yeah, I could eat."

He looked around the kitchen. "Well, I'll make you something, then."

"I thought you couldn't cook."

"I can't."

That gave me a good chuckle.

"I've never cooked for anyone," he said. "But it's your lucky night. Because I'm going to cook for you."

"This should be interesting."

"Actually, it's probably going to be dreadful."

"What are you making?"

"It's a little something called...you'll find out." He winked. "Actually, I have no clue. But I'll figure something out. Sit down and put your feet up in the living room. I'll bring dinner to you. Can I get you a glass of wine?"

"It's midnight. I probably shouldn't."

"It's five o'clock somewhere, Felicity."

"Okay, sure." I shrugged. "Why not?"

He poured me a glass of wine, and I did as he said: put my feet up in the living room as I gazed out the large window at the moonlight over the bay. A warmness came over me. Leo made me feel wanted, special, and safe in a way I wasn't used to experiencing. If I could bottle this feeling forever, I would. I knew it was fleeting, but for the moment, I cherished it.

Over the next several minutes, I heard lots of clanking in the kitchen. I hoped Leo wasn't in some kind of distress. Finally, he appeared at the entrance to the living room.

"Okay, so it turns out, Sigmund pretty much cooked everything decent we had in the refrigerator tonight. I tried to make you an omelet, but I messed with it too much, and now it looks like soggy brains."

I cackled. *He's adorable.* I probably needed to rescue him, even if this was super entertaining. "Do you need help?"

"No. I have a Plan B. I'm going to present it to you, but you need to promise not to laugh."

"I promise." I paused. "Not to laugh...too much."

He wriggled his brows. "I'll be right back."

A few minutes later, he returned carrying a single plate.

My mouth dropped when I looked closer and realized what was on it: SpaghettiOs. The funniest part was the garnish of basil in the corner to make it look fancy.

"Turns out, all I know how to do is open a can and heat the contents."

"But look how nicely you plated everything."

"I was hoping the garnish would distract from the otherwise pathetic offering. Does it count as cooking if it comes out of a can?"

"You know what? I'm going to eat this. And I'm gonna enjoy it. You know why?"

"Why?" He grinned.

"Because you made it, even if that only entailed opening the can and heating it up. You said you'd never made anything for anyone. I'm honored to be the first." I hadn't had SpaghettiOs since I was a kid. I took a bite, surprised to find that they tasted better than I remembered. "This is surprisingly good...tangy."

"Yeah?"

"Or maybe I'm just so hungry that anything tastes good."

"Probably the latter. But I'll take it as a win."

Holding the fork up to his mouth, I said, "Taste."

Leo took a bite and spoke with his mouth full. "It's not terrible."

I ended up feeding him random bites of SpaghettiOs as we talked and laughed.

This night, this "dinner," even if a bit ridiculous, was everything to me. There are some moments you just know you'll never forget, and this SpaghettiOs supper was one of them.

After I finished eating, Leo took my plate into the kitchen.

He returned to his seat on the couch next to me. My eyes fell to his mouth. Licking some remaining wine off my lips, I hoped so badly that he'd kiss me.

It seemed he'd picked up on my signal, because within seconds he leaned in, breathing erratically before taking my mouth with his. I gasped, perhaps a little too loudly, because he laughed against my lips. As he leaned over me on the sofa, pressing his chest into mine, Leo kissed me as if his life depended on it, as if he were making up for all the time this week when he'd held back.

Threading my fingers through his hair, I relaxed into the kiss, forcing away the voice inside my head that was ready to remind me I was setting myself up for a broken heart. I kissed him harder, moaning against his mouth and savoring his taste. He groaned as he took my bottom lip between his teeth and pulled ever so gently before deepening the kiss once again. From the commanding way he kissed, it was easy to imagine what he might be like in bed. I suspected he knew exactly how to please a woman.

As the kiss escalated, somehow I ended up under him. Rather than resist the change, I opened my legs, allowing him to position himself between them. Through his jeans, I felt the heat of his erection as he grinded himself against my throbbing clit. Leo lowered his mouth, kissing down the length of my neck. Then he suddenly stopped, resting his mouth against my skin and breathing against me for several seconds.

He looked up at me in a daze before pulling away. "I... think I should stop."

"Why?"

"Because it started to feel like you weren't going to stop me if I went further."

"You're right. I wouldn't have," I said honestly. My body yearned for his return as a coldness swept over me.

"Felicity..." he whispered.

"What?"

"I was seconds from being inside of you. At least that's where I wanted to be. But I know that's not what *you* want right now, even if you were getting carried away." He leaned his head on the back of the couch and turned to me. "I lose all sense of judgment when I'm kissing you, smelling you, touching you. I am by no means new to this...but *this* level of need *is* new to me. I've never been so drawn to someone I also need to be careful with. I've never *cared* this much before."

He raked his hands through his hair. "You asked me earlier what I ache for. And I wasn't completely specific. I said 'more time', and of course that's true. But I ache for so much more when it comes to you. I ache for everyday, mundane things that I've never yearned for—like date night, going out to dinner, and coming home to curl up on the couch together. I've never longed for that with anyone. Ever. Couldn't have cared less about such things before. But I also ache to lie with you at night...to worship your body, to trace my tongue over every single one of your freckles, to take my time with you and give you the best fucking orgasm you've ever dreamed of. And if you don't think you'll ever be ready for that with me, I need to be careful not to push things. But I can't lie to you. I want that. I want all of that with you, Felicity. So badly."

I was barely able to breathe. "Where the hell did you come from, Leo?" I shut my eyes and exhaled. "This is so fucked-up. I want you, too. I'm just scared."

"You're not the only one."

I sat up, resting my head on his shoulder. "I know I should probably head home, but I don't want to."

"Stay the night with me, then. We don't have to go upstairs. We'll stay right here and talk until we can't keep our eyes open anymore. Just don't leave."

I looked up at him. "Okay. I won't." Nestling my body into the crook of his arm, I said, "Tell me a story."

"What kind of story?"

"Take me to the English countryside. Virtually. Take me home with you. Tell me what it's like. Pretend you've just arrived back. Tell me what happens. Describe for me what it all looks like."

"All right." He rested his chin on my head and wrapped me in his arms. "There are rolling green hills everywhere. It's just finished raining, so I can see a rainbow in the distance as the driver approaches our property."

"Tell me about your house."

"It's very...large, a stately home."

"Like a castle?"

"Not quite."

"Like *Downton Abbey*?"

"Like a version of that, perhaps. Made of brick."

"What happens when you go inside?"

"When I get there, it's neither my mother nor father who greet me, but rather Camila, our house manager."

"What does she do exactly?"

"Oversees the staff."

"How many people work there?"

"About ten."

"Wow."

"It's a bit much, but that's how it's always been from generation to generation."

"Your parents won't greet you when you arrive?"

"If I've arrived during the day, Mum is probably off at some meeting with her friends. My father is likely at his office off site...if he's feeling up to working on that particular day."

"Okay, so it's Camila you see first. What is she like?"

"She's tall and can be a bit scary." He laughed. "She keeps the house in order, though. Older...in her fifties. Blond hair tied back tightly in a bun. Very serious demeanor but manages to break a smile once in a while if I work hard enough at it. I love making her laugh because it's not something she offers very easily."

I smiled. "What's the first thing you do?"

"I drop my things and head to the kitchen with Camila. She and I will have a talk about my travels. I'll give her the abbreviated recap of our trip. I'm probably exhausted, so I'll go to my room soon thereafter."

"What does your room look like?"

"It's large. A four-post bed. Dark-wood crown molding. A little depressing and cold, actually."

"What's the first thing you do when you get to your room?"

"I take a long, hot shower in my bathroom."

"And after?"

"I totally crash, tired from the trip, but completely and utterly depressed to have left you. So, I go to my bed and spend the first of many evenings staring at your photo."

Even though what he'd just said hit me deep in my heart, I made light of things by smacking his chest. "Sap."

"Maybe." He smiled, but it didn't reach his eyes.

Curling farther into his arms, I rested my head on his chest, soothed by the rise and fall of his breathing. Then Leo kissed the top of my head.

We ended up talking into the wee hours of the morning—until the sound of Sig's voice woke us the next day.

CHAPTER 11

Leo

Track 11: "Jealous Guy" by John Lennon and The Plastic Ono Band

"Well, well, well, what's going on here?"

My cousin's voice was grating.

"What does it look like?" I said, squinting at the sun shining in through the windows in the living room.

"To me? It looks like someone went from Hello Kitty to Hello Titty last night."

Felicity's eyes fluttered open.

"It's none of your business, in any case," I said, rubbing her shoulders. "Are you okay?"

She looked up groggily and smiled. "Sure. Why wouldn't I be?"

I was relieved she seemed happy to still be here. We'd been talking for so long last night that we'd both shut down.

"Where are the Marias?" she asked Sig.

"They're coming downstairs. I was going to make breakfast. Are you two hungry?"

I didn't think she'd want to be around Sigmund's harem, so it surprised me when she said, "Yeah. Breakfast sounds great."

Felicity stood from the couch, looking adorable with her hair all messed up from sleep. While I'd often fantasized about lying next to her at night, I hadn't anticipated that our first sleepover would be on the sofa. It wasn't the most comfortable night's rest, but I'd do it every night if it meant she'd stay again.

After Sig disappeared into the kitchen, I placed my hand on her cheek. "How did you sleep?"

"Surprisingly good. When I woke up, it took me a second to realize where I was." She squinted. "What?"

"I want to kiss you," I admitted.

"Kiss me, then."

Just when I'd readied myself to plant one on her, we were interrupted by the sound of Sigmund's girls skipping down the stairs.

Now that our moment was ruined, Felicity and I ventured into the kitchen. The coffee had just finished brewing, so I grabbed two mugs. Sigmund stood at the counter mixing eggs for what I assumed were omelets.

"How do you take your coffee?" I asked.

"Black, like Sigmund's soul," she teased.

"I think you meant *steaming hot* like Sigmund," my cousin fired back.

Felicity laughed, and Sigmund smiled as he continued cooking. It was nice to see them getting along. I'd worried he might have gotten under her skin, though she'd likely never admit it. But if I didn't know better, it almost seemed like she enjoyed his company.

I poured four coffees, serving Felicity first and then the Marias.

Sigmund's girlfriends began talking to each other in Portuguese, and I noticed Felicity blinking rapidly as she listened, like she was trying to decipher what they were saying.

Finally, she blurted, "It's the way I go down on him."

Say what?

"That got your attention, didn't it?" she added.

Both women froze at once.

"I'm lost," I said. "What's going on?"

Felicity turned to me. "They aren't sure what you see in me. I told them it must be the way I go down on you." She looked back over at them. "Kidding, by the way. I haven't done that to him...*yet*. It was just the first thing that came to mind." She placed her hand on my knee. "They've been talking shit about us from the moment they came downstairs."

I didn't know what affected me more—the nerve of these girls or the fact that Felicity had implied she planned to go down on me.

"You speak Portuguese?" Maria One asked, looking dumbfounded.

"One of the foster moms I had growing up was from Portugal. Her mother, whom I called Vavo—which, as you know, means grandmother—used to teach me Portuguese. So, while I don't speak it often, I can understand it *really* well."

"Shite," Sigmund muttered. Even *he* looked embarrassed at the behavior of his friends.

But I was proud of the way Felicity had handled it.

"If you're gonna talk shit about someone, you should probably make sure they don't speak the language," Felicity added. "Not everyone is unilingual."

"I'm sorry. We didn't mean anything by it," Maria Two said.

"You mean, you didn't mean for me to *understand*. You most certainly meant what you said. It's pretty sad when women decide to talk smack about other women before they get to know them. You're lucky I'm smart enough to understand what's really going on when that happens. You do it to feel better about yourselves. I mean, how insecure do you have to be to simultaneously fawn over the same man, right? You're so wonderful that he needs *two* of you? Think about it. It's pathetic." Felicity took a long sip of her coffee. "Anyway, we're even. You said a mean thing. I said a mean thing. Now let's just forget about it and eat some chorizo and eggs. Life's too short for this bullshit."

She turned to me before looking back at them. "Incidentally, I'm not entirely sure what he sees in me, either. But I've been trying to lose the guy since I first met him and can't seem to do it." She winked at me.

God. I wanted to lift her up and kiss her so hard, but I was speechless at the moment. *What did I see in her?* That wasn't a short answer. It was more like I couldn't see *anything else* whenever she was around.

Remarkably, the rest of breakfast went relatively well. After Felicity put the Marias in their place, she spent a good portion of the morning chatting with them. She even asked them to test her Portuguese, so she could prove just how much she remembered.

By the time Sigmund and I had cleaned up everyone's plates, you would have thought the three of them were friends from the way they were laughing together. All was apparently forgotten. It takes a special kind of person to befriend people who were trying to kick her down just moments earlier. Felicity undoubtedly had practice proving herself to people who made assumptions about her.

Later that afternoon, Felicity and I went over to Mrs. Barbosa's to put the finishing touches on the interior before we'd have to pause to let the electrician come in and do his part.

To my dismay, her ex, Matt, showed up to help, along with Bailey and Stewart. He said it was his final day before he was set to return to Pennsylvania.

Things were fairly routine until the end of the afternoon when Matt asked Felicity if he could speak to her privately. She followed him to the backyard, and they sat on the swing where Theo had held me hostage. My blood boiled.

As I lingered in a spot where I could see what they were doing, I muttered, "What does he want?" I hadn't realized I'd asked that question aloud until Bailey answered me.

"He wants her."

I turned to her. "Elaborate."

She looked over at them as she answered. "He's convinced that once she moves to Pennsylvania, they're going to reconcile."

I swallowed. "How far is he from where she'll be living?"

"About forty-five minutes."

Brilliant. Just brilliant. "You know for a fact that he's trying to get back together with her?"

"Yeah. He's told Stewart. I probably shouldn't be telling you this, but I suppose it's good for you to know what you're up against. Not that it matters anyway, right? Since you're leaving."

She had a point. It shouldn't have mattered, but somehow it did. *A lot.*

"Do you think she still has feelings for him?"

"I don't really know. She'd tell you she didn't, if you asked her, but she was completely devastated when he broke up with her. So I can't imagine that she doesn't still harbor some feelings. Although right now, she's really into you. Maybe she won't realize any feelings she still has for Matt until you're out of the picture and she's in Pennsylvania."

Adrenaline raced through my veins. It seemed like Bailey was intentionally trying to push my buttons, like she felt a certain animosity about the fact that I was set to hurt her friend. I couldn't fucking blame her.

"He does care about her," she added after a moment. "I know he broke her heart, but he says he's always regretted it. They were so young. He thought he was doing what was right for both of them at the time. But in retrospect, he said he realizes he's always loved her."

Her words downright gutted me, but I appreciated her candor—until what she said next.

"I don't think he's the only one who still has feelings. Felicity won't admit to anything because he hurt her. But

I wouldn't be surprised if on some subconscious level, she chose Pennsylvania for law school because she knows he's there."

I felt a bit sick.

After their conversation, Matt left for the day, and Felicity was quiet for the rest of the afternoon. The change in her mood made me uneasy because it told me he'd had an effect on her. But perhaps my own reaction to the idea of her harboring feelings for him made me the most uneasy.

During the ride home, she was the first to bring up the subject.

"I'm sorry for leaving to talk to Matt earlier."

I clenched my jaw. "You don't need to apologize."

"It was rude of me."

"You don't owe me an explanation."

"You're probably wondering what it was all about, though."

My pulse sped up. *Fuck yes, I want to know.* "You don't have to tell me, if you don't want to."

She glanced out the car window. "Matt seems to think we should reconnect just because I'm moving to Pennsylvania. He claims he made a mistake when he ended things with me, and once this summer is over and I'm done with what he calls 'my little fling' with you, he'll be there waiting for me."

I wanted to fucking murder him. Clearing my throat, I said, "Is that what this feels like to you—a *little* fling?"

"It feels like more, even if it's temporary."

Reaching for her hand, I brought it to my mouth and kissed it. "It feels like more to me, too. But our situation is what it is, Felicity. You need to do whatever will make you happy after this summer." Admitting that was hard.

"I won't go back to him. I won't ever have peace being with someone who left me in the past. I can never trust him again."

Fuck. My chest hurt. "You can't trust him for leaving you in the past, just like you can't trust someone who's leaving you in the future."

She let out a long breath but didn't respond.

"I just want you to be happy," I whispered, meaning that, even if it killed me to think of her with another man.

"I *am* happy—spending the summer with you. I don't want to think about anything beyond August," she said.

"We have that in common."

This time, she took my hand and kissed it. "Anyway, I didn't mean to make you uncomfortable by going to talk to him."

"You didn't do anything wrong. My unreasonable feelings over it are what I can't seem to grapple with."

"Well, he's gone now. He won't be showing up again. So let's not think about it anymore. Okay?"

Still struggling with my jealousy, I chewed on my lip. "All right, love."

After some silence, I brought up something I'd been waiting to ask. "So...Sigmund told me he and the Marias are planning to spend the upcoming July Fourth weekend in Boston. He wanted to know if we wanted to join them."

She rolled her eyes sarcastically. "As much as I love the Marias, that sort of sounds miserable to me."

"Me, too." I let out a relieved breath. "Good. I thought I'd ask, but I'd much rather stay here and have the house to ourselves—that is, if you want to stay with me for the weekend," I quickly corrected. "You can have my bed. I'll sleep in Sigmund's room. I don't want you to think I'm asking because—"

"Heck yes! I don't even have to think about it. There won't be many more opportunities. We only have so many weekends left, and I'm sure he won't be away for all of them. Not that I dislike him, but—"

"But he can be a pain in the arse, and it's nice to have some privacy, yes?"

"Exactly," she agreed.

Fuck yes. "I'd better stock up on SpaghettiOs."

"Or...we could just get takeout." She winked.

"Don't worry. I was only kidding. I'll spare you."

Her eyes glimmered. "You know what the best part is?"

"What?"

"I don't have to work on Friday night. So we can start the weekend Friday afternoon."

"Brilliant. I think they're heading to Boston around the same time."

"That couldn't be more perfect."

Feeling ecstatic, I paused. "No, it really couldn't."

Felicity had to work that evening, so I dropped her off and returned to the house. My phone rang as I was rummaging through the refrigerator, hoping for leftovers from whatever Sigmund had made for lunch.

It was my grandmother. I pressed a button to put her on speakerphone. "Hey, Nan. It's late there. Is everything okay?"

"Yes. Didn't mean to alarm you. I'm having trouble sleeping, so I figured I'd check in on you. The last time we talked it was a sad state of affairs."

So much had happened since then. "I'm doing quite well, actually."

"You managed to get over the girl?"

I hesitated. "Not exactly. Uh...things took sort of an unexpected turn after we last spoke."

She figured it out without me having to even say anything. "Oh my..."

"Yeah." Over the next several minutes, I filled my grandmother in on the recent turn of events with Felicity. "Anyway, I know what you're going to say—that spending more time with her is a terrible idea. But I can't quit her as long as I'm here."

"I'm not going to give you grief, Leo. After we spoke previously, I suspected it might not have been the last of her. As long as you're prepared for the inevitable outcome, I see no problem with it."

"You're not going to lecture me, then?"

"What good would that do? Unlike my thick-headed daughter, I realize no amount of scolding is going to change things when it comes to matters of the heart. I don't even try. There are times in life when we simply choose to jump into the fire, even if we know we're going to get burned. We've all done it. And I'll have you know, your mother is no stranger to that, either."

"What does that mean? Are you holding back on me?"

"Let's just say, before she married your father, there was a certain groundskeeper I'd spotted far too many times climbing down from your mother's bedroom window."

My jaw dropped. "Really…"

"Feel free to do what you will with that information. Although, if you call her out on it, she'll likely say I'm senile and deny it. But I assure you, it's true."

I laughed. "Thanks for the tip, Nan."

She sighed. "It's a shame you can't take a lesson from Sigmund. He never gets his heart involved in anything."

"I haven't let that happen until now. This is new for me. And I know it would be much easier to be more like Sigmund right now."

She laughed. "The irony, of course, is that your cousin doesn't have the same expectations placed upon him. He'd be perfect for a life of keeping up appearances."

"Well, he's *keeping up* with two women at the same time currently."

"What's new about that?"

"I mean, *literally* the same time. That's what's new."

"Oh. He's too much, that one."

My cousin walked into the room.

"Speak of the devil, Nan. Sigmund just got here. I'm going to let you go. I need to fill him in on some things."

"Okay. Love you, my boy. Tell my other grandson hello and to behave."

"I will." I hung up and turned to him. "Nan says to behave."

"That's why I'm her favorite."

I tossed my phone aside. "So, I ran the Boston trip by Felicity, and we've decided to just stay here."

"Ah. Taking advantage of having the house to yourself so you can have a shagfest in peace, eh?"

"I highly doubt that's going to happen."

"You expect me to believe that?"

"I don't know what will happen. Whatever *she* wants."

"You have no chill about this, and you know it. Stop acting like you're not *dying* to fuck her. It's the only time in your life you've had to wait for anything you've wanted."

"We don't have to have sex in order to enjoy each other."

He examined my face. "All right, I'll stop. It's clear you really like her. And I can't believe I'm saying this, but I'm...starting to as well."

I squinted. "What's that supposed to mean?"

"Relax. I've got my hands full as it is. I don't fancy your girl in that way. I just meant I can see now why you like her. She's grown on me. I still maintain that you're making a mistake and getting in over your head, but I'm not going to give you grief about it anymore."

"I appreciate that."

He left the room, and a few minutes later returned, throwing a box at my chest.

It was a gargantuan box of condoms.

"What the hell? I have my own, thanks. Who needs this many condoms, anyway?"

"The Marias took me to a wholesale store in Massachusetts. It's called BJ's Warehouse. Fitting name, eh?"

"You're insane."

"I got a three-pack of those boxes. You can keep that one."

Shaking my head, I threw the box of condoms and hit him in the chest.

CHAPTER 12
Felicity

Track 12: "Sunshine of Your Love" by Cream

Friday afternoon seemed to take forever to get here. I spent the morning cleaning my room and setting up some more of my planners, just to pass the time. I finally opted to put myself out of my misery and head over to Leo's a little early.

The afternoon sun was shining brightly as I rang his doorbell.

He opened the door with a huge smile. "Welcome home, gorgeous."

"I wish," I said, giving him a once-over.

"Come in."

Wow. He'd apparently just been weightlifting. He wore a pair of black workout tights. I never thought a man in tights could be sexy, but they really showed off the muscles in his legs, which I knew he worked hard on. A sheen of sweat glistened over his chest, and his big feet were bare, which I found incredibly hot.

"Did I interrupt your fitness regimen?"

"I thought you were arriving closer to three, so I figured I'd sneak a workout in, but getting to see you earlier is much better." He looked down at my overnight bag, which was covered in tiny Hello Kitty heads. "You're fucking adorable with that bag."

"Hello Kitty. Did you expect anything else?" It fell to the ground with a thud as I looked around. "Sig already left?"

"Yes. We're completely free. Although, he left you a present."

Leo walked over to a glass cake display on the counter. Sig had baked something and left a sticky note on the front of the glass.

I peeled it off and read it.

A gingerbread for a gingerhead.
I know you'll miss me this weekend. (Not!)
You and Leo will have to try to find a way to entertain each other. I'm sure you can figure something out, eh?
P.S. This is a new recipe. Hope you like it. I suggest adding some "Leo is whipped" cream, which is in the refrigerator.

Fondly,
Your Favorite Ball Buster

"He's a joy, isn't he?" Leo rolled his eyes. "At least it's edible, unlike the majority of the crap he pulls."

"I'm definitely going to devour that later." Somehow my eyes were actually on Leo's body when I said that. And I couldn't help thinking how badly I wanted to devour *him.*

His eyes lingered on mine, then dropped to my chest, which was probably more exposed than he'd ever seen it. "You look so fucking beautiful right now."

I looked down at my cami and denim shorts. "Thank you." I looked over the ridges of his chest. "You should finish your workout since I interrupted you." *Maybe I'll watch.*

"No need. I was pretty much finished. I've been sort of bouncing off the walls all day waiting for you. Nervous energy, I guess."

"Oh my God. I was the same way. Although, I'm surprised *you're* nervous to have me here."

"More like excited—on top of the world. I just want you to have a nice weekend and be happy. That's all."

"I *am*, Leo. I really am. I don't want to overthink anything. I just want to let loose and have fun with you."

"I'm so fucking down for that," he said, lightly pinching my cheek. "On that note, what can I get you to drink?"

"I'm gonna hold off for a bit. The night is young."

"Probably a good idea." Leo smiled. "What do you want to do first? We can go out on the boat for a while, swim in the bay, watch a movie—the possibilities are endless."

"It's pretty hot out. I think a swim would be nice before the sun goes down."

He nodded. "Let me show you to your room so you can change."

I loved that he was being respectful, giving me my own room. I wasn't sure how to tell him I hoped to bunk with *him* tonight. It was probably wise to have the option of separate quarters, though.

He led me up the stairs and into his room. I'd yet to be inside of it.

"This is mine, but I'll be sleeping in Sigmund's room. There's a guest room, as well, but it's not as nice as this, and this room has a great bathroom."

The bedroom was stunning—sleek, black furniture, and gray satin sheets. It looked like something fit for a king, *or a lord*.

"This is so nice. Thank you for giving me your room."

"Anything for you." He took a deep breath. "Anyway, I should let you get changed." But he didn't budge.

I sat down at the edge of the bed and looked over at the bedside table. A necklace I'd seen him wear before was on top. It had a man's gold and diamond ring dangling from it.

"What's the story with the ring on that necklace?"

"It was my grandfather's. It's my most prized possession, so I don't travel without it. It's sort of like a good-luck charm. He gave it to me when I was sixteen. My grandad was ill and knew he didn't have much time left. That was a ring he'd always worn on his pinky finger. He told me to wear it around my neck as a reminder of him. I feel like it brings me strength in times when I need it."

"That's amazing. I'd wondered if it had significance..."

The drawer beneath it was partially open.

"That's quite a box of condoms in there. Can never be too careful, I guess?"

Leo's face turned beet red—like I'd never seen it before.

He gritted his teeth. "Fucking Sigmund."

"It's no biggie. Every guy has condoms in his drawer..."

"Maybe. But not every guy has a box that's large enough for a small village. I didn't put those in there. My idiot cousin bought that box as a gag gift going into this weekend. I gave them back, but he must have put them there and conveniently left the drawer open. Probably hoped you'd find them."

"Where the heck did he even get a box that huge?"

"BJ's, of all places."

"Sig is probably the only person on Earth who might actually need this many." I gathered my courage for a moment.

Leo read my mind. "You look like you have a question."

"I'm curious. Have you been with anyone since you've been in the States?"

Leo blinked a few times. "One person. When we were in California the first month. It was just a one-night thing. No emotional attachment. It didn't mean anything, and I was careful."

"You've said you've been with a lot of women..." I felt my face heat up. "I'm sorry. I didn't plan to have this conversation now. I've just been wondering about it."

Leo sat down next to me. "Look, I've told you before that you can ask me anything, and I'll tell you the truth." He sighed. "I've never counted. But I've never had unprotected sex. Not even once. And I get regular check-ups to be on the safe side."

"Okay," I said, relieved that he'd offered that last bit of information.

He stared off. "I think it's around twenty-five girls I've been with, if I had to estimate. I had the one girlfriend in high school, and there have just been casual hookups since then—mostly women who've wanted more from me or wanted to sleep with me because of my status. I've been ultra careful because I know that for many of the women back home, there are big incentives to trap me. I've been a bit fearful during every sexual encounter, to be honest. I've always insisted on using my own condoms—things like that. I never trusted that someone wouldn't tamper with them. Does that sound crazy?"

"No, it doesn't sound crazy at all. I wouldn't trust anyone, either, if I were you."

"I can't remember the last time I fully let go during sex, just allowed myself to be completely lost in someone. There's always a bit of anxiety putting a damper on things." He paused, his eyes searching mine. "When was the last time for you?"

Ugh. Now it was my turn to stop and calculate. There certainly weren't that many. "It's been a while…"

"Yeah? How long?"

"Well, I've already told you I had two relationships. My first time was with Matt, and then my college boyfriend, Finn. After that ended, I wasn't with anyone for a long time." I paused, my palms getting sweaty. "About a year ago, when I was still living in Boston, I just…really started to miss sex. So I hooked up with someone I met online who said he was only interested in a one-night stand. I was safe, of course, but it had been so long, and I needed it." I exhaled, not sure why that was hard to admit when Leo was far more experienced.

He let out a shaky breath. I couldn't tell if he was upset or turned on by what I'd just admitted. Then he asked, "Did that…scratch your itch?"

"It did, I suppose. But there's been no one since. So, it's been a while." I shook my head. "I can't believe I just admitted that to you." I started to look down but felt his hand on my chin.

He brought my eyes to his. "Why?"

"I don't know. I don't want you to think I take it lightly or something."

"You shouldn't feel ashamed. You're human. You have needs." He lowered his hand to my leg. His voice grew thick. "Do you want to know what I really think about it?"

"Yes."

He squeezed my knee. "Okay. Of course, I don't *love* thinking about you having sex with some strange guy. But I find it incredibly hot that you knew what you wanted and let yourself have it. You come across as a bit reserved, but I think there's a wild side in there somewhere. And I'm here for it. I'm *so* fucking here for it." He leaned in and kissed my neck.

I bent my head back to enjoy it. "I think everyone's libido peaks at different times. I find the older I get, the more I crave sex."

Leo grabbed one of his pillows and placed it over his face, letting out a muffled groan.

"What's that all about?" I giggled.

His hair was a bit messed up as he emerged from behind the pillow. "You realize you're killing me right now, right? I can't remember the last time I was this turned on. And we're merely *talking*. It's too early in the weekend for me to be feeling like this. I'm supposed to be on my best behavior, but fuck, Felicity..." He pointed down to the massive erection threatening to bust through his black workout tights. "Of course, I'd choose the worst pants to be wearing under these circumstances. Look at this. It's bloody pathetic."

"I think it's hot, actually." I forced my eyes up to meet his. "I think *you're* incredibly hot."

He inched closer. "Do you now?"

"Yes."

His pupils seemed to dilate. "Well, the feeling is very mutual."

"You don't need to worry so much about behaving. Regardless of what I might have said at one time, things have changed. I think I'd like to experience you *not* on your best behavior."

His mouth curved into a grin before he planted a long, hard kiss on my lips. Revved up from our conversation, I grew wetter with each second that his tongue swirled around my mouth.

Leo pulled away. "I'm not sure you know exactly what you're signing up for in asking me not to behave, Miss Dunleavy."

I looked down at his hard-on again, and my mouth practically watered. *What is happening to me right now?*

"Seriously..." he said. "Regardless of how badly I want you, there is no pressure this weekend, all right? I hope you know that. And for the record, there are many ways we can explore each other without sleeping together. *Many* options available."

"I'd love to know what my options are." I smiled teasingly.

"They're endless, really."

"Tell me."

"You want me to spell one out for you?"

Biting my bottom lip, I nodded. "Yeah."

"Okay, to be more specific..." Leo's breath tickled my ear as he leaned in and whispered, "There's no place I'd rather be than inside you, Felicity. But if that's not what you prefer, I'd *love* to have you sit on my face and ride the fuck out of it. I can find ways to make you scream. All you need to do is tell me what you want. The ball is in your court, and nothing is off the table. But doing nothing at all is an option, too. I'm just happy you're here and can't wait to spend this time with you."

My legs quivered with anticipation.

"Was that direct enough for you?" He chuckled.

"Mmm-hmm," I muttered, so turned on, I could hardly speak. "Sounds good."

"On that note..." Leo slapped my leg. "I'm going to take a shower. *A cold one.* That will give you some privacy. You get changed. I'll meet you downstairs in a few."

He placed one last kiss on my lips, and I yearned for him to stay on this bed and take me. He deepened the kiss for a few seconds as our tongues collided before he moved back again. "Fuck. I need to pace myself today." He hopped up. "Going to shower!"

He ran out of the room so fast that he tripped on the carpet. "Damn, I'm smooth," he said as he disappeared out the door.

My mouth hurt from smiling. As I got undressed, I realized my nipples were hard as steel. After putting my bikini on, I pulled a cover-up around my body and slipped into some flip-flops.

All that talk about sex had me hot and bothered, but it was *Leo* who made me like this. The way he'd looked at me from the moment I met him. The way he wanted me. The way I wanted him. It had always been this intense. I'd just never let loose long enough to experience the depth of it.

After I ventured downstairs, I found Leo on the phone, looking tense.

"Hang on, Mum," he said. Then he whispered to me, "I'll be right off. It's my mother."

Waving my hand, I said, "Take your time."

I walked over to the French doors leading out to the deck, but I couldn't help but listen to his conversation.

"So they'll just start another round of treatment, then," he said.

My heart sank. *Shit. This must be about his father.* I turned around, unable to pretend I hadn't heard.

He continued talking to his mother for several minutes. At one point, I did finally wander into the next room to give him some privacy. When I returned to the kitchen, he was still immersed in conversation, pulling on his hair as he paced.

"Yeah. Okay. Put him on." He exhaled before it seemed his mother had put his father on the phone. "I thought we had a deal, old man. No getting sick while I'm away." He paused. "How are you feeling?"

Leo spoke to his father for about five minutes before the call ended.

He hung up and stared at the phone for a moment before turning to me. "My dad's cancer is growing. They need to start his treatment regimen again."

"I figured as much. I'm so sorry, Leo." I never seemed to know what to say in horrible situations like this.

"He'd been on a good stretch for the past year. There wasn't any growth of his lung tumor—until now. I was hoping the reprieve would continue."

"I can only imagine. It's got to be so hard on your mother and you."

"He insists that I don't need to come back right now. I feel like I should, but at the same time, I can't leave Narragansett yet. Does that make me a bad person?"

I shoved aside the panic that shot through me at the prospect of his leaving. "I think you would know if you needed to go home. You're a seven-hour flight away, right? Your mother would tell you if anything changed."

He nodded. "That's true. You're right. My father has been very supportive of this trip. I'm gonna try not to feel guilty. Instead, I need to think positive—believe that he's going to make it through this, just as he's made it through all of the other rounds of treatment."

I wrapped my arms around him. "What do you need right now?"

He squeezed me tighter and breathed into my neck. "You. *This*. I just need to touch you."

We held each other for several minutes. I could feel his heart beating against my chest.

"Let's take a dip in the bay," he finally said.

When we got outside, I slipped my cover-up over my head. Leo attempted to make his staring subtle, but I caught him checking me out every chance he got. And I didn't mind one bit, because I enjoyed every minute of ogling his perfect body as he wore nothing but swim shorts.

We spent the next hour playing in the water like two teenagers, even though the bay was pretty cold. We stayed in so long, though, that it started to feel warmer beneath the water than outside of it. I'd feel the chill whenever he lifted me up into the air and threw me. I loved wrapping my legs around him, the feel of his mouth wet from the water as he kissed me.

When we emerged from the bay, he said, "You can go first in the outdoor shower, if you prefer, before we go inside."

"Thank you."

As I walked over to the infamous shower and turned on the water, I was tempted to strip down naked here, as Leo once had. What would he do if I did?

CHAPTER 13

Leo

Track 13: "2 Become 1" by Spice Girls

My heart nearly stopped when Felicity untied the straps around her neck and let her bikini top fall to the ground. She quickly placed her hands over her breasts to cover them. Yes, I'd planned to sit here on this Adirondack chair and enjoy the sight of her showering in her bathing suit. But never did I expect her to undress in front of me. Never did I expect *this*.

What is she doing?

Am I dreaming?

She closed her eyes and let the water rain down on her hair. She then lowered her hands, finally allowing me a clear view of her breasts.

Holy shite.

I'd imagined what they looked like, and the reality only exceeded my expectations. Before I could even process her being topless, Felicity slipped off her bikini bottom.

My heart began to race as I took in her stark-naked body. I was as frozen as I was aroused. Her pussy was clean-shaven. Fucking bare—smooth and flawless. So much for Sigmund's fire crotch jokes. *Fuck. Fuck. Fuck.* Perfect. *She's perfect.*

Felicity gave me a come-hither look when our eyes met, and I felt like that was my cue to join her. At least I hoped I wasn't imagining that signal.

Hard as a rock, I eagerly stood and walked over to the shower.

"An eye for an eye, is that what this is?" I asked, feeling a little breathless.

"Maybe." She flashed an impish grin. "I thought I'd recreate the way we met."

I took a moment to examine her beauty. I'd dreamed of this body almost every night since I'd first laid eyes on her. My imagination hadn't done her justice. As I'd suspected, much more than her face and neck were covered in freckles. My dream of counting them all would be more challenging than anticipated. I wouldn't mind if I died trying, though.

"Christ. You're perfect. Do you have any idea how much I want you right now, Felicity?"

"No...but I think you should show me."

My breath hitched. "Are you sure? I don't know if you realize what you're asking for."

She panted. "Yes. I do."

I groaned, moving my mouth to her neck and sucking before running my tongue down the length of her chest.

I was surprised to find that while freckles covered her upper chest, arms, and legs, there were almost none on her breasts, which were naturally set close together and perfectly round. It was as if God had run out of freckles.

I took her blush-colored nipple into my mouth and sucked so hard I hoped I wasn't hurting her. Then I did the same on the other side. My hand slid lower, momentarily cupping her ass as I continued to suck.

Dropping to my knees, I slid my hands down from her breasts to her stomach, which was also mostly clear of freckles, compared to the other parts of her body.

Her beautiful bare pussy was now at eye level. I looked up at her and noticed the need in her eyes as she stared down at me, her breathing becoming heavier by the second.

Unable to resist, I pressed my mouth to her mound and flicked my tongue against her. My eyes rolled back as I savored the first recognition of her taste. *Sweet heaven.* She gripped my hair as I continued to go down on her.

"That's it. Pull on my fucking hair," I groaned against her. "Use my mouth."

Pressing my thumb over her clit while I licked the tender flesh, I relished every pull and scratch of her hands as she moved her hips to meet the thrusts of my voracious tongue. I ate her out for several minutes until she abruptly retracted.

I stood, afraid I'd done something to hurt her. "Are you okay?"

As the water poured down over us, she looked into my eyes and said, "I almost came."

"Is that a bad thing?"

"I want you inside of me first, Leo."

My eager heart raced. I had no intention of arguing with her or questioning this. I fucking *needed* her.

"Let me go get something," I said, preparing to rush upstairs for that gargantuan box of condoms.

PENELOPE WARD

She grabbed my wrist. "I just want you to know...I'm on the pill. I went on it when we first started seeing each other, just to be on the safe side—in case something were to happen. I never trusted that it wouldn't. You should still get a condom, though, if you want to be extra careful."

She went on the pill for me?

The wheels in my head turned. I wanted nothing more than to bury myself inside of her with no barrier.

"Would it be okay if I didn't...use anything?"

"It's okay with me, but I just figured you'd want to be extra—"

"No. I want to feel you bare. At least once."

Felicity nodded as we stepped out of the shower. I grabbed a towel and dried her off before wiping it over my own body.

"Let's go inside," I said gruffly.

Before she could even nod, I'd lifted her into my arms and carried her into the house, my throbbing cock so rigid it was downright painful. Our lips locked in a kiss as we made our way into the house.

"Let's do it by the fire," she said.

Earlier, I'd turned on the electric fireplace, never expecting it to serve as the backdrop. Maybe my bedroom would have been a more proper place for our first time, but I didn't care.

We practically toppled over each other onto the floor. At least the rug beneath us was fairly plush. As the fireplace roared, I'd never kissed her harder, first down her neck, and then down the entire length of her body.

"Are you sure you don't want to move to my bed?" I muttered over her skin.

169

"No. Please. Just…" Her words trailed off. "Take me here."

Fuck. That was all I needed to hear. Within seconds, I lowered my swim shorts and placed my crown at her entrance, unable to wait even a second to penetrate her. I gasped at how incredible it felt to be inside her pussy. It was hot and wet—everything I'd ever dreamed of and more. I began moving in and out and could barely contain myself from coming.

"You feel so fucking good, Felicity. I'm so goddamn scared."

"Why?" she panted.

"Because I feel like I'm about to break you apart."

"Do it," she panted. "I can take it."

Unsure how we even got to this place so fast, I began fucking her with reckless abandon, the sheer pleasure of her tight pussy enveloping my cock, making it impossible to think about the consequences.

She writhed under me as I bent her legs back and pounded into her, feeling more out of control than I had in my entire life. There was nothing holding me back—no fear of consequences or distrust. That was a first for me: truly letting go. Not to mention, I'd never done this without a condom, and the friction of our bare bodies was *wet ecstasy*. I was so damn happy to experience this sensation with her, this beautiful woman who'd completely taken hold of me—heart, body, and soul.

"You're the first woman I've ever been inside of like this, and it's better than I could have imagined. This feels… so…fucking good."

"I know." She panted. "I know, Leo."

I fucked her so hard that it might have been better that we were on the living room floor, as we could have very well broken the bed. Sensing myself coming undone, I slowed down, hoping to stop myself from exploding too soon.

But the moment I slowed down, Felicity began bucking her hips faster. I had no choice but to pick up the pace, which I knew would be the end of me.

Within seconds, my orgasm rose to the surface and began to shoot through me like a freaking volcano erupting.

"Fuck," I yelled as I started to come, hoping it was okay that I hadn't pulled out.

As my cum filled her, I felt her pussy squeeze around me. Felicity screamed in pleasure as she climaxed.

I lay on the floor, still inside of her, for several minutes as we kissed. Though we were supposed to be sated, I only wanted more. I ran my tongue along the freckles under her neck, and then lowered my mouth, pressing it softly against her breasts. When I looked up, she was watching every move I made.

"You like watching me devour you, don't you? You like watching me come apart, in general."

She smiled. "Guilty. I especially loved watching your face when you moved in and out of me. And the way your eyes rolled back when you came."

"I was so calm and collected."

She laughed. "Just the opposite."

I finally pulled out before lying beside her. "I had big plans for tonight. I wanted to take you out to a nice restaurant for dinner, then perhaps take you back to my room and make love to you properly. Fucking you on the floor was sort of barbaric."

She ran her finger along my jaw. "It was perfect."

"You know what? I think so, too. And is it wrong that I don't even want to get up off this ground? I want to lie here with you forever in front of this fire."

"We should get takeout so we can eat naked."

"You're a woman after my own heart, you know that?"

"I have to give you up at the end of the summer," she said with a shrug. "I don't feel like sharing you with anyone tonight."

My chest tightened as a wave of reality hit. My decision to sleep with her made things much more complicated. As much as I'd never trade the experience, it was still probably a mistake given how much more attached to her I felt right now.

"What are you thinking?" she asked.

I couldn't tell her I'd never felt this way before. It wouldn't be fair to open my heart like that when I was only going to leave.

"I'm thinking about how screwed I am," I finally said.

"You're not the only one."

I got up and offered her my hand. "Come on. I'm taking you to my room next."

Felicity giggled as I lifted her and carried her up the stairs.

After I placed her on the bed, I smothered her with kisses, all over her body.

She placed a dainty hand on my chest, looking contemplative.

"Are you okay?" I asked.

She met my gaze. "Yes. I really am. This is the best July Fourth I've ever had."

"We made our own fireworks just now, didn't we?"

She smiled with an adorable blush.

Today was odd. I'd gone from feeling at peace to anxious in an instant. There was still so much I needed to learn about her, and I was running out of time.

"Tell me something no one else knows about you," I said. "I want one of your secrets that's all mine."

She blinked. "I don't have any sordid things I'm hiding. I just have things I hide *behind*."

I twirled a piece of her red hair around my finger. "How do you mean?"

"I hide behind a façade of strength sometimes, in order to convince myself I'm strong. For the most part, I am. But there are certain lies I tell myself and other people. I've told you the same one. Or at least I've implied it."

"What is it?"

"That I don't need anyone. That's not true. Everyone needs someone. And I wasn't exactly honest when you asked me how I felt about the idea of finding my father. The truth is, I'm scared of rejection. Deep in my heart, the thought of a father who might love me makes me so emotional I can't even think about it. I won't let myself. So, I'm not as strong as I might appear when you first meet me. That's my secret—or maybe that was two secrets."

Her admission touched my heart. "Thank you for sharing that. Although I have to say, it doesn't make you less strong to me. Strength is derived from actions, not feelings. We can't control how we feel inside, our emotions or weaknesses. But we can control how we persevere despite them. In that sense, you're one of the strongest people I've ever met. And your emotional vulnerabilities—least of all your need for love in your life—certainly don't take away from that."

She linked her fingers with mine. "Your turn. Tell me something you've never told anyone."

Oh boy. I suppose I'd asked for this.

Looking up at the ceiling, I said, "Even though on a rational level, I know it wasn't my fault, I often blame myself for the fact that my brother isn't here. When you told me you'd read about his existence on the Internet, I was a little too gobsmacked to say all that much. I wanted to tell you more about it. But it's hard for me to talk about—I really never have."

I shut my eyes. "I'll never get past the idea that my presence in the womb with him basically overwhelmed his system until he couldn't survive. I often wonder what my life would have been like with a brother, you know? He might have wanted all the glory, all the responsibility of pleasing my parents, and I would've gladly let him take it. He might have eased some of the burden on me. His mere existence might have been my ticket out of Westfordshire. Or maybe I would've never wanted to leave him. He might have been my best friend. But I'll never know." I exhaled. "He's part of the reason I've always felt this immense need to please my parents. Sometimes I wonder if God chose wrong." I finally looked into her eyes. "So that's my secret."

She leaned in and kissed me, as if she wanted to take away the pain.

"I obviously hate that you feel that way, and I know it's not always easy to believe people when they tell you it's not your fault," she said. "But I understand. We sometimes blame ourselves for things we have no control over. I often wonder whether my mother would be alive if she hadn't had me. Did the pressure of having an illegitimate child while battling drugs push her over the edge? I'll never know. But I think about things like that, too."

I smiled. "Well, wherever your mother is, I'm certain she's proud of her daughter."

"Maybe not today after I let you fuck me on your living room floor." She blushed. "But in general, yeah."

"Actually, speaking of that, I really want to do it again right now in this bed," I said, grinning like a fool. "But I think we should eat first because you're going to need your energy."

Felicity jumped when fireworks went off outside the window. "Jesus! I thought that was gunfire for a second. Forgot it was the Fourth of July. They sneak up on you."

"The best things in life often do." *Isn't that the truth?* Felicity Dunleavy had rocketed into my world out of nowhere—turning my life upside down in the best possible way.

CHAPTER 14
Felicity

Track 14: "Drunk in Love" by Beyoncé

How did Sunday get here so darn fast? I'd been living in a dream since I arrived at Leo's house. Friday had been all about getting to know each other's bodies—in multiple ways in multiple rooms and on multiple surfaces. The night went by in a sex-induced haze.

Then on Saturday, we ventured out of the house and went down to Newport for the day. I took Leo to see the famous mansions. We had dinner there and returned to Narragansett on the early side, because we were too horny to wait until later to have sex. I'd made a conscious decision not to drink this weekend because I wanted to be present for each of these precious moments with Leo.

But as I stood in the kitchen watching him fiddle with the coffeemaker on Sunday afternoon, the reality of everything washed over me. I'd fallen for this man, and he only had a matter of weeks left. Then I'd never see him again. That had always been the plan, but for some reason that harsh fact only hit me in waves, and this one wiped me out.

After he pressed start on the coffee, Leo walked over. His eyes held a clear affection that matched my own for him. In this moment I realized if I didn't have a drink—and not the caffeinated one currently brewing—the pain would be unbearable. I needed to numb this. I knew it was wrong, but I couldn't afford having my feelings escalate any further.

"You've fallen into a daze," he said. "Is everything okay?"

"I think we should have some tequila."

"Well, that was a very random response."

"I know. But I've been good all weekend. I'm in the mood to get tipsy."

It was going to take more than *tipsy* to forget my worries tonight.

He leaned down and spoke over my lips. "Are you trying to take advantage of me? You know you can do that without the alcohol, right?"

"I've never had drunk sex before. I think we should try it. You make me feel safe enough to let loose in that way."

"You want to get wasted with me?" He flashed a devious grin. "Well, tequila it is, then."

Leo grabbed the shot glasses and the bottle, and we headed out back to enjoy our drinks on the deck overlooking the bay.

Within an hour, we were both pretty sloshed.

The next thing I knew, Leo had lifted me up in the air and was carrying me upstairs to his bedroom. Not only had the alcohol numbed all of my anxiety, it had sparked an adventurous side that didn't otherwise exist.

"Tie me up, my lord," I blurted as Leo threw me down on the bed.

He laughed. "You didn't just say that."

"I'm not sure which part you're asking about. By the way, did it annoy you when I called you that?"

"From anyone else, it would have been annoying, but from you it's kind of hot. Feel free to say it again, but I was actually referring to the tying you up part."

"Can we play Lord Covington does bondage with the peasant girl?"

"You're bad when you're drunk, you know that?" He placed his knees on either side of my body and kissed my neck. "It brings out your devious side."

I shrugged. "At least you can say you experienced both sides of me before we parted ways."

"Don't talk about that right now—my leaving."

"What are you going to do if I defy you?"

"Let me guess...the right answer is tie you up?"

"Maybe."

"Be careful what you wish for, Miss Dunleavy. I have no problem giving you exactly what you're asking for and more. Especially the way I'm feeling right now."

"I'm sort of curious about the 'and more' part."

With a twinkle in his eye, Leo hopped off the bed and went to his closet. He returned with one of his ties.

"Lift your hands over your head," he demanded. His eyes were dead serious, and a thrill shot through me. Leo placed the tie around my wrists and tied it in a knot. "I'd put something over your eyes, but I like looking in them too much."

After he worked to slip my bikini off, he pulled his shorts down, leaving his glistening cock hanging in the air.

"What shall I do first?" he asked.

"Fuck my mouth."

I'd only gone down on him one other time this weekend, a random moment when I snuck up on him in the bathroom. He'd been caught off guard and came in a matter of seconds.

"You discovered my weakness, didn't you? Maybe I'll last more than twenty seconds this time."

I sat up a bit, with my hands still over my head, as Leo knelt before me on the bed and stuck his cock in my mouth. He groaned as his eyes rolled back, surrendering to the gratuitous pleasure as I took him all the way down my throat.

He suddenly pulled out and slid down. "Open your legs wide."

Within seconds, he'd pushed himself inside, fucking me hard. I wished my hands were free so I could grab his hair, but there was something arousing about giving up that little bit of control.

"I'm going to fucking blow my load, Felicity," he groaned. "Damn your pussy and the alcohol making me weak. But I know you're not ready to come."

Bending my head back, I panted, "Come on my chest."

His eyes widened as he pulled out, jerking his thick cock until streams of hot cum shot all over my skin. It was simply breathtaking—the way his mouth fell open as he orgasmed and the sounds he made as he covered me.

"Untie me," I begged, so incredibly turned on.

He did as I said, and the moment my hands were free, I brought them to my clit and circled it with my two middle fingers. Leo watched intently as I pleasured myself. It took a matter of seconds before the muscles between my legs contracted.

"Watching you do that with my cum all over you is just about the sexiest thing I've ever seen."

He lay on top of me and slipped his tongue into my mouth as we once again fell into a deep kiss.

We found the tequila and stayed in our drunken state in bed for the remainder of the day.

The afternoon turned to evening, and we'd just finished having sex again when Leo slowly pulled out of me and said, "I love...fucking you so much."

My heart nearly stopped. For a split second, I thought he'd told me he loved me. Would it have mattered that he'd said it while intoxicated? Likely not. But when he completed the sentence, I felt as much disappointment as I did relief.

Why would I want him to say those words anyway? Stupid.

The room spun a little, but I didn't regret the tequila. It had done its job. I prayed that the thought of him loving me—or not loving me—would go away and forced my mind to something else.

Sinking into Leo's silk sheets, I made another random drunken announcement.

"I wish I had a Shetland pony."

Leo cracked up. "Where in God's name did that come from?"

I hiccupped. "Blame the tequila. But a Shetland pony *is* something I used to wish for a lot when I was younger, and for some reason, I really want one right now."

"Like, right this second?"

"Yeah."

"Would you take it to law school with you?"

"Well, that's the problem."

"We have several horses on our family property, actually."

"See? You're lucky. A Shetland pony would blend right in."

"Pretty sure I take them all for granted." Leo nuzzled my neck. "What is it about the Shetland that you like?"

"Have you ever seen one?"

"Can't say that I have." He reached over to the nightstand and grabbed his phone. "Let me look it up." He scrolled for a while. "Ah. They're from Scotland. It says here that they were originally used as pack horses in the eighteen-hundreds, taken to work in the coal mines in England." He turned to me. "They're basically English. That's why you like them."

I cackled. "That's got to be it."

"Although, I thought you preferred us *hung* like horses. Not the horses themselves." He slapped himself. "Christ, I sound like my cousin. Sorry." He looked back at the image on his phone. "Gosh, they're tiny, aren't they?"

"Yeah. They're so cute."

He tossed the phone and wrapped his arms around me, kissing the top of my head. "*You're* so cute."

I wanted to make the most of the rest of the night, but somehow lying in Leo's arms was the last thing I remembered before drifting off.

A somber air cast a shadow over Monday morning. Our staycation was officially over, and that bummed me out. As expected, I'd awakened with a terrible hangover. Leo drove to Dunkin' Donuts to get bagels, and ended up coming back with not only those, but donuts and other pastries, as well as a giant box of coffee.

"I didn't realize we were sponsoring breakfast for the entire town," I teased.

"Well, I wasn't sure what you liked, so I thought I'd get a variety. And I figured you'd need a lot of coffee this morning."

"That's definitely enough."

He seemed a bit on edge, as he kept checking his phone.

"Is everything okay?" I asked. "Is that Sig? He must be on his way back from Boston soon."

He placed his phone in his pocket. "No, no one texted. I was just checking the time."

"You've been looking at your phone a lot. I assumed someone was messaging you."

He hesitated. "I'm expecting a...visitor."

Before he could elaborate, the doorbell rang.

"There he is now. Stay here. I'll be right back."

Rather than wait, I followed him to the foyer.

When he opened the door, I couldn't believe my eyes. My jaw dropped.

A man stood on the porch next to the most beautiful, gray Shetland pony I'd ever seen.

"Leo, what the—what did you do?"

He didn't answer, and instead took a huge wad of cash from his wallet and paid the man. They exchanged some information, and before I knew it, the guy was gone, but the pony stayed. With my mouth still ajar, I walked over and began rubbing its soft mane.

"Are you crazy?" I yelled at Leo.

"Okay, hear me out. I—"

"What are we supposed to do with him?"

"Last night after you finally passed out, I went online to see if there were any Shetland ponies for sale in the area. As luck would have it, this chap is moving to Florida and needed to unload this little guy ASAP. I figured we'd enjoy him for a few weeks and then find him a permanent home before we both leave town."

"Okay...but where are you going to put him?"

"I'll keep him here."

I looked around. "Here?"

"Yes. Sigmund won't mind."

"What happens if we can't find a home for him?"

"Worse comes to worst, I'll take him back to England. He can join the other horses on our property."

"I can't imagine how expensive it must be to ship a horse to England."

"He's not that much bigger than a large dog. It shouldn't be a problem."

"How are you going to explain bringing a horse back home with you? Your family will think you've gone insane." I pulled out my phone and did a quick Google search. "Oh my God, Leo. Ten-thousand dollars on average. That's how much it costs to ship a horse overseas!"

"It doesn't matter." He walked over to me. "Let me ask you this. Are you happy he's here?"

"Yes. Very, but—"

"Then it's worth every penny." He petted the pony. "I can't offer you the world. I can't even fucking give you myself. Let me give you him until the end of the summer. Then I promise I'll make sure he goes to a good home— even if it's mine."

Tears sprang to my eyes. Too much about what he'd just said made me emotional. And this was the sweetest thing anyone had ever done for me.

"Is it wrong that I'm a bit jealous because he might get to live with you?" A tear fell from my eye.

Leo bent to meet me where I knelt. He wiped my eyes and kissed me long and passionately until the horse neighed, interrupting our moment.

"Does he have a name?" I asked.

"I never inquired." He turned to the animal. "Identify yourself."

The horse neighed again.

I shook my head in laughter. "This is ludicrous."

"Indeed." Leo eyed the animal. "Hmm... That would be a fitting name for him, don't you think?"

"What?"

"Ludicrous."

"You know what?" I wrapped my arms around the pony's neck and hugged him. "Oddly, I can't think of a better name."

Here he was, our new, temporary love child.

We spent the rest of the day buying supplies for him. Ludicrous was just the distraction I needed from my ever-growing attachment to Leo. Although, did I really want to fall in love with both a horse *and* a man I wouldn't be able to keep?

I froze as I realized what I'd just admitted to myself—I was falling in love with Leo.

CHAPTER 15
Leo

Track 15: "Never Say Goodbye" by Bon Jovi

After a full day of horsing around—quite literally—Felicity returned to her house Monday evening. When Sigmund returned from his trip later that night, he was less than amused to discover our new roommate.

"Why in the bloody hell is there a horse in our living room?"

I closed the magazine I'd been looking at. "Oh, you're back."

"Yes. Apparently, I should have stayed in Boston. What the fuck is going on?"

"This is Ludicrous."

"You're telling me."

"No. That's his name. Ludicrous. I bought him for Felicity."

"I would ask why, but there is no answer that could ever make sense."

We'd set up a safety gate to cordon off an area of the living room.

PENELOPE WARD

"She told me she'd always wanted a Shetland pony, so I decided to buy one and keep it here for the rest of the summer."

"Yeah. That makes total fucking sense, Leo. I knew you were a bit daft when it came to her, but this takes it to a new level."

"Don't worry. He'll be spending a good amount of time out in the side yard. I only brought him in tonight because it's raining."

"Did you at least get to shag her before she had you turning this place into a funny farm?"

"That's none of your business."

He laughed. "I'll just check the condom box I left you and see if it's opened."

"That's not going to tell you anything, actually." I immediately regretted my words.

"Why is that? Please tell me you covered it up."

My lack of response and perhaps the look on my face caused him to draw the right conclusion.

His eyes widened. "You didn't use anything with her? Are you fucking insane?"

"She's on the pill."

He raised his tone. "I don't give a damn what she says. You can't trust it."

"Yes, I can trust her. And I do."

"Well, you're stupider than I thought, then."

"You know I don't take things like that lightly. I've always been careful, with every single person."

"Do you realize how easily she could trap you?"

"She wouldn't do that."

"How do you know?"

187

"Because I know her, and I trust her more than anyone I've *ever* known. I trust her more than I trust you, for Christ's sake."

"I think you're officially delusional."

"It's none of your concern, Sigmund. Besides, how is my having unprotected sex with someone I trust who's on the pill any worse than you sleeping with multiple women at once and relying only on condoms? They can break. Nothing is foolproof. You're taking a risk every time you stick your dick in someone."

"With condoms, at least I have some control. You have nothing but her word that she took a pill. What if she gets pregnant? How the hell would you explain that to your parents? You'd be stuck with her."

Stuck with her.

Did he think the idea of being permanently bound to Felicity would scare me? It gave me the opposite reaction—a fleeting thought that maybe getting her pregnant would put me in a situation where I had no choice but to be with her. In that scenario, following my heart and doing the right thing would then be one and the same.

"We don't need to discuss this any further," I said.

"Yes, because clearly there's no talking to you."

I gladly changed the subject. "How was your weekend away?"

Sigmund looked down at his shoes and muttered, "It could've been better."

"Why?"

"It seems having a small harem is only good so long as no one gets attached." He rolled his eyes. "They...started fighting."

"About what?"

"About not having enough alone time with me. They started getting competitive. It got weird, and I was ready for the weekend to end."

"So no more Marias, I take it."

"No."

I'd been enjoying his most recent "relationship," if you could call it that, because it seemed to take his attention off of me. But it probably wouldn't be long before he found someone else to occupy his time.

The following morning, I woke up to a text from my cousin.

Sigmund: Hey, tosser. That damn horse of yours just took a dump on the floor. Come down and clean it before I vomit.

Oh. Not exactly the way I wanted to start my day, but I suppose I deserved it for my rash decision to buy the animal.

After I cleaned up the mess, I took the horse outside and fed him. It was a beautiful day, so he'd be able to hang out in the side yard without me feeling guilty. I did need to start figuring out a permanent home for him. The earlier I lined something up, the better. But certainly finding Ludicrous a good home was the least of my problems. Today, in particular, I felt more down than usual about the inevitability of having to leave Felicity. It was hard to believe we'd only known each other for a matter of weeks, because I couldn't seem to remember a time when she wasn't in my life.

My plans for today were up in the air. On a Tuesday, I normally would have headed over to Mrs. Barbosa's, but the electrician and plumber needed one more day to complete their jobs. So we wouldn't be able to get back to work there until tomorrow, at the earliest. I wasn't sure whether to call Felicity or give her some space after the whirlwind of a weekend we'd had. I felt even more addicted to her now, but I also recognized that if I kept things up at this pace, it would only hurt her more when I left. But part of me had started to wonder whether there was any way we could make this work. It was crazy to even ponder, but I didn't understand how I was going to forget her. It would undoubtedly be the most painful thing I'd ever had to do. Was it possible to just walk away from someone you truly cared about?

I needed to talk to someone. It couldn't be Sigmund, that was for sure. He'd just tell me to rip the Band-Aid off and book my ticket home tonight.

There was only one person I could trust with this situation. I picked up my phone and dialed her.

"Hi, Leo," she answered. "Everything okay? Usually it's me ringing you."

"I'm fine, Nan. But I need to talk to you."

"What is it?"

"It's about…Felicity."

"What's happened? Oh, dear God, she's not pregnant, is she?"

"No, no, Nan. It's nothing like that."

"Oh, thank goodness. You nearly gave me a heart attack."

"I need to ask you an honest question."

"Okay, my darling."

"Do you really think they'd disown me if I found a way to make it work with her?"

Nan paused, and then let out a long breath in my ear. "Your parents..." She sighed. "My honest opinion is that they wouldn't disown you. But that's not to say they wouldn't make your life miserable, particularly your mother. However, do I think they would take anything that's rightfully yours from you? I don't."

"It's not about the physical things to me—the money, my inheritance. That's not what concerns me. My fear is upsetting Dad, especially in his condition. I want to fulfill his expectations of me. But at what cost? I don't feel like I can just...leave her. What if she's the one, Nan? It's only been a little over a month, but sometimes you just feel things in your gut. What if she's the one, and I spend the rest of my life living in regret because I walked away?"

My grandmother sighed. "You've really gotten yourself into a predicament, haven't you?" After a period of silence, she said, "You asked me for my honest opinion, my love. And so I'm going to give it to you, even though you may not want to hear it."

Bracing myself, I swallowed. "Okay."

"I understand how you must be feeling right now, and there's no doubt in my mind that your feelings for this girl are real, even if things moved quite fast. Frankly, from what you've described, she sounds lovely—intelligent, beautiful, self-deprecating, and genuine. Worthy of my grandson, indeed. But it's also the first time in your life you've ever felt this way about someone. First loves have a way of not only sweeping us off our feet but clouding our judgment. As much as you care for her, I think deep down you understand *why* it could never work. Those reasons hold no bearing on your feelings for her, however. And I understand that. But you must look at the big picture. The life she would have to become accustomed to here is so very different than her own, and that would eventually wear on her. The scrutiny from the public, the scrutiny from your mother—do you really think it's fair to drag her into all of those complications at a time where she's about to take the next step in her education? You've described her as a free-spirited woman, one who's used to not depending on anyone. Don't hold her back. That's what you'd be doing if you asked her to come to England. And you certainly know that living in America is not an option for you. The only thing your father truly couldn't forgive would be you abandoning your legacy here at home. So, I feel like there's no choice here, as hard as that may be for you to accept."

I said nothing while I let it all sink in. She was right, but I hated admitting that to myself.

"Sometimes..." she added. "Letting go of someone can be just as important a gesture of love as hanging on to them."

I nodded. My stomach was in knots. Everything she'd said was true. In my heart, I knew I needed to let Felicity go—for her own good more than anything else. I just didn't know how to do it.

I spent the remainder of the day downright depressed and ended up returning to my Bob Ross painting tutorials for the first time in a while. Sigmund had already connected with someone new, so he was out of the house for a hookup with her. Good riddance. That gave me the space to spread all of my things across the kitchen.

I wanted to call Felicity, but told myself I should continue to give her space today, especially after the conversation with my grandmother, which had left me reeling. It had helped solidify what I already knew—that there was no chance for things to work—but the harsh truth was a hard pill to swallow. Regardless of my own feelings on the matter, if I wanted what was best for Felicity, I needed to let her go.

The painting I was working on today reminded me a lot of a scene out of Narragansett. There was a body of water and surrounding trees. And of course, happy little clouds. My eyes wandered from the canvas to the window. A flash of red hair blowing in the wind met my eyes.

Felicity was in the side yard, feeding Ludicrous a long carrot stick. The look of joy on her face momentarily made me forget what I'd been lamenting. After he'd fully demolished the carrot, she wrapped her arms around his neck and gave him a squeeze. When she closed her eyes, looking so content, a wave of guilt hit me. That beautiful spirit would be crushed in just over a month's time.

Putting my brush down, I walked to the back door and ventured out to the yard.

"I never thought I'd be jealous of a horse, but here we are."

She looked up suddenly. "You scared me."

"Were you hoping I wouldn't know you were here? How come you didn't call me?"

"I hadn't heard from you all morning. I wasn't sure if you were busy. But I really wanted to see Ludicrous, so I thought I'd sneak over and see if he was out in the yard, since it's a nice day."

"I'm never too busy for you."

"What were you up to?" she asked.

"I was actually...painting. I've gotten out of the habit of practicing, so I thought I'd take advantage of Sigmund being out of the house, so as not to have to deal with his ridicule. Anyway, I'm happy you're here. I wanted to see you, but I thought I'd give you a little space, since this weekend was quite intense. I figured maybe you needed a breather."

She resumed petting the horse. "Maybe I should feel that way, but I don't. I wish I did. It would make everything easier."

"Yeah. I know." I slipped my hands in my pockets.

Standing my ground when it came to my decision wasn't going to be easy. Whenever Felicity was physically with me, the thought of losing her forever felt even more impossible.

"How are you feeling...after everything?" I asked.

Turning her attention away from Ludicrous for a moment, she said, "I feel good. I don't regret anything we did, if that's what you're asking."

"I guess I was wondering where your head is in that respect, yes. We got very caught up in things. You've been on my mind even more than usual since you left yesterday.

With the days passing so fast, I'm getting more anxious. I don't know how I'm supposed to say goodbye to you."

Felicity wouldn't look at me. "Maybe we shouldn't say goodbye."

"What do you mean?" For a moment, my heart filled with hope.

Still looking down at Ludicrous, she said, "I've been thinking about this a lot, and I think maybe we just pick a time to not see each other anymore—closer to when the time comes—and skip the goodbye altogether. I can't imagine saying goodbye to you, Leo. I know what I just proposed sounds really harsh, but I think in some ways, it might be easier for me..."

"But there *has* to be a goodbye. If we know it's our last time together, how do we avoid it? I can't just walk away from you and not say goodbye."

"Maybe we can't avoid it altogether. I just don't want a *long* goodbye."

I couldn't put this discussion off any longer.

"I didn't want to have this conversation today, but maybe it's for the better." My chest filled with anticipatory anxiety. "We've never discussed logistics. By that I mean, what happens *after* we leave each other? Will we be in contact at all?"

Felicity closed her eyes and hugged the pony closer as she ran her hands along its mane. Then she finally looked up at me. "I don't know that I can handle it."

I swallowed. "Can't handle...keeping in touch with me?"

She nodded.

"You're suggesting we never speak to each other again?" I was shocked. "I don't know if I can do that,

Felicity. At the very least, I need to know you're okay. I can't just erase you."

"This is painful for me, too. I don't know what the right answer is. But I don't think I can handle hearing about you moving on, getting married, having children someday."

In all of the time I'd known her, I'd never once gotten the impression that she would want to lose contact altogether. Maybe that was naïve of me. I knew we couldn't *be* together. But to never see or hear from her again? It seemed unimaginable. Panic washed over me.

"Is this negotiable at all?"

A distraught look crossed her face. "Leo..."

My priority needed to be what was best for her. Maybe my need to keep in touch was selfish. Or maybe it was an attempt to hold on to the last shreds of hope that it wouldn't be the end of us. If my priority was truly to prevent the most damage from my departure, maybe she was right, as painful as it was to imagine never seeing or hearing from her again.

"I will do whatever you want, Felicity. It hurts, but I won't blame you for not wanting to keep in touch. It won't alter the amazing memories I have of you in any way. I will respect your decision, even if it's hard to accept right now."

"You think it's what I want?" She shook her head slowly, her voice trembling. "It's just what I can *handle*, you know?"

"Come here." When she started to cry, I reached out and pulled her into my arms.

Taking a long, deep breath of her scent, I felt my chest constrict. I decided to be honest with her in a way I hadn't intended to up until this very moment.

"This morning I was wracking my brain, trying to figure out a way to make this work."

She pulled away and looked up at me with wide eyes.

"Leaving my family would obviously be difficult. Everything I'm obligated to handle is there. The promises I've made my father won't be possible unless I'm permanently in England. But over the past couple of days, I've wrestled with the idea of begging you to come to the UK with me."

Felicity seemed shocked, her eyes wide. "I'm surprised to hear you say that."

"Then you've underestimated my feelings for you."

"I just never thought you'd even consider that."

Despite all of my grandmother's advice, I needed to know. "Would you say yes if I asked you to take the risk and be with me?"

She blinked, looking tormented. "I honestly don't know."

Her hesitation spoke volumes. If there was apprehension now, once she got to England, the stress that greeted us would only solidify that she'd made the wrong decision. She'd have to be a hundred-percent sure going into it, and she was far from that.

"I spoke to my grandmother this morning about it. I trust her more than anyone and wanted her honest opinion. She helped me see that even though asking you to come home with me might be what I want, it wouldn't be fair to you. To ask you to drop everything and become accustomed to a life so different from what you're used to wouldn't be in your best interest. Not to mention, the vultures would come out and try to make your life miserable—maybe not forever, but definitely at first. I don't know that I could ever forgive myself if I disrupted you in the prime of your life in such a way."

But fuck, if you told me yes, I'd risk it all.

Felicity nodded. "If you did ask me...just know that I would *want* to say yes. But I don't think your grandmother is incorrect. I don't have any clue what I'd be getting into. I wouldn't want to put that kind of stress on you, either—to have to worry about how people treated me. And there's this little thing called law school I'm supposed to be doing. Moving to England would derail that for a while. I just don't know how we could make it work, even if we wanted to."

I pulled her to me again and spoke into her ear. "So how do we handle the weeks we have left? Tell me what you want."

Speaking against my shoulder, she said, "I still want to see you every day. We'll just take it moment by moment... until there are no moments left."

I sighed. There was no other way to handle this. "It's getting hot out, eh?" I reached for her hand. "Let's go inside."

Felicity followed me into the house and stopped short when she saw my easel in the kitchen. "Oh my God. You did that?"

"Yeah. It's what I do when I'm most stressed, apparently." I reached over to a bowl sitting on the counter. "Taffy?"

She shook her head. "No." She walked over to the easel to take a closer look. "The way you described your painting skills made it sound like you were horrible. This is really good, Leo."

"Well, you get the hang of it after a while. I'm getting better at copying his exact movements. But it's not true talent if you have to follow someone else's lead the entire time."

"I beg to differ. I could never do this."

Her feedback actually made me feel quite good. I'd always suspected I wasn't as bad an artist as Sigmund would have me believe. But it's hard to judge your own work.

"This is probably my best one yet. So thank you for the compliment."

"Can I have it when you're done?"

I smiled. "Of course."

"I'll hang it in my room."

"Are you sure you'll be okay with the reminder?"

Felicity placed her hand on my cheek. "There's no way I'll ever be able to erase you, Leo. I'll always want to remember this time. I just don't want to have to see you with anyone else."

Feeling a pain in my chest, I took her hand and kissed it. "Will you spend the rest of the afternoon here?"

"I have to work tonight, but I have a couple of hours before I have to get ready. Can I watch you paint? You obviously have a ways to go."

"If you'd like. Sure."

Over the next hour, my redheaded beauty sat on the floor with her legs crossed, watching me paint as Bob Ross instructed me from the laptop.

It was peaceful. And for now, she was here with me. *What more could I want?* If I could've frozen time, this might have been the moment I chose to pause.

Later that night, after Felicity had gone and taken the painting with her, my cousin found me sitting in the living room with my head in my hands.

"You've gone and done it, haven't you?" he said.

"Done what?" I asked, feeling like my spirit had been plucked from my body.

"You've fallen in love with her."

I turned to look at him. "What do you want me to say?"

He took a deep breath. "I actually feel sorry for you, cousin. It makes me wish we'd never stopped in this damn place."

I knew I would never trade this time I'd had with her, would never trade getting to experience having authentic feelings for someone. Sigmund had never been in love, so I couldn't expect him to understand. You simply don't until it happens to you.

"Did you tell her?" he asked.

"Tell her what?"

"That you love her?"

"No. There's no point. Telling her would only complicate things more. We've agreed to ride out the rest of my time here."

"By ride, I assume you mean fucking each other's brains out."

I didn't dignify that with a response.

Sigmund's tone turned serious. "Okay, so what's the plan after you leave?"

"That's it. She doesn't think we should keep in contact if we're not together."

"Really? Not at all?"

"That's correct. She thinks it'll be too painful."

He scratched his chin. "That's wise, actually. At least one of you understands that nothing good can come of it." He sighed. "For the record, I get no joy from seeing you this down."

"That might be the nicest thing you've said to me all summer."

"Yeah, well, I think I've been poisoned by the residual love vapors in the air."

I rolled my eyes and chuckled. "You're an idiot, you know that?"

CHAPTER 16
Felicity

Track 16: "Never Forget You" by Zara Larsson

Late August

Leo had dropped me off at my house after a morning of putting the final touches on Mrs. Barbosa's garage renovation. As I got out of the shower, I thought about how fast time was flying by. I had to leave for Pennsylvania in a week, and Leo had decided to book his flight for around the same time. *One week left.*

Over the past six weeks, we'd done an excellent job of taking things day by day, throwing ourselves mostly into finishing up the work at Mrs. Barbosa's. The space was now fully functional, and it was so satisfying to watch Theo enjoying his new indoor swing and having his therapy sessions in a corner of the room. Leo and I had done some good this summer while taking our minds off the inevitable.

We'd spent as much of the rest of our time together as possible, enjoying the simple things like clamming, and relaxing afternoons with Ludicrous when I didn't have to work at Jane's by the Water.

A few weeks ago, though, I'd told Leo I thought we should stop being intimate. As much as it had pained him, he agreed that continuing our sexual relationship would only make things harder in the end. So we'd stopped cold turkey, made easier by the fact that I didn't spend the night at his place anymore.

So we were no longer sleeping together, but I often had sex dreams about him that woke me up at night. They were intense and always seemed so real. In one of them, though, I'd had the clear realization that the man making love to me wasn't mine. He was someone else's future husband, someone else's future. I woke up in a sweat, tortured by the emotions the dream had evoked.

But here's the thing. As much as I'd convinced myself that stopping sex was for the better, I couldn't say it made me feel any less attached to him. You can physically separate two people, but if all they want is to be together, in some ways the effort to keep away from each other only strengthens the non-physical connection. If anything, I loved him more, wanted him more. The longing was more powerful than sex could ever be.

As I dried myself off, a text notification snapped me out of my thoughts. I looked down at my phone.

Leo: We need to talk. Should I come there?

That didn't sound right.

Felicity: Mrs. Angelini has a friend over. I can come to you. Is everything okay?

Leo: I'll explain when you get here.

With an unsettled feeling in my stomach, I got dressed as swiftly as possible and drove faster than I should've to Leo's house.

When he opened the door, his face was solemn.

I stepped inside. "What's wrong?"

"My mother just called. My father contracted a bad infection during his latest treatment, and she's worried something may happen to him. I have to leave, Felicity. I booked a flight for tomorrow evening because that was the soonest I could get. I have no choice."

I clutched my chest as if to stop my heart from leaping out of it. He'd only had a week left anyway, but that didn't make this any less jarring.

"Of course, you don't have a choice. You have to go."

"This is killing me," he said. "We were supposed to cherish the last week together. I'm not in any way ready to leave you."

"Where's Sig?" I didn't know what else to say.

"He's packing up some of our things."

"What can I do to help?"

His eyes looked hollow. "Tell me this is a nightmare so I can wake up from it."

Trying hard to remain calm, I knew I needed to forge through this. That approach would be best for both of us. "Do you need me to take Ludicrous?"

Leo had been trying for the past month with no luck to secure a permanent placement for the pony. It wasn't looking good.

"I heard from a farm this morning that seemed interested. It's this place that offers therapeutic rides for children with special needs. I asked if I could drop him off tomorrow morning, and they were going to get back to me. It sounded promising, but if they can't take him, I'll let you know."

"That's no problem. I can figure something out."

"You shouldn't have to." Leo turned toward the window, seeming dazed.

With each second that passed, my heart broke a little more. Instead of shutting down this time, I pulled him close. "Leo, it's okay. It will be okay."

He buried his head in my chest, and we stood holding each other.

When Sig walked into the room, it barely registered. He didn't say anything, which was unlike him, but I was grateful.

Leo spoke into my neck. "I know you didn't want a long, painful goodbye, but I feel like I'm getting ripped away from you, and that's no better."

"You do what you need to, Leo. Your father needs you. We were about to be in this place anyway. It wouldn't have been any easier then." I finally moved back and forced myself to say, "I think it's best if we leave each other now. Take tonight and tomorrow to clear your head and get your affairs in order before your flight. It'll be too tough to drag this out. I can't handle that."

"I can't." He kept shaking his head. "I can't say goodbye to you."

"You don't have to." My chest rose and fell. "I'll just walk away."

"Give me five minutes." Leo shut his eyes tightly before opening them. "Just give me five minutes to hold you."

I nodded, falling back into his arms. His heart beating against mine was like a ticking clock.

I don't know whether it was five, ten, or twenty minutes later that I forced myself to pull away. I suspected Leo wouldn't have let me go if I hadn't been the first to move.

As I wiped the tears from my eyes, I noticed he seemed to be fighting them as well.

"Give me your phone, please," he said.

I handed it to him and watched as he input some information.

"I've entered my email and address in two places—under my name in your contacts and in the notes. If you ever change your mind about keeping in touch with me, you have all my info now. And Felicity, if you ever need anything, if you ever need help in any way, or just *anything* at all, please promise you'll let me know."

Leo brought me in for one last long and painful kiss, and I tried my hardest to block out the magnitude of it.

Taking a deep breath, I took a couple of steps back. "I'm gonna walk away, okay? I'll go out back to say goodbye to Ludicrous and then head home."

Leo nodded and shut his eyes, as if he couldn't bear to watch me leave. That was the final thing I saw before I put one foot in front of the other and made my way out the door, feeling as though my heart had shattered into a million pieces.

The following day, I felt awful. I'd tossed and turned all night, and the achiness in my body was the physical manifestation of my heartbreak. Knowing Leo was still just across the bay, and that he was just as hurt as I was, haunted me.

I did nothing but sulk in my room and look out my window toward Leo's house. I tried to busy myself with packing for Pennsylvania, but I was thinking about him.

Mrs. Angelini wasn't home. She rarely went out for the entire day, but today she'd gone to visit a friend an hour away in Massachusetts. She'd asked me if I preferred that she cancel so she could distract me from Leo's leaving, but I assured her it wouldn't make a difference and convinced her to keep her original plans.

I didn't even know what time his flight was, just that it was tonight. He'd never called me about Ludicrous, so I could only assume the farm he'd found had agreed to take him this morning; at least I hoped so. I would've figured it out if he needed me to.

When 5 p.m. rolled around, I finally made my way downstairs. For all I knew, Leo had already left for the airport. He was already gone from Narragansett.

When the doorbell rang, my heart jumped. Mrs. Angelini wasn't due back until around nine.

I peeked through the peephole to find Leo, a sight that knocked the wind out of me.

When I opened the door, he seemed out of breath. "I'm so sorry, Felicity," he stammered. "I know I promised not to do this, to prolong our goodbye, but I forgot to give you something." He handed me the blue planner he'd taken the first night I'd invited him over. "I wrote in this and wanted to give it to you as a keepsake. I'm sorry if my being here upsets you. I—"

I leaped into his arms. The regret that had been building inside of me all day was unbearable. The short goodbye I'd mandated had been pointless. My emotions were pummeling me—a punishment for ever attempting to stop them. The way things ended yesterday was never what I wanted; I'd just been afraid to experience what I was feeling right now.

He kissed me with such force that I nearly fell back. If yesterday I hadn't wanted to feel anything, this was the total opposite. Breathing him in was the only thing that mattered in the world, even if for one last time. There were no words. Leo lifted me in the air, and I wrapped my legs around his torso. Our hearts beat against each other.

What I needed right now, I knew would be detrimental. But like a drug addict about to take a hit, I just didn't care.

"I want you," I breathed into his mouth, knowing he was waiting for permission to cross the barrier I'd previously set. "Please."

He let out a deep groan that vibrated down my throat.

Within seconds, our pants were down, and he pushed himself inside of me with my back against the wall in Mrs. Angelini's foyer. Pulling on his hair, I bucked my hips to meet his frantic movements. There was nothing gentle about the way he was banging me, nor the way I desperately received each thrust. We took our anger out on each other, a desperate final act. It was the most intense sex I'd ever had and probably the only ending fitting for the passion we'd felt this summer.

It didn't take long. Within a couple of minutes, Leo's body began to shake. I felt the warmth of his cum between my legs as my own muscles contracted around his cock. He continued to hold me as I leaned on him, feeling suddenly limp, too weak to endure yet another goodbye.

"God, this hurts," he whispered.

He slowly put me down and adjusted his pants as I pulled my shorts up.

And then his phone buzzed.

I wiped a tear from my eye. "Is that Sig?"

"Yeah," he whispered, looking distraught.

"What time is your flight?"

"Nine. We're supposed to have left by now. He's giving me hell for even being here."

"Go," I said, waving my hand.

He brushed a tear from my cheek. "I'll be forever grateful that I broke the rules."

"Me, too, Leo." I gripped his shirt. "No regrets, okay?"

He stared at me for several seconds. He took the necklace he was wearing, the one that held his grandfather's diamond ring, and placed it around my neck. I looked down at it in awe. Then he pulled me in for one last firm but chaste kiss before walking away.

He turned around in the front driveway a final time and said, "I will never find another you."

Then he got in his car. And he was gone.

I knew it was real this time. I'd been restless all day because on some level, I knew he would come to me, knew he wouldn't stay away. I'd been waiting for him even if I hadn't realized it. A strange calm came over me now that I knew he'd truly gone. There was no longer a pressure to beg him to stay or do something rash.

It took a while before I built up the courage to open the planner he'd returned to me. Mrs. Angelini still hadn't come home yet when I made some tea and sat down at the kitchen table to read. Inside, there was an entry for every day he'd had it in his possession. It was our entire summer, reduced to a five-by-eight notebook.

June 26: *I'm only going to admit this here, because I'm too cowardly to say it to your face. I was bloody jealous today when your ex took you aside. I envy him for so many reasons; he's experienced things with you that I haven't. How is it right that I don't want anyone else to have you when I can't stay and be the one? It's not fair, so I need to suck it up. But damn, I wanted to strangle him just for looking at you.*

I kept reading.

June 30: *Did you know one of your eyes is a lighter color green than the other? I find it fascinating, almost as fascinating as the freckles that taunt me constantly, begging me to count them. You're beautiful, Felicity.*

Some entries were just descriptions of what we'd done on a particular day, like working at Mrs. Barbosa's or going clamming. But every so often, one of them would break my heart.

July 7: *You've just returned home after our weekend together, and I'm staring at our new horse as I write this, laughing. I've really lost* *my mind—in the best possible way. It was bar none the best weekend of my life. I told myself I wasn't going to say that four-letter word, Felicity. Because it's not fair given our circumstances. But I wonder if you can sense it. Can you see it in my eyes? Can you feel it in my heartbeat? I wonder if I even have to say it at all, or if it's been obvious for a while.*

I wiped a tear from my cheek and read each entry until I got to the last one.

August 21: *You just left for the last time, and I'm empty. If there's one thing you take from our time together, please know that I will never forget this experience with you. I will never forget you, Felicity. But I'm haunted by the idea that you'll think of me as just another person who abandoned you in this life. If I could have one wish right now (besides the health of my father), it would be this: I would want to be with you and know that that decision wouldn't ruin your life. I could never live with myself if I dragged you into a life you'd regret.*

Remember that no matter how far away we are from each other, we'll always be looking at the same moon. At night, whenever you notice it, I hope you'll think of me. I promise to do the same—look at the moon and think of you. And the sun and the stars, for that matter, too. I may be leaving, but you will always be in my heart. That might not be a consolation right now. But it's the truth.

FIVE YEARS LATER

CHAPTER 17

Felicity

Track 17: "Coming Home" by Skylar Grey

So much had changed, and yet everything was the same. Sipping my glass of wine in Bailey's Providence apartment, it seemed like the old days, only now there was a two-year-old hanging out with us. My best friend had gotten pregnant while I was in law school. She and Stewart hadn't planned it, and she'd ended up putting her career ambitions on hold to stay home with little Kayla, while Stewart worked at Brown University's Research Lab.

"So, are you sleeping at the big house tonight?" Bailey asked as she placed her daughter in the highchair.

I nodded. "Probably. It's going to be weird being there without her. But I'd better get used to it."

I had driven straight to Bailey's from Philadelphia because I wasn't ready to go to Mrs. Angelini's empty house just yet. Skylar Grey's "Coming Home" had played on the radio as I drove, and I got so emotional I had to stop at a rest area to get some tissues. All the feelings I'd been hiding from rose to the surface.

But I suppose that made sense. This was my first time back in Rhode Island since my foster mother had died suddenly of a heart attack two years ago—a week after I graduated from law school. I still hadn't absorbed the shock. When it happened, I'd come back from Pennsylvania for the wake and funeral, but wasn't able to spend much time in Rhode Island after. I was studying for the bar and applying for jobs, but mostly, there was no point in staying if Mrs. Angelini was gone.

Since her death, I'd been reassessing what I wanted out of life, and I'd realized I truly missed home, even if Mrs. Angelini wasn't there anymore. I longed to be near her spirit, which represented the only family I'd ever known. Something seemed to be calling me back to Rhode Island now, even if I didn't fully understand it. I also hoped to find a position that felt more fulfilling than the junior-associate job I'd taken right out of school.

About a month ago, I'd quit, with the intention of coming back to Narragansett, even though I didn't have anything lined up. I'd need to pass the Rhode Island bar before finding another position. The next opportunity to take it would be in six months, so this time off would be my opportunity to straighten out the situation with Mrs. Angelini's house, as well as sort through my head. The perfect scenario would be to eventually find a job in Providence—relatively close to Narragansett—so I could live at the house and not have to rent another place. I didn't have the heart to sell Mrs. Angelini's property, and hoped I was never forced to for financial reasons.

"The house is still in good shape, though?" Bailey asked.

I nodded. "Her brother, Paul, and the neighbor, Hank Rogers, have been looking after it. Now that I'll be staying there, they won't need to do that as much anymore. Although, I might be calling them and begging for help when something inevitably breaks."

"You know you can count on us, too. Stewart can always drive over if you're in a bind and can't fix something."

"Hopefully I won't need to bug you guys, but thank you."

She hesitated. "Just a warning—Matt is supposedly coming home for Labor Day weekend. Stewart wanted to have a barbecue, but I don't know how you feel about seeing him."

I sighed. "Whatever. I'll deal if he's there. I haven't seen him in ages, nor do I care to."

I'd learned a lot of lessons in the time since graduating from law school. The first was a validation of something I'd always heard growing up: when someone shows you who they are, believe them the first time. About a year after I moved to Pennsylvania, I'd ended up giving my ex, Matt, a second chance. He'd been coming around for a while, under the guise that we could be friends. He was actually supportive during the time when I was most heartbroken. Although, I never admitted just *how* messed up I was, he knew I was getting over Leo.

Once Matt earned his way back into my good graces, we started a relationship again. It seemed easier to trust him than someone totally new. After Leo, I didn't have the mental energy to start from scratch. At the same time, I didn't want to be alone.

But after the novelty of our reunion wore off, Matt began acting differently. I suspected he was having an affair with a co-worker, but I was never able to prove it. I broke up with him after a year or so—before I could get hurt again. Although, if I were honest with myself, regardless of my suspicions, I simply wasn't in love with him. I tried not to think about Leo during that time, but in my heart of hearts, the feelings I'd still harbored for him made it impossible to give myself completely to Matt. Maybe someday someone would come along who could make me love enough to forget Leo, but it certainly wasn't Matt. And there had been no one else since.

Despite that, and considering how hurt I'd been when Leo left, I thought I'd done a pretty good job of putting him out of my mind over the years. As I'd always done when faced with life's difficulties, I threw myself into school and my failed relationship with Matt. Then when I passed the bar and got hired by the firm where I'd previously interned, I had an even bigger distraction.

Yet over the past six months, I'd started to feel lonely out in Pennsylvania. Giving my all to a meaningless job wasn't cutting it; I needed something more fulfilling. Once I passed the bar here in Rhode Island, I wanted to get back to what I'd always said I wanted—use my degree to help kids who grew up the way I did. That was my ultimate goal.

Bailey poured me more wine. "You've been working so hard for so long. You went right from law school to losing Mrs. Angelini, then passing the bar and starting a job. You deserve this break."

"Yeah, as long as it doesn't go on too long. You know me. I always need something to focus on, or else I'll go crazy. Taking care of the house is not going to be enough."

"How long can you afford not to work?"

"Well, thanks to Mrs. Angelini, I don't have a mortgage. And she left enough money to cover the property taxes for at least five years."

"Good. Try to enjoy this time."

That was the problem. I didn't want *too much* free time. While the memories had brought me back here, I worried that it could all backfire. My biggest fear was becoming depressed while living alone at the Narragansett house with little else to focus on. Not only did I miss my beloved foster mother, the memories of Leo would be freshest here at home. I worried about having to look across the bay and deal with all of the feelings *that* would conjure up.

As if fate were paying attention to my current insecurities, Bailey went over to her cabinet and returned with a can of SpaghettiOs, of all things. That seemed like a strange sign from the universe. My eyes welled up.

"Are you okay?" Bailey asked as she opened the can and placed the contents in a small pot on the stove.

"Yeah. It's just allergies." I sniffled.

It was eerie being back at the house without her. This was part of the reason I'd avoided it for so long.

Upstairs, I went straight to Mrs. Angelini's room, which looked the same as I remembered. Her long, woolly sweater was still thrown over a chair in the corner, as if she might walk in at any second and put it on. I lay on the bed and curled into her pillow, which still held a hint of her smell. How was that even possible after two years?

Opening her side table drawer, I found a half-empty bottle of Fireball.

Smiling, I opened it and saluted the ceiling. "This is for you, Mrs. Angelini." I took a long swig, the cinnamon liquor burning my throat as it went down.

After several minutes and a few more sips, I could feel it going to my head. And it was not having a relaxing effect. Instead, I felt emotional. Thoughts of Mrs. Angelini flooded my senses. I had so much regret when it came to her. I thought I'd have many more years to show her how much I appreciated her—how much I loved her. It wasn't until she was gone that I realized she *was* my mother—in all the ways that mattered, at least.

She never knew I saw her that way. I'd had her in my life longer than the woman who birthed me, and I wouldn't even call her by her first name. It undoubtedly would have brought her joy to know I had opened my heart to her. Looking around her room only validated that. There were pictures of me everywhere: me and Matt dressed for our senior prom, my high school and college graduations, photos of Mrs. Angelini and me on the boat with her brother, Paul.

Why is it that sometimes we only realize how much we love someone once we lose them? It's one of the most unfair things about life, if you ask me. Closing the bottle of Fireball, I tucked it back inside her night table. I could have fallen asleep in her bed, a sobbing mess, but I lifted myself off the mattress and went to my room.

If I thought that would ease my aching heart, I was wrong. The first thing that met my eyes was Leo's painting, the one I'd watched him create the day that we admitted it was essentially over for us. I remembered that horribly bittersweet feeling of watching him paint that afternoon, a mix of hopelessness and appreciation for the moment. And now I was thinking about him again. As if crying over a two-year-old's SpaghettiOs wasn't bad enough.

Walking to my window, I looked out across the bay at the house where Leo and Sig once lived. Thinking about Leo's cousin made me chuckle. He was such a dickhead—but a funny one.

There were lights on at the house. I had no clue who lived there now, but it was easy to imagine Leo and Sig were inside, just like it was yesterday—Sig cooking in the kitchen while Leo got ready to drive the boat across the bay.

I looked up at the moon illuminating the night sky.

"At night, when you look up at it, I hope you'll think of me."

There wasn't a single time I'd looked at the moon in the past five years that I didn't think of Leo. My heart clenched. I needed to stop. But like anything, the more I tried to stop thinking about him, the worse it was.

He's thirty-three now.

He had to have gotten married. I wondered whether he had a child. I wondered what happened when he returned, whether his father had survived the cancer. I wondered a lot of things, even as I tried not to let those questions overtake my brain. Leo was always there in the back of it, though. *Always.*

Once again, my mind turned to thoughts of regret. Not only did I wish I'd told Mrs. Angelini how I felt about her, I wondered what would have happened if I'd answered Leo differently when he asked me if I would consider going to England with him. I remembered the disappointment on his face when I'd expressed my doubts and fears. That was the moment that had truly ended all hope—had ended us.

Had I made the right decision? Sure, I'd gone on to do the "responsible" thing—finished my education, started my career. But where did following through with my plans really get me? I hadn't found a job that made me happy yet. And I certainly hadn't found a man who'd made me as happy as I was during those weeks with Leo.

Would dealing with the scrutiny of half of England have been worse than infinite longing for the rest of my life? At least I would've had Leo by my side. The stress might have been temporary. I could've gotten used to it. But the regret I still held in my heart to this day? That might last forever.

There was a little voice in the back of my head that occasionally said, *Call him.* But every time it spoke, I shut it down. I'd made my decision five years ago. Now I had to live with it. While being apart from him meant constant "what-if" thinking, contacting him might mean perpetual heartbreak. My gut told me he had moved on by now, and confirming that would ruin me. It was better not to know. It was better to imagine that we lived on in his heart than realize he'd all but forgotten me.

Shaking the thoughts from my head and forcing myself away from the window, I reminded myself to focus on why I was here: to honor Mrs. Angelini while I found a way to make a meaningful living. There was irony in that. I'd once told Leo I couldn't relate to having a family or a legacy. And yet with Mrs. Angelini gone, here I was, wanting nothing more than to make her proud, keep this house running, and keep her memory alive. If that wasn't upholding a legacy, I didn't know what was.

CHAPTER 18

Felicity

Track 18: "Please Read the Letter" by Robert Plant and Alison Krauss

The following day, there was a knock at the door. It was the neighbor, Hank Rogers, who'd been so helpful in the two years since Mrs. Angelini's death.

"Hey, Felicity. Welcome home," he said when I opened the door. "Everything kosher?" He wiped his big, construction-worker boots on the mat.

"Yeah." I sighed. "Just trying to get used to being back here. I'm glad you came by. I was just about to head over to your place to see if there was anything I need to be aware of."

He stepped inside, placed his hands on his hips, and looked around. "Nope. Other than the hot water heater being replaced last week, nothing eventful. Of course, you already know about that because you paid for it, but it's all taken care of."

Mrs. Angelini had left me a good amount of money to handle such things, so I'd had Hank send me the bills, even as he graciously handled the logistics in my absence.

"Try not to stress too much," he said. "She'd want you to relax a bit and enjoy being home. You know that."

"Yeah, I'll try. I'm hoping for a laid-back summer and plenty of time to get the house in shape for the colder months."

"Good way to look at it." He grinned.

"Are you sure there's nothing I might need to know?"

Hank scratched his chin. "Oh! I've been checking the mail every few days and bringing it in. I leave it in a pile over on the desk in the corner of the living room. It's not much since you had most of the bills forwarded to you, but there are some cards people sent, a lot that came in around the time she died—sympathy cards and such. I saved them. And some catalogs you probably don't want. I threw anything away that was definitely junk mail. But things still come in addressed to you and her every so often. If I'm not sure what it is, I keep it in the pile since you told me not to forward anything except bills or tax notices."

I nodded. "I appreciate it. I'll go through everything. Thank you again for all of your help. I can't begin to pay you back."

"No need. Eloise was a true friend. I'd do anything for her." He smiled. "And that extends to you. Just let me know if you need anything, okay?"

"I will, Hank."

"The Mrs. wants you to pick a night to come over for dinner this week. She'll make that seafood casserole you like."

"I'd love that. I'll text her and work it out." I smiled.

After he left, I made some lunch and ate it out on one of the Adirondack chairs in the yard. The August heat was a bit much, so I didn't last long.

When I went back inside, I decided to sort through some of that mail Hank had been piling up for the past couple of years.

Like he said, there were several sympathy cards. And I smiled at how many Victoria's Secret catalogs there were. Why Hank didn't just toss those, I wasn't sure. Maybe he'd enjoyed them.

I paused on an envelope addressed to me. Unlike the cards with my name on them, this looked more like a letter. When I caught sight of the name on the return address label, I nearly had a heart attack: *Leo Covington*. I froze, and the envelope slipped out of my hands. My heart kicked into high gear.

As I bent to pick up the envelope, I looked more closely at the line under my name: *Care of Eloise Angelini*. He knew the only way to reach me was through her, since he'd never had my address.

Oh my God. How long has this been sitting here?

I was terrified to open it. My lunch felt like it might reappear, and the room seemed to sway.

My hand trembled as I took the letter over to the couch and shakily opened the envelope. The paper was thick and cream-colored, and the words were written in blue ink.

Dear Felicity,

I don't even know where to begin, but I should probably start with: "How are you? It's been a long time, eh?"

I sincerely hope this letter finds you well. I'm certain you weren't expecting it. I can honestly tell you I wasn't expecting to write it.

But here goes.

As I sit here alone in my room, there are over a hundred people downstairs celebrating me. And all I've wanted to do the entire evening is escape. Thoughts of you are particularly heavy today. That's nothing new— it just doesn't normally happen until I lay my head on the pillow at night and close my eyes. It's always you I'm thinking of in that moment.

I sometimes wonder if it's only me feeling like this. I wonder if you still think about me as much as I think about you. I told myself I wasn't going to contact you, that nothing good could come of it after so long. This isn't the first time I've broken my vow not to try to reach you, though. I tried calling you about a month ago but couldn't get through to your phone.

I had to stop reading for a moment. That hurt my heart so much. A couple of years ago, I'd gotten rid of my old cell phone and switched to a new phone and number my law firm had given me. While I did transfer all of Leo's information into my new phone, if he'd tried to reach me at the old number, I wouldn't have known. When I left my job, I'd kept the number of my corporate phone, but switched to a personal plan.

I continued reading.

I have no other way to reach you, so I'm writing this letter in the hopes that you receive it. Felicity, the truth is I still love you. And in case it wasn't clear that I felt that way, I did fall deeply in love with you that summer. On some level, I knew that when I left. But I hadn't realized the extent of it until we weren't together anymore. There are still moments where I long for you more than for the air I breathe. They happen at very random times—I'll suddenly smell something that reminds me of you. Or see a flash of red hair on the streets of London and think for one insane second that you changed your mind and came for me, only to realize it was just a fleeting delusion.

I'm still in love with you, or at least the memory of you. As for the reasons we supposedly couldn't be together—nothing has changed in that regard. My life in no way fits with yours. I'm all wrong for you in every way—aside from the fact that I love you. If you're still reading this and haven't crumpled it into a ball out of frustration, you're probably wondering why I'm telling you all of this. Why now...after all this time has passed?

Well, here it is: I'm getting married, Felicity. My father is dying. He fought a good battle over the past several years, but there's nothing more they can do. They've stopped all treatments, and he only has about six months left to live, if we're lucky. As was always the plan, I want to give him the peace I know he needs. He wants to know I'm settled and that I'm going to follow through with his wishes, continuing the family name and business.

I'm engaged to a wonderful woman—one who deserves a man whose heart belongs only to her. Her name is Darcie. She was actually one of my friends growing up, and we reconnected about a year ago. She's kind and beautiful, and she knows this life inside and out. But moreover, she's a good person whom I'm very fond of. I don't think I would regret marrying her. The only thing I regret is that she's not you. Once we're married, I plan to take my vow seriously. Part of planning for that is trying to work out these unresolved feelings before I enter into a lifelong commitment.

For all I know, you may be in love with someone else right now. You might have moved on. I've tried to look you up. I've tried to find information, and I've come up with nothing.

I feel like this letter is my last hope in reaching you. I know I'm rambling. And admittedly, I'm a little pissed. (That means drunk, remember?) Having a few Negronis was the only way I could tolerate this engagement party. Which reminds me, I should probably return to it at some point. So, let me get to the heart of this letter.

If there's any chance you've regretted being apart from me as I've regretted being apart from you, I need to know. Reach out to me. I don't know what that will mean for us, but I'm fairly certain the only way I can go through with this wedding is if I know there's no chance for us to reconnect in this lifetime.

I need to know whether you're still thinking of me. I need to know whether there's any chance you would want to see me again. If you don't respond, I'll understand. I will get the message loud and clear. I don't know when *you'll get this letter, but my wedding is set for September 16.*

I had to stop reading again. My heart was going a mile a minute. I looked at the date at the top of the letter: *June 2, 2025. Holy shit.* He'd written it a little over two months ago.

September 16.

I calculated in my head. *Oh my God. That's three weeks from now.*

He'd assumed Mrs. Angelini would be here to tell me about this—which she absolutely would have the second she received it. But now, he must have thought I'd chosen not to respond. I looked at the envelope, and although the date stamp was smudged, it had an Express Mail label on it, which meant it probably took less than a week to get here. It had likely been sitting here for two whole months.

I braced myself to read the last part of the letter.

I don't want to hurt Darcie. I have every intention of honoring the commitment I'm about to make. But I would be doing myself a great injustice if I didn't at least reach out to you before it's too late.

Again, you don't need to respond if this letter in any way upsets you. I can't begin to imagine where you are in your life right now and whether receiving this news is disruptive. But Felicity, if there's any chance you would want to see me again, that you would want to throw caution to the wind as we figure things out together, I need to know.

With love (always),
Leo

With the letter in hand, I must have paced for three hours straight.

I have a chance to stop him before he gets married.

However, he had probably already assumed I wasn't going to respond and had come to terms with his plans. Contacting him now would be cruel. It would turn his world upside down. Was that fair? But how could I not? I did still love him. This was my chance to tell him— something I'd never done. Hadn't Mrs. Angelini's sudden death taught me about leaving things unsaid?

Speaking of Mrs. Angelini, I would have given anything—*anything*—to have her advice right now. Sure, I could've called Bailey, but I didn't always trust that she had my best interests in mind. I loved her, but she was way too reckless. She'd tell me to hop on a plane and go there tonight.

I looked up at the ceiling and said a silent prayer. I probably should have been talking to God, but it was Mrs. Angelini I tried to reach.

"What would you tell me to do?" I whispered.

I forced myself to take a shower, figuring running water might bring me some clarity. But it didn't help.

As I got dressed, I felt more and more panicky, like my life now had a timer attached to it, and the ticking sound was deafening.

Needing something in my stomach before I passed out, I made my way to the snack cabinet. There wasn't much in there, but I noticed an old blue can of butter cookies and wondered if they were still good. If so, I'd probably demolish the entire thing.

When I opened the tin, though, there were no cookies inside. Instead, I found something I hadn't laid eyes on in over five years: Leo's necklace—the one with the diamond ring that had belonged to his grandfather. It was probably worth the price of a small house, and I'd been too afraid to take it with me to Pennsylvania. I'd worried something might happen to it, and it had been too painful to look at. I'd told Mrs. Angelini to put it in a safe place, and she'd assured me she would take care of it. I knew why she'd put it in this canister. If someone were to rob the house, this would be the last place they'd look for jewelry that cost a fortune.

Placing it around my neck, I remembered exactly what it felt like when Leo had put it on me. I'd been devastated because he was about to leave, but also confused as to why he was entrusting me with such an important family heirloom when he wasn't ever going to see it—or me—again. It had seemed like some strange form of insurance and left me a little unsettled. I couldn't imagine him wanting me to keep something so important forever.

When it hit me, chills ran through my body. *This is it.* This was the sign I'd prayed for. Mrs. Angelini had led me to where she kept the necklace, but only I could interpret what that meant. I closed my eyes and knew she wanted me to follow my heart and go to him. That's what I wanted, too, even though I was scared.

Fiddling with the sparkler around my neck, I picked up the phone and dialed Bailey to fill her in on everything that had just happened.

"Have you Googled him at all?" she asked.

"No. I don't want to see photos of him with her. And I've managed to not Google him all these years. I'm not going to start now. I wouldn't even know what to believe."

"Okay. So what's your next step?"

"Do you think I should call him?"

"What if you just went there?" Bailey suggested.

"With no warning?"

"Maybe you need to see him to know whether you want to go through with stopping a freaking wedding. Don't you feel like you have to be there to know whether the connection is still there? If you call and fuck everything up for him, it might be premature. This kind of thing has to be done in person. I say get your ass on a plane and go. Look him in the eyes, and I think within seconds you'll know whether it's right. And if it's not, at the very least, you can have one final goodbye."

If I allowed myself to overthink things, nothing would ever get done. And I didn't have the luxury of time in this instance. I needed to make a decision before I could even begin to waffle.

My stomach started churning, not because of my internal debate, but because I knew I'd decided to go.

CHAPTER 19
Felicity

Track 19: "Long Long Journey" by Enya

Riding through the English countryside seemed like a dream, more picturesque than I could have imagined—animals grazing off the sides of the road, beautiful stone architecture, sprawling green fields for miles. Chills ran through me almost the entire length of the car trip.

My driver finally dropped me off at the cottage covered in vines where I'd be staying.

The little old woman who ran this bed and breakfast greeted me at the door. "Welcome to the Bainbridge Inn."

She stepped aside to let me enter. I'd chosen this place because it was only two miles from the Covington estate in Westfordshire.

By the time my flight landed, it was too late in the day to go straight to Leo. I would go in the morning. I needed time to find my bearings. It had been a long flight, and the stress of anticipation left me mentally exhausted. I didn't want to see him like this. I needed a good night's sleep and then, come hell or high water, I'd go to his house in the morning.

"I'm Lavinia," the woman said. "I'm at your service for the length of your stay."

She was short and frail. Asking her to do anything for me seemed wrong.

"You've provided me with a safe place to sleep, and that's all I need."

"Serving my guests is what I live for." She smiled. "And I very much enjoy the company. Let me make you some tea. I'd show you to your room, but stairs and I haven't been getting along lately. I try to limit the number of trips I have to make."

That made me feel bad. She was too old for this shit.

"Tea sounds great," I told her. "And no worries at all. I don't need you to accompany me. Just tell me where it is."

"First door on the left as soon as you reach the top."

The upstairs room had an old-school charm. With floral wallpaper and an iron bed frame, it looked like a life-sized version of a 1970's dollhouse bedroom. The bed was creaky and a bit uncomfortable, but it would obviously have to do.

After I situated my bags in a corner, I went back downstairs.

Lavinia had already set the table in the kitchen. The tea water began boiling on the stove.

"Are you hungry for a meal, my dear?"

"No, thank you. I ate something at the airport when I landed."

She placed a plate of cookies in front of me. "What brings you to Westfordshire?"

She had to know who Leo Covington was, so no way was I going to mention his name. I kept things generic.

"I've come to reconnect with a man from my past," I said as she poured the tea.

She leaned in. "Well, that might be the most exciting thing I've heard around here in a while."

I took a sip and laughed. "It's more terrifying than exciting, actually."

"Tell me the story."

Without getting into specifics, I told her about the summer I fell for a handsome, charming British man from Westfordshire who swept me off my feet. I ended with the gist of the letter.

"It's just so romantic," she gushed.

"It is, but equally scary. I wish I'd gotten the letter when it arrived two months earlier. At this point, he's likely assumed I received it and chose not to answer him. It's going to be quite a shock to see me." My heart sank. "This might not end well, Lavinia."

She pushed the plate of cookies closer. "Have hope. If it's meant to be, all will work out in the end." Lavinia tilted her head. "Is there a reason you chose not to call him first?"

"I decided it would be more meaningful if I just came. This seems too important for a phone call. If he doesn't see me in the flesh, he won't truly know whether the feelings he *thinks* he has are really there. I need to see the look in his eyes, you know?"

"I think the poor bloke might have a heart attack."

I cringed. "I hope not."

"That wouldn't be a very good ending to the story, now would it?" She carefully stood from her chair. "Well, if I'd known what you were about to embark on, I would have offered you something a lot stronger than tea."

I chuckled, remembering my first tea with Leo and Sig, which turned into tea-quila.

"Can I interest you in something to calm you before bed?" she asked.

I was just about to refuse, because it was way too late to be drinking, but then I noticed what was in her hand: a bottle of Fireball.

My eyes widened. "You drink Fireball?"

"Well, I have a few different options. But this is my favorite, yes. Do you not like it?"

"That's not it. It's... Well, someone who was very special to me who's since passed away—that was her favorite drink. I can't help but think you taking that out was a message from her."

"Well, see, now you *must* have a drink before bed." She poured some Fireball into a small glass for me.

"Thank you," I said as I gulped it down.

"There you go." She laughed.

There was nothing like that spicy burn. Definitely not my favorite, but it would be forever special because Mrs. Angelini had loved it so much.

I took my glass to the sink. "I'm really grateful to have found this place. It has the comfort of home that I appreciate tonight. I'm so nervous, and it's nice to know I have a place to come back to tomorrow if all doesn't work out in my favor."

"Well, for the record, I don't have anyone else booked for the foreseeable future. So, even if things don't work out, I hope you'll stay a while and enjoy Westfordshire, enjoy the reprieve from home."

I smiled, but if Leo sent me packing, I'd be leaving this countryside faster than a bat out of hell.

The following morning, my nerves were completely shot. Lavinia made me some tea and eggs. I forced everything down so I'd have some energy. I'd called a car service to drive me to Leo's property, and my ride would be here any minute.

I'd chosen a simple black dress for the occasion of either getting my heart broken or reuniting with the love of my life. I'd also opted to wear Leo's grandfather's ring around my neck. I hadn't taken it off since I found it in Mrs. Angelini's cookie canister.

When my car pulled up, Lavinia gave me a hug, and I greeted my driver and got in. As he took off down the road, I gave him the address of my destination.

"Do you have an appointment at Covington Manor, miss?" he asked.

"I'm…going to visit a friend."

"That's not what I asked. Are they expecting you?"

"No."

"You don't have an appointment?"

Shit. I hadn't thought about the logistics of this. It wasn't like I was visiting Leo at a normal house. It hadn't occurred to me that I might have trouble gaining access. "Um…I'm just going to wing it."

"With all due respect, madam, I don't want to be privy to your antics if this is some sort of stalker situation."

What? I shook my head. "I promise it's nothing like that."

He sighed but kept on driving. Eventually, we arrived at what I assumed was the Covington estate. There was a long road that served as a driveway and then a fountain at the end of it. The brick property was surrounded by rolling, green hills and looked like something out of a movie—otherworldly.

The closer he drove to the main building, the harder my heart beat. There was no going back now. I just wished I'd realized sooner that this was going to be more complicated than ringing a doorbell and having Leo answer. I might have gone to Harvard and graduated law school, but sometimes I wasn't very bright.

The driver pulled up to the front, and with wobbly legs, I got out of the vehicle. After I shut the door, he took off. I'd planned to ask him to wait for me, but he never gave me the chance.

Shit! He really did think I was a stalker and didn't want to be associated with me. *Thanks for your support, asshole.*

With my pulse racing, I ascended the steps to the massive and ornate front door, flanked by two gigantic pillars. I rang the doorbell, which almost mimicked church bells.

A few seconds later, a man dressed in a black suit opened it. "May I help you?"

The words hardly came out. "Yes. I'm here to see Leo Covington."

His brow lifted. "I trust he's expecting you?"

"No, actually. I don't have an appointment. But he knows who I am and would want to know I'm here."

His eyes narrowed. "Your name?"

239

I cleared my throat. "Felicity Dunleavy."

He pulled a device from his pocket that looked like a walkie talkie and spoke into it. He was so quiet that I didn't understand what he said.

Then a much larger man appeared in the doorway. "Miss, we don't let anyone into this house who does not have an appointment. If he were expecting you, he would have notified us. We keep a list of guests who are expected to arrive each day, and you're not on it."

"I understand. You have security measures you need to abide by. I'm not asking that you let me in, only that you let him know that I'm here."

"If we bothered him whenever a random stranger showed up and tried to gain entry, surely neither of us would have a job," one of the men said.

My heart began to race. "Listen, I'm an old friend of his. I absolutely guarantee if you tell him I'm here, he will not fire you."

The two men looked at each other. A sheen of sweat formed on my forehead. This was not a scenario I had anticipated, despite the many ways I'd imagined the moment I showed up at his door.

"If you're truly an old friend," the smaller man said, "you should be able to contact him directly. He would then put you on an approved list of people allowed to enter this home. Until then, I'm going to have to ask you to leave the premises."

This was not good. I did still have Leo's number, and I supposed I could call him. But that seemed like a brash and informal way of letting him know I was here.

But it seemed I had no choice. I went to lift my phone from my purse, but after much patting at the bottom, I realized it wasn't in there. I was so discombobulated this morning that I must have left it at Lavinia's.

Shit! What do I do now? I looked up at the men blocking my path. "Listen, I really need your help. I've come all the way from the United States. I understand that he doesn't know I'm here, but I promise you he won't be mad if you just tell him—"

The door shut in my face.

The silence was deafening.

I can't believe this is happening. I looked around and debated whether to scream. Somehow, I didn't think that would go off well around here. But how else was I supposed to get to Leo?

Without a clue what else to do, I rang the doorbell again.

The larger man immediately answered. "Shutting the door was your cue to leave with some dignity. I didn't want to have to use force to remove you from the property. But I'm afraid if you continue to insist on entering, I will have no choice but to carry you off the premises."

That rubbed me the wrong way. I raised my voice. "You will do no such thing. You won't lay a hand on me. Do you understand?"

"I'm afraid you'll give me no choice."

"Standing at someone's door is not a crime. I haven't pushed past you or tried to enter. If you touch me, I will kick you straight in the balls!"

That didn't seem to scare him. The next thing I knew, two more men appeared, and I began to worry for my safety. *What exactly are they planning to do?*

My instincts told me to yell. "Leo! Help!"

I had no clue if he was even home. But I continued to scream, repeating his name. Would these guys call the police? I pondered leaving, but I didn't have a phone to dial a driver. I'd have to walk the two miles back to Lavinia's house.

And then, just when I thought I was going to lose my mind, I heard his voice.

"What the hell is going on here?"

I looked up. "Leo. Oh my God."

He hadn't looked me in the face until I said his name. He turned white as his eyes met mine. He just kept blinking, as if he wasn't sure I was actually standing in front of him.

"Felicity..." he whispered.

"I'm so sorry I made a scene. But they wouldn't tell you I was here."

Leo stared at me incredulously as one of the men tried to explain.

"Do you know this woman? We didn't think—"

"Please leave us be." Leo held his hand out. "Go back inside."

The man stammered, "Your Grace, we were just—"

"Leave us be!" Leo shouted.

The air fell silent. The man nodded, and the other guys followed him back into the house. The door didn't completely close behind them, but at least we were alone now.

Leo seemed neither happy nor upset. His was an expression of pure shock.

"What are you doing here?" he finally asked.

My heart nearly stopped. *Why is he asking me that?* My voice shook. "I got your letter. Two months late. I'm so sorry I didn't respond, but I only saw it sitting there in a pile a few days ago."

His eyebrows knitted. "My letter...?"

"Yes." I fished inside my purse for the envelope. "The letter you wrote me back in June. You said you were getting married in September—which is less than three weeks away. And you needed to know if I still had feelings for you before you took that step. I was so shocked to receive it, but honestly, Leo, I haven't stopped thinking about you over the years, either. I would have come sooner if I—"

"Let me see it, please." He held out his hand. "The letter."

Confused, I handed it to him.

What's going on?

Then a feeling of dread came over me. The letter mentioned he'd been drinking.

Oh no. Panic squeezed my chest.

"Do you not remember writing it?" I asked with a lump in my throat.

He seemed to be in disbelief as he stared down at it. "Of course, I do."

"Why are you acting like you don't?"

"Felicity..." He took a few steps toward me and handed the letter back. "Look at the date."

I looked down and read. "It says June 2, 2025."

"That's not a five." He paused. "It's a three. I wrote this letter to you over two years ago."

A few seconds went by as I processed what he said. It felt like all of the air left my body. Then my heart dropped to my feet. "How can this be?" I looked down at it again, the letter shaking in my trembling hand. Three... Five... Everything looked blurry right now.

"I can't believe you're here," he whispered.

I cleared my throat. "Wait…so, um, if this was written two years ago then…you're…"

He finished my sentence. "Married."

The sun seemed to disappear in that moment. It felt like the world was closing in on me. I wanted to run, but I couldn't move. "Oh."

"Why is it that you only saw the letter now?"

My eyes closed. "Mrs. Angelini passed away after a heart attack about two years ago. This letter must have arrived around the time she died. It got mixed in with a bunch of sympathy cards. I only just found it when going through all the mail at her house recently, and that's why…" My words trailed off.

"Oh, Felicity. I'm so sorry to hear about Mrs. Angelini."

"Thank you."

"I know how much she meant to you."

You meant a lot to me, too.

As we stood facing each other, light raindrops began to fall.

"You look beautiful," he said.

Those words were like a knife to my heart.

"So do you. Handsome." I nodded. "Healthy."

Healthy? I didn't even know what I was saying at this point.

He kept shaking his head. "I don't know what to say. I'm speechless right now. I can hardly breathe, let alone speak."

"I can relate."

He looked beyond me, as if to check for a vehicle. "When did you get here? Are you staying somewhere?"

"Last night. I'm staying at a bed and breakfast two miles down the road."

I looked over and noticed a group of people inside the house staring at us from the window.

"What's the name of the place?" he asked.

"The Bainbridge Inn," I answered, still focused on the window.

"We need to talk," he said. "I'll meet you there later."

"I guess I don't need to ask why you're not inviting me in. Not sure there's anything left to say. Honestly, I should just go back to the States, Leo." My eyes began to well up.

"Please don't leave Westfordshire." His tone was urgent. "At least not until we've had a chance to talk properly in private, all right?"

Just then the door opened. An attractive woman around my age stood in the doorway. She wore a pink dress that accentuated her tiny waist. Her hair was blond, pin straight, and cut to just above her shoulders. Based on her look of disdain, it didn't take much to figure out who this was.

She looked me up and down. "What's going on here?"

Leo opened his mouth, but I didn't give him the chance to respond.

"Nothing," I said, straightening my posture and feigning a smile. "I'm an old friend of Leo's. I met him when he was visiting the States years ago and thought I would come say hello while I was here visiting England. I would've called, but I left my phone at the place I'm staying. Also, stupid me didn't realize I needed an appointment. I made a bit of a ruckus with your security people. Leo came out when he heard the racket."

Her eyes moved between the two of us. "I see," she said, looking skeptical.

I wondered if she could sense the shakiness in my voice, if she could see the lingering tears in my eyes. Could she see that she'd interrupted the moment my entire world turned upside down? The moment my heart was ripped out of my chest?

For Leo's sake, I hoped not. He didn't deserve the position my stupidity and inability to decipher a simple number had put him in.

I can't breathe.

I need to get out of here.

Forcing composure, I said, "Leo, it was nice seeing you. I hope you have a great rest of your day."

As I turned to walk away, he called, "Felicity, wait."

His plea was painful. Refusing to turn and acknowledge it, I kept walking down the long pathway until I was off the Covington grounds. Only as I turned the corner to the main road did I allow my tears to fall.

I wasn't even sure I knew how to get back to the damn inn. And it wasn't like I had a phone for navigation.

Here in this rainy countryside was the lowest point of my life.

CHAPTER 20

Felicity

Track 20: "Someone Like You" by Adele

If I'd known I was going to be walking two miles, I would've worn sneakers. My flats were now covered in mud. However, this now-soaked black dress was perfect for mourning all hope of a future with Leo Covington.

As the rain poured down, I figured I had about a mile more to go. Thankfully, I'd stopped and spoken to someone who gave me precise walking directions back to Lavinia's.

At one point, a car began driving slowly alongside me. *Great.*

"Christ, you're a mess," the male driver said.

Picking up my pace, I turned to him. He had a beard and wore what looked like a beret.

"That's what happens when you're walking in the rain."

"Get in."

Just what I needed—to be attacked and left for dead in the English countryside.

"I'm sorry. I don't get into cars with strange men, particularly ones with abrasive tones."

"Ginger, get in the car. You're soaked."

I stopped in my tracks. *Ginger?*

But it couldn't be. It looked nothing like him.

I squinted. "Sig?"

"You're telling me you didn't know it was me? I assumed that's why you were being a bitch."

"No, of course I didn't know it was you. Since when do you have a beard...and wear hats?"

"Since when are you walking around England in the rain looking like you're heading to a funeral? Although, you never did have fashion sense."

"How did you know where I was?"

"Leo called. He said you took off on foot and asked me to make sure you got back to your place safely."

"I'd ask why he didn't come himself, but I'm pretty sure he's putting out a major fire at home right now." A slightly angry laugh escaped me. "You must have been amused when you found out about all of this."

"Get in, Ginger."

I decided to take him up on his offer. Once inside, I fastened my seatbelt. "Thank you."

He drove off without a word, but he finally huffed, "No, for the record, it doesn't make me fucking happy to know you're hurting. I might be a snarky bastard, but I'm not heartless."

My chest tightened. "I'm sorry for implying you were. It's been a rough day."

He glanced over. "Dumb question perhaps, but are you okay?"

"Honestly?" I sighed. "No."

"Understandable."

I stared out the window for a moment before turning back toward the windshield wipers.

"Does he have a child?"

Sig shook his head. "No."

Relief washed over me. Not that it changed anything, but I didn't have to handle that on top of everything else.

"Did he tell you everything? How I ended up here?"

"Yeah. Pretty freak mistake, if you ask me, but anyone could have made it."

I examined him from top to bottom. "Why do you look so different?"

His jaw tightened. "Let's just say you're not the only one going through a rough time."

Hmm... "Do you want to talk about it?"

"No, I absolutely don't."

"Okay."

After several minutes of silence, he pulled up in front of Lavinia's.

"This is the place, right?"

"Yes."

He put the car in park and got out.

"What are you doing?" I asked.

"I'm coming in with you."

"Why?"

"Because I've been given instructions not to let you leave the country yet and to make sure you're okay. You admitted you're not. I assured Leo I would look after you."

I rolled my eyes. "I'm not alone. Lavinia, who owns this place, is with me. And why are you at Leo's beck and call anyway?"

"I owe him quite a bit."

Hmm...

As I walked toward the door, he followed.

"Are you really coming inside?"

He nodded.

I'd definitely entered the British version of *The Twilight Zone*.

Lavinia beamed when she opened the door. "This must be the lovely man you've told me all about!"

"No, no," I was quick to correct. "This is Sig. He just drove me here. It's a long story, but things didn't work out today at all." I shook my head. "Turns out, I misread the date on that letter. It was actually written two years ago, not two months ago. He's married, and I pretty much made a fool of myself."

"Oh, dear." Her mouth dropped as she pulled me in for a hug. "I'm so, so sorry. That's devastating." She looked over at Sig. "Your driver is staying?"

"Sig is actually Leo's cousin. He's...looking after me."

"Lovely to meet you, Lavinia." Sig extended his hand.

She took it. "I sense a very handsome face behind that grizzly exterior. You're welcome to stay as long as you like."

Sig looked around. "Where's the alcohol? Ginger's going to need it."

Alcohol? I couldn't stomach anything right now, let alone that.

"I'm fine."

He ignored me as he turned to Lavinia. "What do you have in the house?"

"Fireball and whiskey."

Sig balked. "Disgusting. I'll head to the store." He turned toward the door. "Lavinia, you need to make sure she doesn't go anywhere in my absence."

I looked down at myself. "Do I look like I'm in any condition to leave the house again right now? It would take me at least an hour to get cleaned up and more time to arrange for a getaway car. So you're good. I won't run."

After Sig left for the store, Lavinia tried to get me to tell her more about what happened, but I wasn't ready to rehash it. Instead, I lay on her couch and closed my eyes, trying to rid myself of this pounding headache.

When Sig returned, I pulled myself off the sofa. He was carrying two paper bags. In short order, he unloaded the stuff to make margaritas on the counter, plus lots of food.

"I didn't realize we were having a party," I said.

"A pity party."

"This is sort of ridiculous, you know."

He paused. "What's the alternative? Sitting in the corner, crying about it all? Do you want him to come here and find you in that state?"

Sig was right. Leo had said he would come see me. I wasn't sure about the purpose of that, but it would be better if I weren't a mess. So maybe having a couple of drinks would keep me from totally losing it.

"Can I help?" I asked.

"No. But you can help yourself. You still look like a swamp monster. Go take a shower and get out of your funeral clothes."

I nodded and went to have a good cry under the hot shower, which left me feeling a bit better. I threw on my favorite T-shirt and jeans and felt a heck of a lot more comfortable.

When I reemerged in the kitchen, Sig looked at my T-shirt from his spot at the stove. "Oh, Hello Kitty. So nice to see you again."

"Some things never change, Sig." I laughed.

"Like your dreadful style."

"Not sure you're one to talk about style right now, Sigmund."

"Touché, love."

He was stirring something in a large pot.

I leaned my head over the stove. "What are you making?"

"Tears of Unrequited Love Soup."

I slapped his arm. "Jackass."

"You're smiling, though." He winked. "It's the beginnings of chili con carne, actually." He pointed to the other side of the counter. "There's a margarita waiting for you in that red plastic cup."

"Wow. Thank you."

Lavinia entered the kitchen, margarita in hand. "These are quite good. I've never had one before."

That made me laugh. She looked so cute holding that big cup.

A spoon dropped to the floor, and Sigmund bent to pick it up. The beret he'd been wearing slipped off his head. I was shocked to see his thick mane of hair gone, replaced by a short, cropped cut. *Strange.* I didn't say anything, but I certainly wondered why he'd cut it.

Over the next hour, Sig made corn bread in the toaster oven and put out an array of toppings for the chili: sliced avocadoes, shredded cheese, sour cream, and jalapeño peppers.

I helped set the table as he carried the pot over, placing it on a trivet.

As we dug in, Lavinia sang Sig's praises. "Such a handsome man who can cook is hard to find."

"Are you hinting at something, Lavinia?" he asked.

She blushed. It was freaking adorable. "If I were forty years younger, perhaps."

"Age is just a number." Sig looked over at me. "Sort of like 2023 versus 2025."

I dropped my spoon and glared at him.

"Too soon?" He smirked.

Then, amazingly, I burst out laughing until I cried. I didn't know if my tears were happy or sad, but it felt good to let it all out after the day I'd had.

Sig had checked his phone a lot during dinner. I wondered if Leo was texting him, but I was afraid to ask.

He pointed to my empty cup. "You want another drink? You only had one."

"No, I'd better not."

"You might need one."

"Why is that?"

"Because he's on his way over."

Shit. My stomach dipped. "Okay, yeah."

"Thought so."

Sig stood and poured the last of the frozen margarita into my cup.

"Go prepare yourself. I've got the cleanup covered."

"Are you sure?"

"I've got nothing else to do."

"Thank you, Sig. Truly." It turned out this dinner had been exactly what I needed to calm down. Who would have known that at a time like this, Sigmund Benedictus would be my savior? Life is funny—when it's not excruciatingly sad.

Ten minutes later, the doorbell rang. I let Lavinia answer, because after the scene I'd made earlier, there was no way I was going to rush to the door. Never again would I put myself in such a vulnerable position.

I lifted myself off the couch but didn't move from my spot. I just listened.

"I know you," came Lavinia's voice from the doorway. "Oh my. You're...Your Grace? What are you doing at my house? Have I done something wrong?"

It hadn't occurred to me that she would freak out.

"No, madam. I'm sorry to alarm you. I'm here to see Felicity. And please, call me Leo."

"She said her lost love's name was Leo, but I never imagined." She looked back at me for a moment. "You're... oh my dear. It's you. You're the man who broke her heart."

His eyes met mine, and suddenly the margaritas were no match for my emotions. So much for that plan. The look of pain on his face made me sad, not only for me, but for him. I knew it hurt Leo to know he'd hurt me. He hadn't meant to. Neither of us had meant for this to happen.

Because Lavinia was still frozen in shock, she hadn't invited him in.

Sig came to the rescue. "Lavinia, earlier you were telling me about that game you wanted to show me how to play. I've cleared the table. Why don't you get the cards?"

"Oh...yes." She snapped out of her stupor. "Let me get them." She rushed away.

Once they exited the room, Leo stepped inside and walked toward me. Everything in me felt electrified. He looked at me for a few seconds before he reached out and pulled me into his arms. I could instantly feel his heartbeat.

I hadn't expected him to touch me—earlier he had kept his distance. In the warmth of his arms, I let my guard down for a moment, allowing myself to experience the comfort of his embrace and his familiar smell, even if it was bittersweet. Still, I never wanted him to let go.

"I'm so sorry about today," he whispered. "And I'm sorry it took me so long to get here."

When he pulled away, I wondered if that had been the last time I'd ever feel him against me.

He looked down at my chest. "Look at you, here in England in your Hello Kitty shirt."

"Well, Sig was kind enough to point out that I looked like a swamp monster in my drenched outfit from earlier."

Leo forced a smile. "You mentioned you didn't have a phone. I felt terrible when you walked away in the rain. I'm glad he was with you until I could get here."

"You assumed I would flee?"

"Yeah, actually. And I wouldn't have blamed you."

"You were probably right. I might have." I looked down. "What happened after I left you today?"

When he exhaled, the brief touch of his breath against my skin felt torturous.

"I explained everything to Darcie. Though the moment she saw you, she knew who you were."

My eyes widened as I looked up. "She did? How?"

"Years ago, I told her about you. She took one look and figured it out."

"You told her about me?"

"Darcie and I were friends when we were younger, long before we became a couple. Her father is a dignitary and a friend of my dad's. When she and I reconnected as adults, I confessed that I was still in love with someone. The one thing she didn't know until now was that I'd written the letter. But I explained that today."

"I'm surprised you would admit that to her."

"I didn't *elaborate* on the content, just said I had reached out to you before the wedding because things were left unsettled between us. I didn't have to detail it. I think she put two and two together—enough to realize the inappropriateness of my actions."

"She must have been upset that you came to see me."

"She wasn't happy. But I think she understood."

"Well, she's a better woman than I am. I would have beaten your ass if you left to go see some tramp who showed up at our door."

"Darcie's not thrilled, to say the least, but I had to be honest." After a long moment of silence, he shook his head. "I'm sorry. I think I'm still in shock. I thought I'd come here with a million things to say, but I'm...speechless."

"I understand that."

Leo reached out and touched the ring hanging around my neck. The brush of his hand against my chest sent shockwaves through me.

"I noticed you wearing it earlier." He put his hand by his side.

I ran my fingers over the ring. "I wore it for strength. I thought it would be a good luck charm. Apparently, it had the opposite effect."

"Yeah," he whispered.

I couldn't keep staring into his eyes, so I suggested we sit on the couch.

Leo took a seat at the opposite end. "I want to know everything," he said. "Tell me about the past five years."

Taking a breath in, I composed my thoughts. "Well, after you left, I went straight to Pennsylvania. I was really broken up about us, but I focused on school and tried to block it out." I paused, looking down at my fingers. "About a year into it...I started dating Matt again."

Leo swallowed.

"To make a long story short, it wasn't meant to be. It never was. I broke it off with him. I never got involved with anyone else after that. Soon after I graduated law school two years ago, Mrs. Angelini passed away."

"What happened?"

"She died in her sleep. It was a heart attack."

A look of sadness crossed his face. "You never got to say goodbye. That's fucking hard. I'm so sorry."

Tears threatened as I nodded. "There's not much to say after that. In the time since she's been gone, I've thrown myself into my job. But I quit last month because it was so unfulfilling. Something was calling me back to Rhode Island, even though Mrs. Angelini wasn't there anymore. I used to think I wanted to live in the big city. But all I've wanted recently was to be back in Narragansett. I found your letter as soon as I got there, and everything started to make sense—why I felt such a pull to return. Or so it seemed." I shook my head. "Now nothing makes sense at all."

He looked tormented, and his hands were restless. My heart clenched at the jarring sight of the gold band on his finger. *My Leo is married.* Married. I remembered so vividly how that hand felt on my body. But no part of him, neither his gorgeous hands, nor his heart belonged to me anymore.

I cleared my throat. "Tell me how these past five years have been for you. I mean, obviously I know one major thing that happened."

Leo blew out a breath and settled into the sofa. He stared off. "When I returned home, my father was in better shape than I'd expected. He bounced back fairly quickly from that infection. So that was a relief, of course. But aside from that, I felt...lost. The trip to America was supposed to have helped me clear my head, but all it had done was make me more confused about things. I struggled through that first year. Until I couldn't take it anymore." He looked up and met my eyes. "So I left and returned to the US."

Adrenaline rushed through me. "What?"

"I realized letting you go was a huge mistake. I went to find you at Drexel."

"What?" I repeated. My mouth hung open. *He came back for me?* "I don't understand, Leo."

"I planned to beg you to reconsider finding a way to be with me after you finished school. Mostly I just needed to see you again."

"What happened?"

"I was staying at an Airbnb near the Drexel campus. I wasn't sure how I was going to approach you, so I decided to get to town first and then figure it out. But before I had a chance to find you, I saw you."

"Why didn't you come to me?" I could hardly breathe.

"Because you were with him."

My stomach sank. "You saw me with Matt..."

"Yes. He had his arms around you. And you seemed happy. I realized I was too late, that you'd moved on. I felt entirely out of my league at that point."

That tore my heart out. Despite what things might have *looked* like with Matt, I would have dropped everything for Leo in a heartbeat. My entire reconciliation with Matt had been a vain attempt to get over Leo anyway.

"So, you just went back to England?" I asked, willing my tears away.

He looked down. "Yep."

My eyes stung. "I hadn't moved on from you, Leo. I was *forcing* myself to try."

Leo looked back up at me. "Only after that was I able to force *myself* to try to move on—because I assumed *you* had. You can see how well that went by the rambling letter I sent you before my wedding. Even knowing you were with someone else didn't change how I felt."

I wiped my eyes. "God, we're a mess."

"A mess with impeccable timing, I might say." Leo stood up and ventured into the kitchen, returning with a tissue. He handed it to me.

I sniffled. "Thank you."

He watched as I wiped my face.

When I finished, I looked up at him with clear eyes. "Are you in love with Darcie?"

Of course, he was. He'd married her, for heaven's sake. But I needed to hear him say it.

Leo blinked. "I do love her. But it's different. I can't say that it's the same kind of love I felt for you."

Felt. Past tense.

"I trust her," he went on to say. "And I care for her deeply. We have a mutual respect for one another. She's deserved better than me from the very beginning, but I was honest with her. I told her about you. She herself had gotten her heart broken by a man she loved shortly before we reconnected. We bonded over our mutual heartbreaks, though they were different situations."

Leo pressed his fingertips together. "Darcie wasn't you, Felicity, but she was someone I felt comfortable with and could relate to. She came into my life at a time when I needed incomplexity and companionship. She and I never had the insane chemistry you and I did. The evolution of my relationship with her was different. It started with genuine friendship and grew from there."

He paused, as if to figure out how to soften the blow of what he was about to say.

"It did evolve into a romantic relationship. She knew the situation with my father and understood what I was up against. Due to his health at the time, I asked her to marry me before either of us was ready for that. And she knew the reason—because I wanted my father to bear witness to it. That's not to say I didn't want to marry her. If not you, there was no one else I could have imagined myself with." He exhaled. "Felicity, when you didn't respond to my letter, I was certain my assumption that you'd moved on with Matt was correct. I forced myself to move on with my life."

"And now?" I braced myself. "How is your marriage?"

"At this moment, with me being here talking to you? Not very good."

"Obviously I meant before today…"

"I know what you're asking." He sighed. "It hasn't been perfect. We've had our issues."

"Like what?"

"She wants to start a family soon."

"And you don't?"

"I haven't felt ready. So that's been a point of contention."

I shook my head. "I'm sorry for all the questions. What happens in your marriage isn't any of my business."

"You can ask me anything, Felicity. I've always told you that."

"She must hate me."

"She knows you meant no disrespect in coming here and that you didn't know I was married."

Married.

Married.

Married.

The word felt like it was choking me.

"I think I should go back home," I blurted.

"Stay for a week," he said immediately.

"Why?"

"Because I'm not ready to say goodbye to you yet. I don't have a better reason than that."

"What—are you going to invite me over to dinner at the estate? I mean, come on, Leo. What purpose will my staying serve? I can barely look at you right now with this pain in my chest."

"You think I want to hurt you?" he shouted, then quickly lowered his voice. "That's not what this is about. I just need time to process this before you leave." He paused. "One week, Felicity."

He stared into my eyes. I had to remind myself that this situation was just as shocking to him as it was to me. And it was the fault of no one but fate.

"How are you supposed to see me, given that your wife knows who I am?"

"I don't plan to lie to her." He paused. "And I'm telling Sigmund to stay here at the inn with you."

"Why? He doesn't need to do that."

"I need to make sure you're okay, since I can't be here with you. You don't know your way around Westfordshire. And he could use the distraction as well."

"What's going on with him, anyway?"

"I'll explain when we have more time. That's not a conversation that should be rushed."

That left me unsettled.

"It's late," he said, standing. "I'd better get back, but I'll see you tomorrow, okay?"

He walked to the door. He looked so painfully handsome, his golden brown hair slicked back off to the side. At thirty-three, Leo was sexier than ever. If anything, he was more physically fit than I remembered. His periwinkle blue sweater hugged his broad shoulders and muscular chest.

"Try to get some sleep tonight," he said before walking away.

He didn't hug me again. It seemed surreal to have been standing across from the man I still cared so much about and not be able to touch him. It was as close to pure torture that existed.

CHAPTER 21
Leo

Track 21: "Goodbye My Lover" by James Blunt

The moon was bright against the dark, night sky as I pulled onto our property. Dread mixed with guilt followed me inside as I opened the front door.

Darcie waited for me in the foyer, which likely meant she'd been watching from the window until I arrived.

I don't fucking blame her.

Her arms were crossed protectively over her chest. "That took long enough."

"I'm sorry."

"I still don't understand how she didn't Google you and figure out you were married."

"I understand your confusion." I removed my jacket and hung it up in the coat closet by the door.

"So then explain," she demanded.

"Come sit with me for a moment."

She followed me into the adjacent living room. We sat down.

"When my relationship with her ended, we agreed not to keep in touch if we weren't going to be together. She must have chosen not to search the Internet for information on me."

"And somewhere along the line, she realized she'd made a mistake and wanted you back? So she just hops on a plane without calling first? Who does that?"

There was no good way to spin this situation. I could already see the wheels turning in Darcie's head. I reached my hand out and placed it on hers. "I know you're upset."

"What now?" She pulled her hand back. "Is she going home?"

"She's staying for a week. She and I need to talk through some things. Nothing more. I don't want her to return to the US so shocked and hurt. We just need to process this before she goes."

She gritted her teeth. "I want to tell you to go fuck yourself right now, Leo. But I'm not entirely sure that's the answer. Whatever you still apparently feel for this woman isn't going to go away, even if I take that stance."

"I wouldn't blame you if you told me to fuck myself, Darcie. I really wouldn't. I'm sorry to have put you in this situation. But I need you to trust that I would never cheat on you, if that's what you're worried about."

She let out a long, frustrated breath. "So when are you going to see her again?"

"Tomorrow."

"Jesus," she muttered. "I suppose this is what I get for agreeing to marry you so hastily. You told me yourself when we first got together that you were still in love with her. I should've known better."

"If you recall, you'd barely gotten over Gabriel when we started dating."

That was irrelevant now, but I was desperate to take some of the attention off me.

"Gabriel? You're going to bring him into this? I've long moved on from him. Gabriel is not going to be showing up at my door unannounced years later. For God's sake, Leo."

"You're right. I shouldn't have brought him up." I looked at her with pleading eyes. "Darcie, I've never lied to you. And I don't plan to start now, all right?"

She tapped her foot against the floor. "What time are you seeing her tomorrow?"

"Probably the afternoon. I'll only be gone a couple of hours. And Sigmund will be with us, if that makes you feel better."

She raised her voice. "Actually, it doesn't. You point that out as if I would have a reason to worry if he *weren't* with you."

"That wasn't how I meant it."

My wife stood. "I'm going to bed. I waited up long enough."

"Darcie…"

She whipped around. "Please just let me be."

Feeling completely beat and emotionally drained, I sat in silence, alone for a while. I deserved every bit of her attitude.

After a few minutes, I ventured into the kitchen, where Camila was still awake making some tea. While most of the staff lived off-site, Camila had always been a live-in employee.

Years ago, before my return trip to the US, I'd confided in Camila about falling in love with an American girl. While I hadn't opened up to her like I had my grandmother, Camila certainly knew more about my life than my parents did.

"I've been worried about you," she said.

I pulled out a chair and sat down. "As you should be."

"I've tried to tame the vultures. They've been gossiping all day. That girl made quite a scene. But my God, Leo. I never imagined she was the *same* girl you told me about—Felicity."

I put my head in my hands. "I'm a terrible husband, Camila. Really. I should be shot for my behavior today. But I just—"

"You can't let the redhead go home."

"Not like this, no." I pulled on my hair. "And it's not fucking fair to either of them."

"Leo, I've known you since you were a young boy. I've observed a lot. You've always tried to do the right thing. By your father, by your mother, by Felicity, by your wife. Sometimes even when we're trying to do the right thing, we still muck it up. Just give yourself grace and do the best you can. But also, don't expect your wife to have too much patience with this situation. No sane woman would allow it."

"I hear you."

Camila slid a cup of tea toward me. "Not to pour salt in your wound, but your mother somehow got wind of the situation. Seems we have a mole here in the house. She called looking for you while you were out, and I expect she's going to be after you tomorrow for an explanation."

Years ago, that might have seemed like a nightmare. But I was numb to it at this point. After hurting two people

I cared about today, dealing with Mother seemed like nothing.

I exhaled. "I'll face her when I have to."

The following morning, I decided to grab the bull by the horns after all and confront my mother before she had a chance to call me. After my father died, Mum had moved to a separate residence so Darcie and I could have our independence in the main family property. My mother's house, on the other side of Westfordshire, was nearly as large, with a staff of its own.

"Hello, Mother," I said as I met her out in the garden.

I could see from her stark expression that she was seething.

"What's this about some American girl showing up out of nowhere? Who is she?"

There was no point in skirting anything now. I told her the full story, holding nothing back. My mother's reaction was everything I'd always imagined it to be.

She was practically shaking. "You would've given up everything, Leo. Thank the gods for intervening and making it impossible for you to wreck your life!"

"And you wonder why I've never told you anything over the years..."

"Your father is likely rolling around in his grave right now."

"I highly doubt that. For all he knew, I did right by him." I lifted my brow. "Anyway, what's the point of this lifestyle without a little scandal to shake things up from time to time, right? Like father, like son?"

Immediately I knew alluding to my father's rumored infidelities was uncalled for. "I'm sorry, Mother. Just trying to point out that I'm hardly the first imperfect person in this family."

My mother took a long sip of her mimosa and slammed the champagne flute down. "What are you going to do about this problem? Is she still here?"

"She's not a *problem*. She's a *person*. One who had no idea what she was walking into. And I think what I'm doing at this point is none of your concern. I don't owe any explanations from this point forward to anyone but Darcie."

"Why did you run over here this morning to talk to me if you don't value my opinion?"

"Because I knew your head was likely ready to explode, and I wanted to put you out of your misery."

My mother screamed in frustration. "If your nan wasn't already on her deathbed, this might just put her there."

That was almost laughable.

"That goes to show how much you know about Nan..."

"What are you talking about?"

"Nan knew about Felicity from the beginning. She was the only person besides Sigmund who knew about our relationship back then. Nan knows more about me than anyone, actually."

That should leave my mother's knickers in a knot.

As her jaw dropped, I chose that moment to walk away.

A few hours later, I picked up Felicity and Sigmund at the Bainbridge Inn. They hadn't killed each other yet, so that was good news. The sweet, old woman who owned the place stood outside and waved us off.

Felicity fastened her seatbelt. "Where are we going?"

While she was next to me in the passenger seat, my cousin sat in the back.

"There's something I want to show you," I said.

"I'm sure that's not the first time you've said that to her," Sigmund cracked.

I glared at him in the rearview mirror. "Why am I taking you along again?"

"Oh, I don't know...because your wife will have your arse if you don't? Because you think I'll drink myself into oblivion if left alone? Because you can't get enough of my charming personality? Because you don't trust yourself to be alone with Felicity? There are multiple answers to that question."

Ignoring him, I turned to her. "We're taking a ride out to one of my properties, actually."

My stomach churned with excitement and nerves for what lay ahead. I tried to limit my looking over at Felicity because it was painful. I knew I wouldn't cross any lines, but my unwavering attraction to her was unnerving. As a married man, I shouldn't ache to kiss another woman. I shouldn't so instantly remember what she tasted like and yearn to taste her again. But nothing ever went as it *should* when it came to Felicity Dunleavy.

Her eyes widened when we arrived at the property known as Brighton House. My father's widowed sister lived here most of the year, but she was currently in France on holiday. My aunt Mildred loved animals and kept a large farm on the estate. Her house manager, Nathaniel, happened to be a longtime friend of Sigmund's. I knew my cousin would likely head inside to have a drink with him, and that would allow me some alone time with Felicity.

Sure enough, Nathaniel came out to greet us, and Sigmund disappeared inside. I'd introduced Felicity as a friend I'd be showing around the farm. Although Nathaniel looked confused, I was certain Sigmund would have a field day filling him in on the soap opera my life had become.

"Let's take a tour of the farm, shall we?"

"I'd love that." She smiled.

It was a relief to see her at least momentarily happy.

"My aunt is an animal lover, like you, and this is her farm. She's away on holiday right now, so her staff tends to the animals. Mildred lost her husband when she was in her thirties. He died in a car accident."

"Oh, I'm sorry."

"She never remarried and never had children. The animals are like her kids."

As we walked toward the barn, excitement built in my veins.

Several ponies congregated behind a wooden partition.

As she looked over at them, Felicity beamed. "Oh my God. Is that a Shetland?"

"Yeah." I couldn't contain my smile.

"He looks just like Ludicrous."

I arched my brow. "Just *like* him, huh?"

"Yeah."

"Look closer."

There was nothing better than the look on her face when she realized it.

She pointed in disbelief. "That's not him…"

"It *is*, Felicity."

"What?"

I opened the gate, and she ran toward him. Felicity wrapped her arms around his neck and hugged him. Honestly, few things in life had brought me greater joy than witnessing this moment. I could certainly relate to the feeling of seeing someone after believing you'd never see them again in this lifetime—because that's what I was experiencing right now.

Leaning her head against him, she said, "I don't understand. I thought you found a farm in Rhode Island to take him? I told you to let me know if you couldn't find a place for him. You didn't say anything, so I assumed that was all set. How did he end up here?"

"No way was I going to leave you with that responsibility. I just never got back to you before I left. I did get that farm in Rhode Island to agree to keep him until I could transport him back to England. But that was all they were willing to do, since they didn't have the space for him. About a month later, he was here. And he's been here ever since."

Ludicrous neighed.

She began to tear up as she petted him. "I told myself I wasn't going to cry today."

"As long as I'm not the one causing your tears, I'm good."

"I'd considered trying to find him," she said, running her fingers through his mane.

"Little did you know…"

"I can only imagine what your aunt must have thought when you brought him to her."

"She was thrilled, actually, and considered it more a gift than a burden. My one condition was that I asked her to keep his name."

Felicity looked up at me. "Well, this trip certainly has been full of surprises."

She spent about twenty minutes with her precious pony before I suggested we take a walk; I was running out of time with her, and we needed to have our conversation.

"We'll circle back around and spend more time with him before we leave," I told her.

I'd arranged to have a late lunch laid out on a table overlooking the hills. We walked for a few minutes until it came into view around a bend.

When she noticed the spread, she said, "What's all this?"

"Well, I can't take you out for the day and not feed you. Don't worry—I had nothing to do with cooking any of it."

"Well, thank God for that." She chuckled.

"Not a can of SpaghettiOs in sight."

We fell into an easy and comfortable conversation over the meal. She told me more about the job she'd left at the law firm and why it had burned her out. As she spoke of the life she planned to lead when she returned home, I felt myself longing to be back at that serene house on the bay.

After we ate, Felicity looked out into the distance, and I stared at her profile, stopping myself from counting the freckles. *Old habits die hard.*

When she turned to me, I lowered my eyes to the table so as not to get caught.

"Even though things didn't work out the way I'd hoped, I want you to know I'm proud of you, Leo. You're doing everything you set out to, everything you promised your father you would. I'm sure he's very proud, too."

"Thank you. I appreciate that. But now tell me what you *really* feel."

"What do you mean?" She blinked. "I meant every word."

"I know you meant what you said about me. But I want to know what's going on in your mind right now—about *us*, this situation—even if it pains me to hear it."

"What I'm thinking or feeling when it comes to us doesn't matter anymore."

"It matters to me. I want to hear it, even if it hurts. We need to let it out."

Felicity's cheeks turned pink. "What do you want me to say? You want to hear that I'm in love with a married man? Because that's not really a good look." Her eyes glistened. "You want to know how I *feel*? I'm...angry. I'm confused. I'm frustrated. I'm scared. I'm jealous. I'm a mess." She wiped a tear from her eyes. "At the same time, I'm still so grateful for this moment, even if it won't last forever. Because it's one more moment in time with you than I was supposed to have."

My heart felt heavy. Her words mirrored my own feelings. I wanted to say so much, but my fear of seeming disrespectful to my wife paralyzed me. I was a married man, which gave me no right to open my heart to someone else, even if I wanted so desperately to tell her she wasn't alone.

Just when the words at the tip of my tongue were ready to choke me, she changed the subject.

"Will you tell me what happened to Sig?"

I nodded and exhaled, gearing myself up. There was no good way to tell this story, so I just dove in. "He fell in love."

CHAPTER 22
Felicity

Track 22: "Tears Dry On Their Own" by Amy Winehouse

M y eyes widened. "He fell in love? Sigmund? Of Sigmund and the Marias fame? *That* Sigmund?"

"Hard to believe, I know." Leo flashed a gorgeous smile that hurt to look at.

"What happened?"

"He decided to take a trip to the States again. He'd connected with some woman online and flew out to New York for a week."

"He ended up falling in love with her?"

"Hardly. That woman was only out for a good time, as was he. He got bored with her quickly enough."

I blinked. "So, then...who did he fall in love with?"

Leo settled into his seat. "He was delayed at the airport on the way home. While there, he started bickering with this girl who was waiting for the same flight as him. They were the last two people to check in. The airline had overbooked the flight and was short one seat. Neither of them wanted to give up theirs."

I laughed as he continued.

"Finally, some poor bloke intercepted and agreed to take a later plane so neither one of them had to move their flight. But Sigmund and Britney kept bickering. He teased her about everything from her height to the Birkenstocks on her feet. She was tiny—only about five feet. So he picked her apart, chewed her up, and spit her out. You know Sigmund."

I shook my head. "Oh, yes, I do."

"Well, she dished it back to him even harder—like no woman he'd *ever* met before. She called him every name in the book: giraffe, player, imbecile..." He laughed. "She was younger—twenty-five to his thirty-two. Anyway, the flight got delayed. Somehow, they ended up wandering the airport together. He realized she sparked something in him that he'd never experienced before. She called him out on his crap, challenging every word that came out of his mouth. Sigmund was so taken by her. The longer they were stuck in that airport together, the more attracted to her he became. As he put it, he'd never been *harder* for a woman in his life. Ironically, for once I think that had nothing to do with looks, although he did find her quite attractive."

I was on the edge of my seat now. "Did they end up flying to England together?"

He nodded. "Once they boarded the plane, they were able to switch seats so they could sit next to each other. They talked the entire flight. You know how my cousin can be. He's not very good at opening up about his insecurities—always dodging questions whenever you ask him about his career path and whatnot. She apparently had a way of seeing through his tactics. She got him to talk to her."

"Wow." I grinned.

"He almost ruined it."

"How?"

"In typical Sigmund fashion, he challenged her to join the mile-high club."

"Oh, Sig." I chuckled.

"She told him where he could stick that proposition. He said in that moment, he knew he was never going to be the same again."

"What happened after the flight?"

"Remarkably, even with all the talking they'd done, she wouldn't tell him why she was in England or where she was going. He only had her first name—Britney."

"Huh…"

"Once they landed, he begged for her number. But she told him if he knew what was good for him, they should part ways."

That actually made me feel bad for Sig. "Oh my goodness. Why? He must have been devastated."

"Totally gutted."

"I assume this is not the end of the story, though."

Leo shook his head. "He kept following her around the airport. She couldn't get rid of him. And even though she said she wanted him to leave her alone, he could see in her eyes that she didn't. He suspected there was something more going on, something she just didn't want to tell him."

"Like maybe she was married?"

Leo glared at me.

"I swear that wasn't a dig at you." I laughed.

"Actually, that did cross his mind," Leo explained with a smile. "Anyway, out on the platform where she waited for her ride, he told her she wasn't going to lose him unless she gave him a good reason why. She just kept telling him he'd be better off not knowing, that they would *both* be better off just remembering the hours they'd had together and going their separate ways." He stared off. "But Sigmund couldn't let her go."

"What did he do...get in her cab?"

"That's *exactly* what he did. She told him he'd be sorry. But the more she said things like that, the more intent he was on sticking with her." Leo chuckled, but then his expression turned serious. "When they got to her hotel, in the lobby there were two older people waiting for her."

I leaned in. "Who were they?"

"Her parents. They'd flown in from the States and had arrived in England before her."

I was confused. "Why didn't they travel together?"

"She apparently had some business to take care of at home first. So they met each other in London."

I cocked my head. "So...they were vacationing?"

"I wish." Leo blew out a breath. "Britney was forced to tell Sigmund everything then and there—that she wasn't in England on vacation at all. She had traveled here to seek an experimental treatment...for her cancer."

My heart sank. "Oh no."

"Sigmund was gobsmacked. He'd had no clue she was sick."

I felt like I was going to cry. Leo looked like he might do the same.

"Holy shit," I whispered.

"With her parents standing there, watching it all, she angrily asked him if he was happy now—couldn't he understand why she'd preferred to leave well enough alone. He told her that actually, yeah, he was happy. That he'd never been happier in his life, and the fact that she was sick didn't change how he felt."

Oh my heart.

"She begged him to ditch her, but he wouldn't. Before her treatments started, they holed themselves up in a hotel room together and made the most of that time. Then, he spent every hour of every day with her during her treatments at a hospital in London. Her parents were really taken with him and grateful that he gave their daughter joy during such a difficult time."

Dread crept over me as Leo took a deep breath.

"One night," he continued, "Sigmund came straight to my house from the hospital. He looked exhausted, and he told me he finally understood. When I asked what he was talking about, he said, 'I understand how you felt about Felicity—why you refused to give her up. When you're in love with someone, you just can't.'" Leo smiled. "It was like my cousin had finally grown up. But it was a damn shame that he had to endure such pain along with it."

I braced myself. "What happened to her, Leo?"

"The treatments didn't work. She died six months after arriving in England, and my cousin hasn't been the same since. He likely never will be."

I couldn't stop the tears from falling now. Leo gave me a minute to compose myself.

"How am I supposed to look at Sig today?" I asked.

"I know. I was hesitant to tell you the story, but you asked."

"Was she his first real girlfriend?"

"She was his wife, actually. He married her a month before she died."

That cut like a knife. "I'm devastated for him."

Leo looked out toward the hills. "In a strange way, as devastating as it was for him to lose her, I think she saved his life. He says he'd experience the suffering many times over again, as long as he got to know her. He even used to shave his head to match hers."

It hit me. "That's why his hair is so short."

"Yeah."

"How long ago did she die?"

"It was only three months ago, Felicity."

Oh my God. "Where are her parents?"

"They went back to the States, but I know they're forever grateful that Britney spent her last days here with Sig."

I'd thought losing Leo was heartbreaking, but clearly there were far worse ways to lose someone. Hearing this story made me realize how fragile life is.

Leo stood. "Come on. I think we need a change of pace before we see him again."

We walked back to where the animals were located, and a farmhand brought out two horses. We each climbed atop one and took a leisurely ride around the estate.

"I'm still thinking about Sig," I said as we rode.

"I figured as much—probably the one thing to take your mind off of us, eh?"

I sighed. "Yeah."

After several minutes of riding in silence, he said, "Talk to me, Felicity. Forget about what's appropriate and what's not. Tell me what you're thinking right now."

The horses neighed in unison.

"I'm thinking you reap what you sow in life. Every bit of pain I'm feeling right now is my own doing."

Leo seemed taken aback. He pulled on the reins to stop his horse. So I did the same.

"Tell me what you mean," he demanded.

"Leo, how could I have let you go? You asked me flat out if I would consider coming here, being with you, and I shot it down faster than you could even blink. I don't know what I was thinking. I was scared—scared of how strong my feelings were, maybe. And taking a chance on you back then would have meant putting someone else first for the first time in my life, and that's damn scary when you grow up believing people will always hurt you and you should never depend on anyone. But the truth is, *I* made that decision. So, *all of this*—the situation we're in, the situation I put *you* in right now—it's *my* fault."

His face reddened. "Your fault because you weren't willing to throw yourself into a world you knew nothing about for a man you'd known only a matter of weeks? And don't forget, I was the one who left *you*, Felicity. Not the other way around. And I walked away again like a coward when I saw you with Matt in Philadelphia because I assumed you were happy. I could've said something. I convinced myself the trip had been a momentary lapse in sanity and that you were where you were meant to be— happy with him in the big city, just like your vision board. So you see, I walked away not once, but twice." He reached out and cupped my cheek. "None of this is your fault, beautiful. Do you understand?"

I closed my eyes, relishing his gentle touch, allowing myself to feel the comfort in it for a few moments without letting guilt creep in. "It is what it is now, Leo. Fate just hasn't been on our side," I whispered.

After that, we rode in silence until we returned the horses.

Once they'd been led back to the barn, we paid another visit to Ludicrous so I could say goodbye. It had to be about time for Leo to drive me home. I was sure Darcie was counting the minutes.

We were almost back at the house when Leo stopped walking and faced me.

"Look at me, Felicity."

I looked up into his eyes.

"I know so much has changed..." he said. "But it's still me. I'm here. You can tell me anything. I want you to tell me what to do. How can I fix this?"

I said the first thing that came to mind, heeding the warnings in my gut and the voice inside my head. "Tell me to go home."

He shook his head. "I can't seem to do that."

My heart was raw after everything I'd learned today. "The only thing more painful than saying goodbye to you once is standing in front of you right now, feeling all the same emotions and not being able to touch you. And I wish you didn't still look at me the same way you always have, on top of it all."

His eyes wandered down my neck. He then shut them abruptly, as if to punish himself. The fucked-up thing was, the sexual chemistry between us felt stronger than ever. We'd always had an intense spark, but it seemed a thousand times worse, fueled by the inability to satisfy it.

Needing an escape, I looked down at my watch. "How long did you tell her you'd be gone?"

"A couple of hours."

"It's well beyond that. We should go."

He bit his bottom lip. "All right."

We continued walking back to the house without saying anything further.

Sig bid his friend goodbye before joining us out front.

"I suppose everything is all sorted between you two, yeah?" Sig teased. "Did you at least see your horse... Ridiculous? Is that his name?"

Still congested from crying earlier, I sniffled then laughed. "Ludicrous."

"Ah, yes. Still the dumbest thing my cousin has ever done."

It was hard to look at Sig the same way, but I tried not to let on that Leo had told me anything. I was totally spent after the day's emotional ride.

As Leo drove me home, we stole glances at each other. Every time I got the urge to reach over and touch him, I forced my eyes to the wedding ring on his hand. It never got easier looking at it. This day had done nothing to bring me closure. Quite honestly, it took everything in me not to burst into tears.

I exited the car before Leo could even say goodbye. I couldn't look at him anymore.

"Will I see you tomorrow?" he called.

"Sure," I said, not wanting to argue about it, which would only prolong him staying. He wanted me here a week, but I didn't know how much more I could take.

After he drove away, relief washed over me. If I lost control now, at least he wouldn't witness it.

Lavinia had left a note on the kitchen table, letting Sig and me know a neighbor down the road had invited her to dinner.

Sig found me in the kitchen and grabbed Lavinia's bottle of Fireball along with two glasses. He pulled up a seat and pointed to the one across from me.

"Sit, Ginger. We're going to drink." He looked down at the bottle. "I'm feeling a bit too lazy to make margaritas, so this will have to do for now."

I was in no place to argue against a stiff drink tonight.

After he poured one, he slid the glass toward me.

I took a long gulp and appreciated the burn.

Though I hadn't said anything about my feelings to Sig, he seemed to read my mind.

"I don't know what the fuck he's doing either, Felicity. I think he's hoping to figure this mess out somehow, but there's no quick solution when you're married to one person and in love with another."

My eyes shot up.

"I'm not saying he doesn't love Darcie, but he most certainly is still *in love* with you."

"He hasn't said that. How would you know?" I asked.

"Because I can see it. I know what it looks like now."

I paused as I debated whether to tell him I knew about his tremendous loss. Ultimately, I couldn't hide it. "I'm so sorry about Britney."

Rather than say anything, Sig opened the bottle and poured himself another drink. He downed it and slammed his glass against the table. "Thank you," he finally said. "He told you the saddest story to ever exist, eh?"

Shit. I could feel tears forming again in my eyes. I did *not* want him to see me cry. But tears had a mind of their own. I sniffled. "I'm sorry. I think I've cried more today than I have in my entire life."

"It's all right, Ginger." Sig poured me another drink, sliding it toward me. "So he told you all the crazy details of how I met her, too?"

I smiled through the remaining tears. "Yeah."

"I bet he forgot to mention how beautiful she was." Sig reached into his pocket for his phone. He scrolled through and turned the screen toward me.

Wiping my eyes, I smiled at the sight of them together. Britney was indeed tiny, especially next to Sig who was well over six feet tall. She had short, blond hair that might have been a wig and the most beautiful, delicate features. Her smile lit up her whole face. She reminded me of Tinkerbell. I doubted Sig had ever run across anyone more beautiful. The fact that she was obviously very sick didn't take away from that.

He looked down at the image and smiled. "That's Britney Benedictus."

"She's beautiful. And I'm so sorry. I can't imagine."

"She was the love of my life. It doesn't matter that I only had her for a matter of months. No one will ever replace her." He pressed his hand to his chest. "She'll live in here forever."

I shook my head. "I couldn't understand why you were so different. It makes sense now."

"Makes sense now why I'm a walking disaster..." He chuckled. "Thanks."

"I didn't say that."

"It's all right. It's the truth." He exhaled and put his phone down. "I'll bounce back eventually. Because that's what she would have wanted. So I'll force it. For her."

"You will," I assured him.

It surprised me that rather than sweeping the subject under the rug, he continued talking.

"The treatment she was getting—because it was experimental, it wasn't covered by insurance. Her parents ran out of money. The treatment wasn't really helping, but the idea that something *might* give us hope kept her spirits up. So when it came time to decide whether we had to stop due to finances or find a way to continue paying for it, Leo came to the rescue. He paid for the rest of her treatment and her parents' accommodations. I'll never forget that. And I'll never be able to repay him."

"That's why you're working for free as my watchdog." I smiled.

Sig swirled his glass. "I finally understand why my cousin couldn't get over you, no matter how many times I gave him crap about it. It's not something you understand fully until it happens to you."

"So then you can also understand why this is so hard for me...being here."

"You're a better person than me, Ginger...for sticking around."

"I don't want to. I'm doing it because he asked me to, but after today, I don't think I can do it anymore." My voice trembled. "I can't say goodbye to him again. Because I know this time, it will be forever. There was always a glimmer of hope before, that somehow we might find our way back to each other. But I know when he lets me go this time, that's it."

"What are you telling me?"

"I'm saying I need to go home. I don't want to feel this hurt anymore."

Sig blew out a long breath. "Felicity, if you want to leave, you know I'm not going to stop you, right? He'll just have to understand. And he will. Because he loves you. If there's one thing I know, it's that. He knows you're in pain. He just can't be the one to tell you to go."

I wiped my eyes for what felt like the hundredth time today. "Will you drive me to the airport?"

"You're trying to get me killed, aren't you?"

Looking down at the table, I shook my head. "You're right. That was too much to ask."

"Ginger, I'm kidding. Of course, I'll take you."

Relieved to have his support, I nodded. "I haven't decided yet. I need to think on this tonight."

The thought of leaving made me sick to my stomach, but not nearly as much as the thought of staying. It wasn't like Leo was going to leave his wife for me. This wasn't going to end well, and there was no reason to prolong it.

Later that evening, Sig ran to the grocery store before it closed, and Lavinia was still out, so I was alone for the first time today. After much ruminating, I was pretty sure I'd made my decision to book a flight for the morning. I'd just opened my laptop to reserve my ticket when the doorbell rang.

I knew Lavinia had given Sig a key, so the only person it could have been was Leo. Butterflies swarmed in my stomach as I went to the door. Except when I opened it, it wasn't Leo.

It was Darcie.

CHAPTER 23

Leo

Track 23: "American Girl" by Tom Petty & The Heartbreakers

After leaving Felicity, I couldn't in good conscience face Darcie yet. There were too many feelings bombarding me, and I knew the moment she looked at me she'd be able to see them all. I needed to calm down before going home. So I called my wife to let her know I'd dropped Felicity and Sigmund off, but that I was going to visit my grandmother on the way home. Nan was in an upscale rehabilitation center, and we'd been told she didn't have very much time left. I visited her often, and every time was different in terms of her condition. Today I prayed she would have enough energy to talk to me, because I needed that more than ever.

My grandmother looked half-asleep when I entered her room.

"Hello, Nan."

Opening her eyes, she held out her quivering hand. "Hi, my boy." Her voice was frail.

"How are you feeling?"

"Well, I've certainly had better days, but this is not the worst one."

"Good." I smiled. "I need to speak to you, but I don't want to deplete your energy."

"Nothing makes me feel more alive than talking to you, my grandson. I might be weak, but my ears are still perfectly fine."

I took a seat at her bedside. "Has my mother told you anything over the past couple of days?"

"No, I haven't spoken to her."

I was surprised, but perhaps my mother knew she wouldn't have been able to address it without upsetting her. In Nan's current state, that wouldn't be wise. I was proud of Mum for containing herself in her mother's best interest.

"Remember Felicity?"

My grandmother's eyes widened. "Of course. The American girl. What about her?"

"She's here."

Nan squeezed my hand. "Oh my."

I filled her in on the last couple of days. While Nan knew I'd gone back to the States after that first year to find Felicity, I'd never told her about the letter I wrote before marrying Darcie. So I started there and ended with Felicity showing up here.

My grandmother seemed deeply affected, to the point that I almost regretted telling her. She couldn't afford to get too emotionally worked up.

"That's absolutely devastating, Leo. For all involved."

"I know. I obviously never saw this happening."

Nan struggled to breathe. "My love, you know I don't have much time left. So I'm particularly careful with anything I tell you, because I never know if it will be my final word." She tried to straighten her body. "I need you to listen to me very carefully." She stared into my eyes. "I was wrong."

"What do you mean?"

She swallowed. "When you asked me years back if I thought it best that you abandon all ideas of being with a girl you clearly loved, I encouraged you to disregard your feelings for the greater good of your reputation. I worried that despite how strongly you felt, the scrutiny you'd receive would be far worse than living without her. What I didn't know then that I've realized the closer I get to death…is that nothing matters more in this life than love."

I remained silent, stunned as she continued.

"You've always been so afraid of displeasing your father. But I can assure you, wherever he is right now, he sees things from a different perspective. Your dad is no longer part of this material world, no longer concerned with money or power. He understands now that the universal purpose of our entire existence is love." Her tone grew urgent. "My advice to you today is not the same as it was then. If I could go back, I would tell you to follow your heart." She paused. "That said, you married a wonderful woman. She doesn't deserve this. It's not fair either way— to leave her high and dry or to stay when she doesn't have your whole heart."

She spoke again before I could respond.

"Leo, you need to understand that your decisions don't change what lies in your heart. You can choose to remain married to Darcie in order to protect her, but that won't change the fact that you clearly love Felicity."

"How do you know I still love her?" I asked. "I haven't told you that."

"You don't need to, my love. You have the same look of passion and fear in your eyes that you did when you told me you were going back to the US to find her. The same look of sadness as when you returned and told me she'd moved on with someone else. This torment is love in disguise. The only difference now is that you're married and some time has passed."

"All the same complications exist today..." I said. "All the reasons we decided not to be together in the first place."

"And yet here you are, feeling the same way. What does that tell you? Is this something you can control or a lie you've been telling yourself?" She let out a shaky breath. "Look, my dear, I can't tell you what to do. I can only tell you what I've learned as I make the transition to the next phase in my journey. I've said all I can say about it. I'm just sorry I didn't realize back then that my advice to you was wrong."

It killed me to think she had any regrets at this point. "I love you, Nan. I can't tell you how much it's meant to have you as my sounding board."

She smiled. "I lied... I do have one more thing to say."

"Okay, tell me."

"I'm proud of you no matter what you decide— whether that's to follow your heart or to keep your vow to your beautiful wife. There's no wrong answer. It's about what you can live with. But you're a good man, Leo. Far more conscientious than your father ever was. And even though you've never said so, I know you live with guilt because of how you came into this world—the death of your twin brother. But rest assured, he, too, is looking down on you, as proud as I am."

My grandmother's words repeated in my mind the entire way home. How was I supposed to face Darcie when this storm of emotions was still brewing inside me? The raw feelings from earlier hadn't waned in the least. And Nan hadn't told me anything I didn't already know, deep inside. But would I choose to live my life ignoring these feelings for the sake of my marriage?

I entered the house feeling completely unsettled.

Before I could head upstairs to face the fire, I noticed a text had come through from Felicity. Looking at its length, my gut immediately told me it was a Dear John letter.

I couldn't consume it fast enough as my heart raced.

Felicity: I have to go home, Leo. I'm sorry to have to leave like this, but I can't endure yet another goodbye with you. Spending time with you today was truly magical. Getting to see Ludicrous again, getting to ride those beautiful horses with you, getting to look into your eyes and see into your soul for the last time. As painful as it's been, these past couple of days have also been a gift, because there was

a time when I thought I would never see you again. Even after everything, I don't regret coming here. I've never regretted a single moment with you, not even the most painful ones. But my feelings for you are suffocating me. To care so deeply for someone and not be able to freely love them is torture. You're a married man. The longer I stay, the worse this will end.

As you read this, I am already headed to the airport. I was able to get on a flight that leaves at midnight. Please don't be mad at Sig for letting me out of his sight. He understands what it feels like to want someone and not be able to have them. Who knows what my life would be like right now if I had just taken a chance five years ago. Please know that I will always love you.

I fell into a panic. *She's gone.*

Chasing after someone to get her to stay in a foreign country while you're wearing a wedding ring isn't exactly fair. But knowing that didn't stop my urge to do it. But why? Why force her to stay when I couldn't offer her anything as things currently were?

Before I could go upstairs, Darcie came up behind me.

"The text you're reading is from her, I assume."

I turned around and gulped. "Yes."

"She told me she was leaving earlier than planned."

My heart palpitations got worse. "You...spoke to her?"

"I went over to the inn tonight while you were visiting your grandmother."

Fuck. "You did?"

"Yes. I had a very difficult time while you were out with her today, and I felt like she and I needed to have a talk."

Trying to remain calm, I asked, "What did you talk about?"

"Don't worry. I'm not the reason she's leaving. She'd already decided that by the time I arrived. She told me so."

"Yeah. She got a flight out tonight. She's already at the airport."

Darcie nodded. "I just needed to see her, Leo. I wanted to look into her eyes and see what you see, to better understand this thing I'm up against. I also wanted her to know that I don't really blame her for her mistake. But most of all, I wanted her to know how committed I am to you and to this marriage, how much I've grown to love you, even though our courtship took a different path than most. Maybe in the beginning we forced things a bit. But over the past year, in particular, I've realized everything is the way it was meant to be." Tears filled her eyes. "I love you, Leo. I truly do. And nothing has made me prouder in this life than to be your wife. I'm terribly scared to lose you, and you need to know that."

My heart broke to see her cry, to see her so vulnerable when she'd been feigning strength. Guilt and torment twisted inside me as I brought her into an embrace. Darcie had been nothing but an amazing wife. She didn't deserve this situation I'd put her in. But I had no words that would comfort her tonight. I couldn't lie and say Felicity's leaving hadn't shaken me to my core. So, I didn't say anything. I just continued to hold her.

That night we slept turned away from each other in bed as my mind raced.

The following day, I headed over to Sigmund's. He'd texted me to make sure I wasn't upset at him for driving Felicity to the airport. I'd told him not to worry, that I understood why he'd aided and abetted her departure from England.

"You look like shite. We're twinsies now," he said as he opened the door.

"Except I've shaved my face in the past few months. You haven't," I snapped.

"Are you here to ream me out? I don't trust for one second that you're not angry about me taking Ginger to the airport."

"I'm not angry, Sigmund. I just hate that this entire thing happened at all." I reached into my pocket and took out a piece of taffy.

He watched me unwrap it. "Not the taffy again. Now I *know* things are bad."

I chuckled. "I happened to find someone selling it in town this morning. Isn't that weird? I hadn't had it in years. Couldn't pass it up." I popped it into my mouth and chewed.

"The taffy gods were watching everything go down, apparently." My cousin walked to the fridge, took a beer out, and handed me one.

I swallowed the last of the candy, took a long sip of the beer, and exhaled. "I don't want to hurt Darcie. But I've hurt her already, haven't I? I've hurt them both."

"Yeah. That's how life works sometimes. Shite happens. Terrible things happen," he finished on a whisper.

"I know this is nothing compared to what you've been through, mate."

He pulled up a chair and stared at the ceiling. "Do you know what I would give for just one more day with her? One more hour?"

I walked over and placed my hand on his shoulder. "I do."

"The reason I helped Felicity leave is because I could *feel* her suffering," he said. "I know what it feels like to need someone so desperately but be unable to have them. Granted, it's two different situations—apples and oranges, in a sense. But I *can* imagine now what it would be like in her position."

My chest felt tight. "Was she okay?"

"Yeah, I mean, she wasn't in tears at the airport or anything. She's strong. She's just trying to protect herself from any further harm."

I nodded. "Thank you for being there for her when I couldn't."

"I figured I owed her for all those times I was a complete dick."

I chuckled. "Well, that's probably true."

Sigmund stood and walked over to take something out of his jacket pocket.

"She gave me this to give you." He held out my grandfather's ring on the gold chain.

It killed me that she'd felt the need to return it after all this time. It signified the final ending to our story. The diamond sparkled as I took it from him. "Did she say why she gave this back?"

"No. But I think it's pretty obvious, don't you?"

"Yeah." I looked down at the shimmering metal.

It had been a long time since I'd had this in my possession. But I'd never forgotten the day my grandfather gave it to me when I was sixteen, encouraging me to use it as a pillar of strength when I needed it. In that sense, it was ironic to be getting it back now when I probably needed it most. Maybe Felicity knew that. Or maybe it was simply closure for her, the final nail in our coffin.

"You know what you can always count on from someone like me, who's lost everything?" Sigmund asked.

"What?"

"The truth. I have no fucks left to give."

I looked up. "Lay it on me, cousin."

"Nothing else matters, Leo. You're in love with Felicity. You're afraid to hurt Darcie, but you know what? You already fucking are. You already fucking did—the moment you ran to Felicity the first chance you got. You think Darcie doesn't know? You think she's stupid? But she's willing to put up with it because she loves you." He shook his head. "You can't let her do that."

All my life I'd been enduring my cousin's frank advice. But it had never mattered more than this moment. He'd put things in a way I hadn't considered—that Darcie wanted our marriage to work badly enough to *put up* with my being in love with someone else.

"I needed to hear that," I told him.

"Good. That's what I'm here for."

Rubbing my temples, I said, "I have a lot to think about."

"Take your time, Leo, but don't take *too much* time. If there's one thing I know, it's that time is never guaranteed."

CHAPTER 24

Felicity

Track 24: "I Have Nothing" by Whitney Houston

"I hope she'd be okay with this," I said, holding one of Mrs. Angelini's ceramic bunny figurines.

"Come on," Bailey said. "What are you going to do with a hundred of these things?"

"I know. But I feel like she might have wanted me to keep these."

"You can't keep everything, Felicity. She would want you to have space to make this place your own. You're keeping more than half of her stuff as it is."

I'd decided to run a yard sale to raise money to replace the roof of Mrs. Angelini's house. While she'd left me some money to be used for that kind of thing, it wouldn't last forever. The property taxes were bad enough. And with me not working right now, a yard sale seemed like a reasonable idea. Along with smaller items for sale were some larger antiques.

She held up one of my Hello Kitty T-shirts. "This is yours, right? Why are you getting rid of it? I thought you loved these T-shirts."

That was true, but the shirt she held was the one I'd brought to England. It had to go. It wasn't like I didn't have a dozen others. And in the likely event there were no takers, I'd donate it.

"That one reminds me of Leo, so I'm parting with it," I told her.

Bailey hesitated. "Have you heard from him?"

"No. He hasn't called since that one time."

After I'd landed back in the US three months ago, Leo had called to let me know he fully understood why I'd left, and to make sure I knew there were no hard feelings about my decision. He said my coming to England had made him realize he had a lot of soul searching to do when it came to his marriage and his life, in general. He'd asked if he could contact me again. He said he couldn't live without knowing how I was doing, that he needed to make sure I was okay.

Now I felt like I'd already experienced the worst of what life had to offer me where Leo was concerned. I'd met his *wife*, for heaven's sake. I didn't think I could hurt any more than I already had. So, I'd agreed that he could reach out from time to time.

But he hadn't contacted me since that day, and I certainly had no guarantee that I'd ever hear from him again. I was trying my best to move on from what had happened this past August, but not a day went by that I didn't think of him. I still loved him as much as I ever had. A love that's interrupted is a love, nevertheless. I just hoped someday the pain and longing would lessen.

In the meantime, I was doing what I always did: burying my face in books. I'd be taking the Rhode Island bar exam in February, which was only a few months away. I needed to make sure I passed so I could find a job here and get my life on track once and for all.

The yard sale earned me just over three-thousand dollars, which was about a fourth of the cost of the roof replacement, but it was better than nothing.

It was too cold now anyway to start those repairs. Hopefully, I would find a way to save more money by the time I scheduled the roof work in the spring.

My life as of late was a solitary one. Aside from occasional visits to Bailey in Providence, I spent my days alone, studying and slowly fixing up the house. My morning routine was breakfast, followed by reading law books and quizzing myself. Then I'd break for lunch and coffee before spending the afternoons doing house stuff. I'd follow that up with a daily trip to the market for fresh produce before returning home to cook something for dinner that would leave me with leftovers for lunch the next day. Then, I'd spend the rest of the evening setting up my planners or watching some TV. *Repeat.*

November was always a beautiful time on the bay. Even though it was too cold to enjoy the water, the last of the fall foliage season was in full swing. The gorgeous orange, yellow, and red leaves on the trees surrounding the property and across Narragansett were stunning.

Lately, I'd been throwing on a heavy coat and sitting out back with my afternoon coffee each day. The sunshine helped to offset the otherwise brisk air. I'd take my binoculars outside to admire the foliage across the bay. The trees over there were even more colorful than the ones on this side. And yes, of course, each and every time my eyes passed over Leo's old house, I would think of him. That never changed.

This particular afternoon of leaf peeping, though, was unlike any of the others. As I held the binoculars to my eyes and admired the trees in the distance, I nearly dropped them at the sight of someone staring back at me. At first I thought I was hallucinating.

This can't be.

I am absolutely seeing things.

But then, holding his own binoculars to his eyes, he waved.

This time my binoculars did slip out of my grasp and land on the grass below. My hand went to my chest as I tried to contain my pounding heart.

I ran into the house, turned on the sink, and splashed my face with water. I had to be seeing things that weren't really there.

Then my phone chimed. I looked down at the screen to find a text.

Leo: Where did you go? Come back.

Oh my God.

What. Is. Happening?

With shaky hands, I picked up the phone and typed.

Felicity: I thought I was hallucinating.

Leo: It's me, Felicity. You're not seeing things.

Felicity: I know that now. I just don't understand what you're doing here.

Leo: I have a lot to explain, don't I?

Felicity: Uh, yes.

Leo: Can I come across the bay to see you?

My hands continued to shake as I typed.

Felicity: OMG. What are you doing here???

Leo: It's better if I explain in person, don't you think?

Rather than respond, I just stared at the screen. The dots danced as he typed.

Leo: I'll take your silence as a yes?

When I still didn't respond, he sent another text.

Leo: Is it okay if I come to you now?

I finally typed a response.

Felicity: Sorry. Yes. I'm just in shock.

Leo: Heading over.

I had no clue what to do with myself as I waited for him to arrive. I grabbed a towel and started wiping the table to distract myself from my nerves. There wasn't even anything to wipe.

When the doorbell rang, my pulse raced even faster.

I put one foot in front of the other and opened the door to find my long-lost love towering over me. My heart leaped.

Leo wore a black peacoat, and his hair was a bit longer than the last time I'd seen him, the scruff on his chin a bit more grown out. He smelled amazing, just like always, and I couldn't believe he was standing in front of me in the flesh. *Why is he here?* I didn't dare even let myself hope.

"Oh my God, you're shaking," he said, squeezing my arms and sending shivers through my body.

"Leo, what are you doing here?"

He let go of me and flashed a hesitant smile. "Surprise?"

"I would have loved a warning."

"We've never been good at those, have we?" He smiled into the silence. "Are you going to invite me in?"

Shaking my head, I stepped aside. "Oh. Of course."

His eyes wandered over me. "You look absolutely gorgeous, Felicity."

I looked down at myself. I was still wearing my bulky black parka and jeans.

"You're not that hard to please, then. But thank you. And you..." I pressed my hands to my stomach. "I feel like I'm gonna throw up."

"I make you want to vomit." He sighed. "Great."

"I'm sorry. It's nothing personal. It's just...I can't believe you're here. When did you get here?"

"Yesterday."

"You were across the bay all this time?"

"Yes. The same people own it as when Sigmund and I rented it. They still rent out the property in the summers, but it's typically empty this time of year. So I booked it."

"I can't believe you were across the water last night, and I didn't even know."

"I was jetlagged and needed to gear myself up before I threw this on you. So I waited until today. But I found the old binoculars in the house, decided to look across, and there you were."

"How long are you staying?" I asked, willing my heart to slow down.

He blinked several times. "That depends."

This was getting us nowhere. "Leo...what happened at home? Why are you here?"

He raked his hand through his hair. "I just...left, Felicity. I left. And I don't have any plans to go back until I legally have to."

What?

"What do you mean, you left?" I looked down at his hand. He wasn't wearing his wedding ring. "What about Darcie?"

"Darcie and I are getting a divorce."

"Oh my God," I muttered, looking momentarily down at his black shoes, then back up at him, my eyes likely reflecting the shock I felt.

The first thought that came to me was: *What have I done?*

"And before you go there, Felicity, it's not your fault. Darcie and I rushed into marriage, and there were warning signs long before you showed up on my doorstep." He looked over toward the living room. "Can we sit, please?"

"Yes, of course."

We walked together to the living room. Once we sat down, he immediately started talking.

"After you left, it forced me to open my eyes and take a good look at what I wanted out of life. And sometimes recognizing that means hurting others, something I've avoided since the day I was born. I knew if I decided to stay married, I would be living a lie." He paused. "I love Darcie. But I'm not *in love* with her. The fact that I couldn't bite the bullet on starting a family is very telling. Deep down, I knew that would bind me to her forever, and that was the reason I was never ready."

An immense sadness for her came over me. "Where's Darcie now?"

"She's still living at the house. We've started the process of divorce, but it takes a while to be finalized. I'm legally still married, but we're not together anymore."

"She must be devastated."

A sad look crossed his face as he nodded. "She's accepted it. This didn't happen overnight. Since you left, there have been many heated discussions, many tears... many sleepless nights while we figured everything out. But she's better now with it than she was in the beginning. I knew she'd fight for the marriage, but I couldn't let her. I'm doing what's best for her by letting her go and allowing her the freedom to receive the kind of love she deserves from someone else."

My head spun. "What about everything else...your work?"

"I left things in disarray, but honestly? The business, the properties, they'll be fine. Nothing is going to crumble. I have associates to help with all of that. The only thing I can't buy is happiness."

I shook my head. "Your mom must have flipped."

He cringed. "She's not happy. But that's her problem. I'm not letting it affect me." Leo frowned. "Nan passed away a couple of weeks after you left."

Oh no. "I'm so sorry. I know how close you were to her."

"She left me with some life-changing advice there at the end. I'll forever be indebted to her for helping me to see the light. Sigmund, too."

He paused and then leaned forward, seeming almost desperate. "Are you with anyone, Felicity?"

It had only been a few months since I left England. The idea of my having met someone during this time when I'd been incapable of focusing on anything besides Leo was laughable.

"No."

He exhaled. "I know you're in shock that I'm here. And I know I have to be careful. I can't expect to just jump into your life after everything I put you through. I've been through a lot myself. And I really just..." He looked into my eyes, his voice strained. "I just need a fucking hug right now."

No way was I going to deny this man the hug he desperately needed—the one I needed as well. I moved to sit next to him and wrapped my arms around him. He brought me to his chest and held me close. All of the fear inside of me faded away as I melted into his body. Our hearts pounded against each other. This was the most surreal moment of my life.

When he pulled back, he looked in my eyes again. "We've been apart far longer than we were ever together, yet I haven't been the same since I met you. I don't care how we make this work...only that we try."

"Where do we start?"

"How about dinner?"

"Only if you're not making it."

His face lit up. "I missed you so fucking much."

Leo brought me into his arms again and held me even more tightly than before. This felt different from any other time. Until now, I hadn't realized the tension that had marred every past embrace. I was always afraid to exhale. I'd always believed I'd lose him. But I wasn't tense this time. I let myself feel safe in his arms without worrying about the future—for the first time ever.

A little while later, Leo went back across the bay to give me some time to grab my bearings before dinner. We agreed that I would come over around eight that evening. Alone in the house, adrenaline continued to course through me, even though I was supposed to be calming down. I felt like I was in the middle of a dream.

He was still technically married. I wished I had a better understanding of his expectations for tonight, but I guessed I'd find out soon enough.

When evening came, I drove myself to Leo's rental. A feeling of déjà vu hit me the moment I pulled up to the house. Everything about this moment looked and felt the same as five years ago, aside from the fact that I now drove a small SUV rather than my old Fiat.

I had the jitters as I approached the door. Before I could ring the bell, he opened.

Leo wore a fitted black sweater that looked like it had been painted onto his broad chest. He'd dabbed on cologne, and his hair was damp from the shower. I'm sure it was partly how much I'd missed him, but he'd never looked more gorgeous.

"Come inside from the cold, beautiful."

Leo took my coat and hung it in the closet. I wore a brown sweater dress that showed off my curves.

He smiled as he took me in. "You're wearing a dress."

"You say that like it's a shock." I batted my eyelashes.

"Well, I can count on one hand the times I've seen you in a dress, and this would be number three. The first was the red one the night we had clams—the night you devastated me when you told me we shouldn't see each other anymore. Then there was the black dress you wore when you showed up in England. I suppose that was the day I devastated *you*."

"Gosh, I probably shouldn't wear dresses, should I? They're bad luck."

He flashed his gorgeous teeth. "Come. I have a surprise."

I followed him to the kitchen. On the counter, he'd laid out a seafood feast. There was a tower of shrimp cocktail, oysters, and lobster.

"Did you rob a fisherman?"

"I know you love seafood. But I wasn't sure what you'd be in the mood for, so I ordered multiple things."

"This is your MO. It reminds me of the time you went to Dunkin' Donuts and came back with every pastry under the sun."

"See?" he said. "I'm not the only one who remembers the details of when we were together."

"Most of it's ingrained in my memory."

"Yeah," he said. "I've struggled to hold onto all of it, not wanting any of those memories to disappear."

My eyes returned to the food. "This feels so surreal, Leo. I keep thinking I'm going to wake up, and you're gonna be gone again."

"It feels surreal for me, too, but in a good way. I feel free for the first time in my life. And on cloud nine. But still, I'm so hesitant to do anything that might hurt you or to presume that you're ready to start over with me so easily, given everything that happened in England."

"It's funny that you use the words *start over*. For some odd reason, that's what this feels like—a first date," I said.

"In a way, it *is* a new beginning."

"You've given up a lot to be here."

"My showing up now is far from a fairytale. I know that. This is real life, a bit different from the whirlwind summer we once had. But you know, I'd rather have *this* than that. Because back then, there was always the feeling of dread that I'd have to leave you. And that's gone now. I have my freedom, and I'm determined to live my truth— not to let anything or anyone get in the way of what I want in life. Despite all the money and power I have back home, from the moment I met you, Felicity, there was nothing I've wanted more than to be your boyfriend. And nothing ever changed that." Leo reached for me. "You know what else never changed?" He took my hand and placed it on his chest. "The way my heart beats for you."

I smiled. "If that's not proof of how you feel, I don't know what is."

Leo lifted my hand to his mouth and kissed it. Such a simple thing, yet I burned up all over.

He let go of me. "Let's eat while the food is fresh, shall we?"

After we plated our dinner, we took our dishes to the dining room, and Leo poured the wine. We reminisced a bit, and Leo updated me on Sig. He said his cousin would be enrolling in an MBA program in the spring. The long-term plan was that he'd work for Leo and take on some of the responsibilities of the Covington estate.

"That will be so good for him. It will give him something to focus on, at least."

Leo's phone chimed a few seconds later.

He looked down at it. "Speak of the devil…"

"Sig?" I laughed.

"Yeah."

"What did he say?"

He rolled his eyes. "I'm not sure you want to know."

"Oh boy. Show me."

Leo reluctantly flipped the phone around.

Sigmund: Are you muff diving in the Red Sea yet?

My cheeks flamed as I sighed. "Is it weird that it makes me happy whenever he acts like his old self?"

"It's been coming out a bit more. I'm proud of him for picking himself up and going back to school."

I nodded. This was such good news.

I ate a few more bites of the delicious dinner. "So… you said Darcie is still living at the house. Where were you living?"

He took a sip of wine and nodded, as if to ready himself for the fact that I was *going there*.

"For the last month, I've been staying with Sigmund. There were other properties I could have moved to, but I chose to crash with my cousin."

"Does Darcie get the house in the divorce?"

"I'm giving it to her, though our prenuptial agreement doesn't require me to. My mother thinks I'm insane. Everyone's criticizing me for it. But I don't give a fuck. I left her. She doesn't deserve to lose her home. Let her have it. It's the least I can do."

"I respect you for that."

A serious look crossed his face. "Do you? Respect me?"

"Why would you doubt it?"

"I've often wondered if the fact that I left Darcie would influence how you saw me as a man. Like maybe you would have more respect for me if I'd honored my commitment. Or maybe you'd think, if I could marry someone and leave them, I might do the same to you one day."

I shook my head. "I don't see it like that at all, Leo."

Relief warmed his features. "Good."

The wine buzzed through me as I looked into his azure eyes, wishing more and more that he would reach across the table and kiss me.

"Care for dessert?" he asked, dropping his cloth napkin to the table.

As good as the food was, my stomach was full of butterflies. I could think of little else besides what might or might not happen between us tonight.

I managed a smile. "No. Actually, I'm pretty full."

After we took our plates into the kitchen, Leo turned on the electric fireplace in the living room, and we sat together on the same couch where we'd fallen asleep the very first night I'd slept at this house.

We fell into comfortable conversation. "Sitting here reminds me of the night we stayed up talking, only to be woken by Sig in the morning," I said.

Leo rested his arm on the back of the sofa. "I remember that night very well. You asked me to take you virtually to the English countryside, remember? Little did you know your actual visit there wouldn't be quite the perfect fantasy."

"Despite everything, I found it to be just as breathtaking as I'd imagined. And seeing as though we're sitting here together now, I would say it wasn't a wasted trip."

Leo stared into my eyes, but continued not to touch me. I got the sense that he might be overwhelmed and perhaps still jetlagged. The right thing to do was to give him space and go back to my place—though I didn't want to leave.

"I could stay up all night talking to you and reminiscing," I said. "But it's late, and I think I should head back. You've had a long trip, and you must still be tired." I hopped off the couch, trying to convince myself this was what I wanted.

He stood up suddenly. "Are you sure?"

"We can have breakfast in the morning at my place."

Leo's chest rose and fell as he walked me to the front of the house.

Standing at the door, I leaned in and planted a chaste kiss on his cheek. "Sweet dreams."

Even as my body reacted to the contact, I swiftly turned for my car. Leo must have thought I was crazy for rushing out so abruptly.

He stood in front of the house, looking understandably confused. Just as I opened the car door, I realized I'd left my coat behind. Before I could even consider whether to return and get it, Leo held his index finger up and rushed back in.

A few seconds later, he came running out to my car.

"You forgot your coat," he said, a bit out of breath.

I reached for it, but he didn't let it go.

Our eyes locked as he finally released the jacket. "Why are you really leaving me like this?"

I fumbled for an answer. "I didn't...want to make you uncomfortable by assuming I was spending the night."

"Why on Earth would that *ever* make me uncomfortable?"

"I don't know what you're ready for. Your wounds are still fresh from the end of your marriage. I didn't want to presume anything or freak you out."

PENELOPE WARD

"Freak me out?"

"Because it's hard for me to hide how much I want you. I feel like it's written all over my face."

He let out a long exhale before caressing my chin. "Oh, my beautiful girl. The only thing *freaking me out* is how desperately I want to make love to you. But I've been hesitant to kiss you or even touch you, afraid I'll take things too far. It seems we were both experiencing the same fear. I'm not officially divorced yet...so you might think this is inappropriate. I also thought maybe I'd need to build your trust again first." His breath was visible in the cold air. "I don't just want you. I *need* you."

Relief and desire washed over me. "You think I don't trust you? You left your entire world behind to come here for me."

"Make no mistake..." His eyes bore into mine. "My entire world is *you*, Felicity. Without you, I have nothing."

I closed my eyes. "I feel the same way. And for the record, a legal technicality means nothing considering all you've given up to be with me."

"Communication, you know?" He smiled. "We should try it sometime."

Shrugging, I chuckled. "We're better than we used to be?"

"Get back inside," he said, taking my hand.

Following him back into the inviting, warm house, I somehow knew it would be a long time before we spent a night apart again.

As the door closed behind us, Leo wrapped his hands around my face and kissed me for minutes on end, igniting my entire body.

When he finally let go, he ran his thumb over my bottom lip. "This mouth...how I missed it." He slid his hands down my hair. "This beautiful hair. How I missed running my hands through it." His lips enveloped mine again as he spoke. "This beautiful woman, missing you for so long was fucking unbearable." He breathed out. "Please let me take you to my room now."

I nodded, and he lifted me up. We kissed the entire way up the stairs, only breaking long enough for him to place me gently on the bed. Piece by piece, we undressed each other. I marveled at how damn good his hard body still looked, the same bronze, sculpted perfection. Though the need for him felt urgent, I willed myself to slow down, to take in every second of this.

He echoed my thoughts as his naked body hovered over mine. "I'm gonna try to go easy on you, but I'm not sure I can. I feel like I've been waiting my whole damn life to have you again."

I didn't want to interrupt this incredible moment, but I had to. "There's something I need to tell you."

His eyes narrowed. "All right."

"I'm not on the pill anymore. So, we need something."

Leo froze. "Ah." He scratched his chin. "I'm sorry. I wasn't thinking straight and didn't come prepared." He swore under his breath. "Never thought we'd end up in this place."

"I don't have them at home, either."

He collapsed over me, his voice vibrating against my neck. "I'm fucking throbbing for you. I'll do anything to be inside of you tonight—break into a house, rob a store if it's not open this late, give my left arm...Grandad's necklace, perhaps. Whatever it takes, I *will* return with condoms."

He hopped up, his beautiful, hard cock bobbing up and down. Then he turned to open the side table drawer, allowing me a glorious view of his muscular ass.

Leo turned to me, his eyes wide. "You're never going to believe this."

"What?"

"Are you kidding me?" He laughed into his hand. "Sigmund's gargantuan box of condoms from BJ's is still bloody here! I just checked this drawer out of desperation. I never expected to find anything."

I sat up. "Oh my God."

He opened it. "It's half empty, so clearly people have been partaking over the years. But there are still some left."

"Who knew it would take five years to finish that box. What's the expiration date?"

Leo checked the side of the box. "This past summer. I guess these guys held out for five years, like we did."

I laughed. "Wow."

"They're probably still okay. It's only a few months past the date. I'm willing to take the risk if you are."

"I am."

He took one off the strip and threw it on the bed, tossing the box onto the table. "I'd put fucking plastic wrap over my cock right now if I had to."

"Thankfully, it won't come to that." I was wet and ready and didn't care what he put over himself at this point, as long as he was inside me.

Leo ripped the condom package open and sheathed his rock-hard shaft. I watched as he squeezed the tip and stroked himself, slow and rough, as he looked down at me.

That, combined with the look of desire in his eyes, was so freaking sexy.

"I've missed this beautiful pussy so much."

That was the last thing he said before he lowered himself, spread my legs wide, and penetrated me, closing his eyes until he was completely inside. We both let out unintelligible sounds of pleasure.

What started off slow soon became a frantic and desperate race to consume each other. We'd had sex in many different positions, but this one—missionary, with all of Leo's weight on top of me, holding me down while he fucked me as hard as he could—was my absolute favorite. There were no words for how it felt to have the man I loved inside of me again.

"Fuck, this is even better than I remembered," he groaned. "Tell me if I'm being too rough."

As the bed shook, I dug into his back with my nails, holding on to him for dear life. I wasn't anywhere near ready for this to be over, but as his balls slapped against my ass, I felt myself about to orgasm much faster than I anticipated.

He searched my eyes to confirm I was indeed losing it. "Yeah?"

I breathed out, "Yeah."

"I can fucking feel it," he said, his eyes rolling back as he started to come, banging me harder to the finish line.

The heat of his load through the condom was the cherry on top as my muscles pulsated around him. No one could ever make me climax the way Leo did.

We panted over one another, neither of us wanting to let go. After several minutes, Leo left to dispose of the condom before returning to bed.

We faced each other as he looped his fingers with mine. "Not only do I not want you to leave me tonight, I don't want to spend another night away from you ever again, if I can help it."

"That can be arranged."

"I have to say something," he said, his expression turning serious.

My eyes widened, but I managed a nod.

"I love you, Felicity Dunleavy. Even though I've written it to you and said it in so many roundabout ways, I've never *told you* to your face. And I'm so very sorry for that. I promise to make it up to you."

I melted into his arms. "Just make sure cooking is not involved in that plan."

His shoulders shook as he laughed. "It won't be."

"I love you, too, Leo. So much." I placed my hand on the side of his face. "Losing you hurt so badly. But finding you again made it all worth it."

"Listen to me…" He pressed his forehead to mine. "You never really lost me, not for one single, excruciating moment."

CHAPTER 25
Leo

Track 25: "Yellow" by Coldplay

The past few months here on Narragansett with Felicity had been the closest to a normal life I'd ever had.

After a week at the rental house, I moved in to her place. We spent every waking minute of the day together, making up for lost time, aside from the hours when she needed to study. Whenever she was busy, there was plenty for me to do between home repairs and taking care of the vast land, which now—in the dead of winter—required snow removal nearly every other day.

I kept in touch with my subordinates in England to make sure our properties had everything they needed. It was amazing, really, what I was able to get done remotely. The only major complication was that my mother was still not speaking to me. I knew she'd come around eventually, so I wasn't sweating it. If for some reason she didn't, it would be her loss.

Thankfully, my attorney back home was able to expedite the divorce, which had just been finalized.

It sped up the process when I didn't dispute anything Darcie wanted financially. I never believed she'd married me for my wealth or a title, but Darcie felt she deserved something substantial for the pain I'd put her through. I didn't disagree. Thankfully, as a result, she and I were in as good a place as we probably ever were going to be. While she'd likely never forgive me, she had come to terms with the end of our union. She seemed to be looking forward to the future and a fresh start. I'd even heard through the rumor mill that she'd started dating. I only hoped she was careful. There would be no shortage of men looking to capitalize on her newfound inheritance.

Although my days in Narragansett thus far had been bliss, always lurking in the background was the fact that eventually I would have to return to England, at least part time. I couldn't stay away forever. But the picture of what that would look like was still fuzzy. Felicity and I hadn't really hashed out the logistics of our future. It was a conversation I'd been putting off for far too long.

One afternoon after she'd come in from food shopping, I couldn't hold it in any longer.

I found her in the kitchen. "We need to talk, love."

Felicity searched my face. "I don't know if I like your tone. Is everything okay?"

"Yes, of course. I just want to talk about our plans for the coming months. Each day, I haven't wanted to look beyond tomorrow, but I think the time has come that we need to discuss it."

She placed her items in the cupboard. "I'm glad you brought it up. I hadn't wanted to put a damper on things either, because we've been having such a great time living in denial."

"You know I've always wanted to protect you from the stress of being in the public eye. The drama of my divorce with Darcie has tapered a bit, but the moment I show up in Westfordshire with another woman on my arm, the shite's going to hit the fan. It was a miracle no one leaked anything to the gossip rags when you were there before. We dodged a bullet."

"Are you feeling like it's time to return to England?"

"Not quite yet. I'm definitely not ready. And when I do, it will be on a part-time basis. But when you come back with me, which I hope you will, it's going to be like stepping into the fire, for a while, at least. Are you okay with that?"

She took a deep breath. "I ran away from you once in fear of what people would think. I'm not gonna do it again." Felicity took both of my hands in hers. "Being apart isn't an option. I'll walk through that fire. Hell, I'll dance through it with both middle fingers up. I'll do whatever I have to, because I'm not letting anyone take this away from us again."

There wasn't anything sexier than hearing a woman say she'd walk through fire for you.

I kissed her so hard. "Thank you, my beautiful. I won't let you give up your dreams for me. I'll travel back and forth if I have to. I don't expect you to live there full time. But in an ideal world, you and I would spend time in both places—Narragansett and Westfordshire—even if it's not right away."

"My goals in life aren't what they used to be," she said. "I'll still practice law. But it's going to have to be on my own terms, because I won't take a job that's going to require me to live apart from you for any great length of time. I've been there and done that. Career is important to me, but not as important as family." She paused. "You're my family, Leo."

There was nothing more I'd ever wanted to be. For weeks, I'd worried about this conversation, worried that she might feel threatened by my mother or the prospect of returning to the UK with me. But I should have known better. I should have known my girl was tough as steel. That was something I'd always loved about her.

A week later, Felicity arrived home to find me in a seemingly precarious place—the kitchen.

"What's going on, Leo?"

"Don't be alarmed," I said as I sliced some lemon. "But I'm cooking."

She laughed. "Has hell frozen over?"

"I'm determined to learn so you don't have to prepare every meal. You've been busier than ever with studying lately, and with the bar exam coming up, I want to ease some of the burden. We've had takeaway every other night."

Felicity still seemed skeptical as she looked over at the laptop on the counter. "Okay, so tell me what you're doing here."

"Remember how I used to watch those Bob Ross painting tutorials?"

"Yeah..."

"Well, this is my new friend, Micheline, on YouTube. She's teaching me how to steam clams without overdoing them. We're having pasta and clams tonight in a lemon butter sauce. I figured boiling water and steaming clams sounded easy enough."

"Did you tell Sig you're cooking for me?"

"Yes. He suggested you have 911 on standby."

She chuckled. "Well, I don't know what to do with myself now. I was all prepared to spend the next hour cooking dinner."

I put my knife down. "I have an idea. Why don't you go take a bath instead, love?"

"That sounds like an amazing plan."

"Let me show you to the bathroom."

She narrowed her eyes in suspicion as we made our way up the stairs.

When we arrived, her mouth dropped. "What did you do?"

"Today is the three-month anniversary of the day I came back to you."

"It is? I didn't realize."

"Yep. I've been keeping track."

She took a closer look at the yellow flowers and candles strewn about the bathroom. "Are those..."

"Peeping Toms. Yeah. Just like my beauty."

She covered her mouth. "I can't believe you..."

"I figured they were more fitting than roses."

Felicity picked one up and smelled it. "This is amazing."

"You've worked so freaking hard lately. I just want you to have a nice evening. Relax, and I'll call you when dinner's ready."

"Thank you, Leo."

The look of joy on her face made me so happy.

Back downstairs, I got to work following my video tutorial. First, I had to soak the clams to push the sand and salt water out of their shells. Then I melted the butter and threw in the garlic and herbs before adding wine and lemon juice. After it all came to a boil, I added the clams and leftover butter. I covered the pot and let the clams steam in the fragrant sauce. After I turned on a timer, I got to work on a special side dish just for Felicity. I told her not to come down until I texted.

Once everything was ready, I placed the skillet of clams on the table, along with a dish of linguini cooked al dente. At least, I hoped it wasn't undercooked. As I looked over my work, I wondered if maybe hell would freeze over after all, because I thought I'd managed not to fuck up this dinner. Turned out all I'd needed were step-by-step instructions.

When I finally called her down, Felicity emerged looking adorable in one of her signature Hello Kitty shirts over leggings. Her long, red hair was damp, and there were a couple of wet spots at the front of her shirt, allowing me a peek at her nipples through the material.

She sniffed the air. "I could practically taste the garlic all the way upstairs. Everything smells so good."

"I'm glad you think so. This is *my* supper," I teased. "I've made you your own plate of something else." I gestured to her seat. "Sit."

As she squinted in confusion, my heart raced. I lifted the metal cover off the special plate I'd prepared and placed it in front of her.

She broke out into laughter. While I'd cooked a feast of clams and linguini allegedly just for me, Felicity's plate contained SpaghettiOs with a single clam in the center. Of course, it was garnished with basil.

"Why, thank you. This is mine?"

"I figured you'd like this more, no?"

"Well, maybe if you had burned dinner. But this was so not necessary."

"Okay, I'll spare you. You don't have to eat the SpaghettiOs. But have a taste of the clam on top. Let me know what you think."

Felicity cracked the clamshell open, and I waited for the moment of realization. The second her eyes bugged out, the two-carat, yellow diamond ring I'd slipped inside the shell fell in the middle of the SpaghettiOs.

Her mouth was agape as she stared at the plate. That was my cue to come around to her side of the table and get down on my knee. I reached over and grabbed the ring, wiping the sauce off of it first.

Here goes. "Felicity, you told me you would walk through fire for me. I want you to know, there's nothing I wouldn't do for you, either. I love you more than anything in this world. I used to think I was born to continue my family name. But I wasn't. I know now that I was born to be your husband. And the only heir I ever want is one that comes from you. You're the only woman I want to share that experience with. You once told me everyone who's ever mattered in your life left you. Those days are over. You will always have me. I want to live out the rest of my life with you. It doesn't matter where we are or whether I have a shred of clothing on my back—which is ironic considering how you met me." I winked. "Anyway, what I mean is, I don't need anything but you."

I wiped a tear from her eye. "Felicity Dunleavy, you are the love of my life. Will you do me the honor of being my wife?"

My gorgeous redhead's eyes were still filled with tears as she nodded, seemingly unable to speak. She wrapped her arms around me as I squeezed her tightly.

Her voice trembled as she moved back to look me in the eyes. "Yes. Of course, I'll be your wife! I love you so much, Leo."

I slipped the ring on her finger and lifted her up out of her seat, into my arms.

After endless kisses and many tears, we finally sat back down. The clams were a bit cold by now, but it didn't matter. Nothing mattered aside from the fact that I loved this woman, and she was going to be legally mine forever.

My phone rang in the middle of our celebratory dinner. I wasn't going to answer it, but I saw it was Sigmund.

I immediately put him on speakerphone.

Before I could say anything, his voice rang out. "So... what happened?"

"She said yes!" I proclaimed with a huge smile.

"Hi, Sig!" Felicity smiled from ear to ear.

"That's brilliant," he said. "But I was referring to whether or not she survived your cooking."

We all got a good laugh out of that.

After dinner, I had one more surprise for my girl.

"Get your coat on, we're going out back."

"Really? It's so cold."

"Don't worry. I've got that covered."

I'd hired some local guys to set up outdoor heaters and a firepit in our yard while we were eating dinner.

After we put on our black parka coats, we stepped outside.

She immediately noticed the flames. "When did you do all this?"

"I had some help."

On a table next to the two Adirondack chairs was a bottle of Fireball and two small glasses.

"In honor of Mrs. Angelini, we're going to enjoy some Fireball outside tonight. I know she would have loved to be here and celebrate with us."

Felicity's eyes sparkled with tears. "I didn't think I was going to cry another time tonight, but you managed to make me."

I pulled her in for a kiss. After I poured us each a glass of Fireball, we saluted Mrs. Angelini in the sky and clanked our glasses together, chugging the liquor.

Through the fire, I pointed to the house across the bay. "I much prefer being on this side of the water with you. But I'll always be grateful for that house. If I hadn't chosen it, we would have never found each other."

She jumped as the first set of fireworks burst into the night air.

"You're just full of surprises tonight!"

"I thought this would be a fitting ending to our evening," I explained. "Fireworks are exactly what I've felt from the moment I laid eyes on you."

"This is incredible," she said, gazing up at the sky in wonder. Felicity moved her chair closer to mine and leaned her head on my chest as we watched the rest of the spectacular display.

Perhaps the only thing less than perfect was that the heaters were just not cutting it. It was damn frigid outside.

When the fireworks finally ended, Felicity straddled me in my seat and covered my face with kisses. When her lips landed on mine, I could still taste the cinnamon from the Fireball on her tongue.

Her teeth chattered as she announced, "This night has been a dream. Thank you so much for everything. But…"

"But?"

"Can we go inside and have sex now?" She laughed. "I'm freezing my nutsack off!"

EPILOGUE
Leo

Final Track: "All You Need Is Love" by The Beatles

FOUR YEARS LATER

Westfordshire, England

"Do like Daddy." I dipped my brush in the yellow paint and demonstrated how to draw the sun.

It was a gorgeous, sunny day in the countryside, and I'd set up two easels in the back of our estate, deciding to give our three-year-old a painting lesson today.

Unfortunately, instead of following my lead, Eloise dunked her entire hand in the paint before slapping it against the paper.

"That's amazing, darling." I laughed.

She giggled and flashed her adorable baby teeth, her red curls blowing in the breeze.

"I wonder what time Mummy's coming back. Must be soon now," I said as I filled in my sun with more yellow paint.

Sigmund appeared out of nowhere, interrupting our painting lesson. I'd invited him over for birthday cake.

He smiled at the mess my daughter was making. "Lady Eloise, your painting talent is just as magnificent as your father's."

Sigmund lifted her up, not seeming to care that she got paint all over his shirt—just another testament to how much he'd changed over the years.

He closed his eyes as she dabbed some on his face. "You're adorable, Eloise. You know that?"

"Miraculously, she looks nothing like Ed Sheeran, now does she?" I teased.

"No. She looks like you with a small dusting of freckles and Ginger's hair. The two of you have finally morphed into one another. Congratulations."

I chuckled. "How are things over at the Bettencourt project?"

"We break ground on Wednesday."

"Good," I said, putting the paintbrush down.

After getting his MBA two years ago, Sigmund was now managing a good portion of my properties, which allowed me more time to spend with my family.

"Do you have any plans for the weekend?" I asked him.

He gave Eloise one last kiss on the cheek before placing her down on the grass. "No. Why?"

I hesitated. "You know how Felicity's been working part time teaching American law at the university?"

His brows drew together in suspicion. "Yeah..."

"She said one of her female colleagues is really attractive and single with a nice personality. She wants to invite her out here to dinner."

He glared at me. "No."

"Okay, but hear me out—"

"No."

"All right. All right. Can't say I didn't try." I sighed. "And I'll keep trying."

"Oh, I know you will."

Sigmund had had a few meaningless one-night stands over the years since losing Britney. But he hadn't dated or met anyone he'd connected with. Everything had to happen in its own time, I supposed.

Eager to drop the subject, he pointed in the distance to where Felicity was approaching on one of the horses as she returned from her morning ride. "Ginger seems to be enjoying farm life."

It was hard to believe we'd been living in England full time for a year already.

Our daughter, Eloise Leonora Covington, had been born three years ago today, in fact. We'd moved to Brighton House on her second birthday.

Not long after Felicity and I got engaged four years ago, she found out she was pregnant. Fortunately, it was just after she'd passed the bar. She'd been switching to a new kind of birth control, and we hadn't been careful enough. But honestly, it was the best news I could have received. We got married shortly thereafter in a small ceremony on the bay in Narragansett. Sigmund flew to the States to be my best man, and Felicity had her best friend, Bailey, by her side. We celebrated after with a clam bake by the bay and fireworks. It was perfection—everything coming full circle.

I decided to take control of the situation with the local press back in Westfordshire, cutting a deal with a paper to print a photo from our Rhode Island wedding to announce that I'd gotten remarried. I donated all the money from that article to Mrs. Barbosa and her foster children. After the story went to press, I didn't bother to monitor the situation online. I just let everyone have a field day while I stayed in America. I no longer cared what anyone said or thought about me. My mother still hadn't been speaking to me at that time, so she saw the photos in the paper along with everyone else. The only person I'd contacted with a warning was Darcie. She deserved at least that and appreciated the heads up.

Shortly after Felicity and I got married, she took a part-time job working as a legal advisor for the Department of Human Services in Rhode Island. She was finally doing what she'd always wanted to: advocating for children. She continued working there until we moved, and she vowed to look for a way to continue that work as soon as we were settled in the UK.

The first time I heard from my mother was right after Eloise was born. She asked if I would be willing to come back for a visit with Felicity and the baby. So that's what we did when our daughter turned six months old.

My mother did the best she could. She was cordial to Felicity and tried to pretend we'd never been estranged in order to be in her grandchild's life. Eloise was the game changer. Things weren't perfect with Mother even to this day, but they were better than they had been.

When we moved here last year, Felicity decided to keep the house in Narragansett and was now renting it out to a family. We knew that as Eloise approached school age, we would have had to pick one location, and we'd agreed that England made the most sense. The timing had been right, since Aunt Mildred had decided to move to France around the same time, leaving her beautiful farmhouse vacant. I purchased it from her. Surrounded by animals, which included Felicity's beloved Shetland, Ludicrous, Brighton House was the perfect permanent home for us.

Felicity truly seemed happy here, never wanting to venture away from the farm much, aside from her teaching job or volunteering at a foster home in London.

After her morning ride around the grounds, my wife stepped down off of the black stallion. "Your mother will be here soon. She's coming for Eloise's birthday cake."

"Quick, hide the paint, Eloise! We wouldn't want your grandmother to have a heart attack," Sigmund quipped.

"She's actually loosened up quite a bit, thankfully," I said.

Felicity went inside to shower, and I got Eloise cleaned up for the small family birthday party. We were planning a kids' party later in the week.

Since my wife never wanted a huge staff, we had one part-time housekeeper, Mary, who was now setting up balloons in the dining area.

It was nearly noontime when Sigmund kicked back with a beer in the living room to watch the football game. The doorbell rang, and I went to answer it while Eloise played on the floor next to Sigmund's feet.

My mother stood at the door, holding a gargantuan, wrapped box.

"Hello, Mother." I kissed her on both cheeks.

"Hello, my darling. Show me to the birthday girl."

After Mother joined Eloise and Sigmund in the living area, I noticed my gorgeous angel descending the stairs.

Felicity looked divine in a simple white dress with an empire waist. She and I had an announcement to make at the party. Yes, she was pregnant again, and that was *part* of the announcement, but the other bit made me equally nervous and excited.

I took her aside. "You look so beautiful right now."

"I do? I don't feel it."

"Trust me," I said as I placed a soft kiss on her lips. "I swear you're even sexier when you're pregnant."

Felicity blushed. The fact that I still had that effect on her pleased me to no end.

She went to the living room and greeted my mother with a standard, formal kiss on each cheek.

Mum was still fairly close to my ex-wife, which I knew made Felicity a bit uncomfortable—not because she had anything against Darcie, but because my mother's relationship with my ex was stronger than with her. Technically, under the peerage rules, both Darcie and Felicity were allowed the title of Duchess of Westfordshire, although Felicity still couldn't get used to it. She'd smile awkwardly with a hint of a grimace anytime anyone called her "Your Grace." But she handled it *with* grace, in any case.

As for Darcie, she had recently reconnected with her former lover, Gabriel Davies, who himself was now divorced. He confessed that he'd always regretted ending things with her and wanted a second chance. Given that she'd still had lingering feelings for him when we first got together, one might say everything ended up the way it was meant to.

After lunch, we all moved to the dining room and gathered around Eloise as she blew out the candles on her Hello Kitty cake. (Her mum had a tiny bit of influence on that choice.) My daughter squealed in joy and clapped along with us as we applauded her. She loved attention. In that sense, she wasn't anything like her mother.

After the cake time was over, I looked at Felicity, and she nodded, giving me the go-ahead.

Clearing my throat, I said, "So, we have some news." I took her hand.

My mother placed her teacup down. "Oh?"

I took a deep breath in. "We're having another baby."

Mum's mouth dropped, and I knew what she was thinking: *Please God, let it be a boy*.

Before she could get her hopes up too much, I announced, "And it's a girl."

I paused to allow my mother a moment. My entire existence for so long had been about producing a male heir to carry on the Covington name. I'd come to terms with the fact that it might never happen. It didn't matter to me, although I knew it had mattered to my father. I tried to hold on to the advice Nan had given me—that wherever my father was now, he saw things from a different perspective and understood what truly mattered. Carrying on one's family name for vanity's sake ultimately wasn't the purpose of life.

"You found out already?" my mother asked.

"Yes," Felicity said. "We had an ultrasound. I'm actually about four months along, but we wanted to wait until we were sure everything looked okay before we announced it."

Sigmund came around to our side of the table and offered us each a hug. "Congratulations, guys."

When he returned to his seat, Felicity and I once again glanced at each other.

"I'll tell him," she whispered. "We were thinking about naming her Britney." She paused. "If that's okay with you, Sig. We wouldn't want to upset you in any way. We only want to honor her if it would bring you joy and not sadness."

My cousin sat speechless. Then his eyes began to glisten. He stood from his chair. "Excuse me a moment."

The only time I'd ever seen him cry was right after his wife died. But I suspected he was doing that very thing right now in the bathroom.

Felicity looked a bit panicked. And honestly, I wondered whether we'd made a mistake.

Even my stone-cold mother looked as if she were about to cry.

I knew time hadn't really healed his wounds. I wondered whether he'd be able to give his heart to anyone else in this lifetime. Maybe that didn't matter. Maybe we only get one great love. I knew if something were to happen to Felicity, I could never love another person the same way, and no one would ever replace her. Why would Sigmund be any different?

That reminded me of something I'd once told Felicity, back when we first met: "*a connection between two people is no less valuable if cut short by circumstances*." Perhaps Sigmund and Britney were the greatest example of that.

My cousin finally emerged, and while his eyes were a bit red, there wasn't a tear in sight.

He smiled. "Thank you for wanting to name your daughter after her. Despite what my nearly losing it might imply, there's nothing in the world that would make me happier."

Felicity placed her hand on his arm. "Are you sure?"

"Absolutely. I can't wait to tell her parents." He grinned. "And if the doctors were wrong and it turns out you're having a boy, I fully expect you to name him Sigmund."

Everyone burst into laughter.

If the Covington name ended with me, so be it. I'd die a happy man, surrounded by my beautiful, redheaded angels. Or perhaps my daughters would go against the guard and refuse to change their names, remaining Covingtons after all.

So much had changed over the past nine years since Felicity Dunleavy first came over for tea. My life had turned out nothing like I'd envisioned it, and that was a damn good thing. Sure, I'd made mistakes. People had been hurt along the way, myself included. But amidst the pain of heartbreak, separation, and sadness, I'd learned firsthand what Nan had told me about love before she died.

The purpose of life is to love with all of your heart and soul. No matter when the end of my days came, I would be able to say I'd done just that. My daughters would know their father loved them. And *that* would be my legacy.

OTHER BOOKS BY PENELOPE WARD

The Anti-Boyfriend

RoomHate

The Day He Came Back

The Crush

Just One Year

When August Ends

Love Online

Gentleman Nine

Drunk Dial

Mack Daddy

Stepbrother Deares

Neighbor Dearest

Jaded and Tyed (A novelette)

Sins of Sevin

Jake Undone (Jake #1)

Jake Understood (Jake #2)

My Skylar

Gemini

Park Avenue Player (co-written with Vi Keeland)

Stuck-Up Suit (co-written with Vi Keeland)

Cocky Bastard (co-written with Vi Keeland)

British Bedmate (co-written with Vi Keeland)

Playboy Pilot (co-written with Vi Keeland)

Mister Moneybags (co-written with Vi Keeland)

Rebel Heir (co-written with Vi Keeland)
Rebel Heart (co-written with Vi Keeland)
Hate Notes (co-written with Vi Keeland)
Dirty Letters (co-written with Vi Keeland)
My Favorite Souvenir (co-written with Vi Keeland)
Happily Letter After (co-written with Vi Keeland)
Not Pretending Anymore (co-written by Vi Keeland)

ACKNOWLEDGEMENTS

The acknowledgements are always the hardest part of the book to write. There are simply too many people that contribute to the success of a book, and it's impossible to properly thank each and every one.

First and foremost, I need to thank the readers all over the world who continue to support and promote my books. Your support and encouragement are my reasons for continuing this journey. And to all of the book bloggers who work tirelessly to support me book after book, please know how much I appreciate you.

To Vi – You're the best friend and partner in crime that I could ask for. Without you as a sounding board, I would undoubtedly have gone crazy a long time ago. Well, crazier. ;-) I'm a lucky girl!

To Julie – Thank you for your friendship and for always inspiring me with your amazing writing, outlook, and for always being just a click away.

To Luna –Thank you for your love and support, day in and day out. You continue to be an inspiration in showing me that anything is possible if you put your mind to it.

To Erika – It will always be an E thing. I am so thankful for your love, humor and summer visits. Thank you for always brightening my days with your messages of encouragement.

To Cheri – An amazing friend and supporter. Thanks for always looking out for me and never forgetting a Wednesday. Can't wait to hopefully see you this year!

To Darlene – I am so grateful to have met you, and

it has nothing to do with the delicious Medjool dates you send me, but rather your valued friendship.

To my Facebook reader group, Penelope's Peeps – I adore you all. You are my home and favorite place to be.

To my agent extraordinaire, Kimberly Brower – Thank you for everything you do and for getting my books out into the world.

To my editor Jessica Royer Ocken – It's always a pleasure working with you. I look forward to many more experiences to come.

To Elaine of Allusion Publishing – Thank you for being the best proofreader, formatter, and friend a girl could ask for.

To Julia Griffis of The Romance Bibliophile – Your eagle eye is amazing. Thank you for being so wonderful to work with.

To my assistant Brooke – Thank you for hard work in handling all of the things Vi and I can't seem to ever get to. We appreciate you so much!

To Kylie and Jo at Give Me Books – You guys are truly the best out there! Thank you for your tireless promotional work. I would be lost without you.

To Letitia Hasser of RBA Designs – My awesome cover designer. Thank you for always working with me until the finished product exactly perfect.

To my husband – Thank you for always taking on so much more than you should have to so that I am able to write. I love you so much.

To the best parents in the world – I'm so lucky to have you! Thank you for everything you have ever done for me and for always being there.

Last but not least, to my daughter and son – Mommy loves you. You are my motivation and inspiration!

ABOUT THE AUTHOR

Penelope Ward is a *New York Times, USA Today* and *#1 Wall Street Journal* bestselling author.

She grew up in Boston with five older brothers and spent most of her twenties as a television news anchor. Penelope resides in Rhode Island with her husband, son and beautiful daughter with autism.

With over two million books sold, she is a 21-time *New York Times* bestseller and the author of over twenty novels.

Penelope's books have been translated into over a dozen languages and can be found in bookstores around the world.

Subscribe to Penelope's newsletter: http://bit.ly/1X725rj